FORBIDDEN

FORBIDDEN

Megan Paul

This Large Print edition is published by BBC Audiobooks Ltd, Bath, England and by Thorndike Press, Waterville, Maine, USA.

Published in 2004 in the U.K. by arrangement with the author.

Published in 2004 in the U.S. by arrangement with Dorian Literary Agency.

U.K. Hardcover ISBN 0–7540–7690–3 (Chivers Large Print)
U.S. Softcover   ISBN 0–7862–5978–7 (General)

The text of this Large Print edition is unabridged.
Other aspects of the book may vary from the original edition.

Set in 16 pt. New Times Roman.

Printed in Great Britain on acid-free paper.

British Library Cataloguing in Publication Data available

Library of Congress Control Number: 2003110367

PROLOGUE

So this was what a forbidden kiss felt like?

Kitt's lips were hard and demanding, punishing not tender—yet they had every magical quality that Chloe had longed for. She felt weightless and nerveless and, at the same time, more keenly alive and in her skin than ever before. Blindly, she answered Kitt's every prompt. Sighing beneath his lips, she coiled her arms around his broad, linen-clad back, opening her mouth to him and surrendering everything that she'd always denied other men. Kitt responded with a cross between a gasp and a groan, as if he were as adrift as she was, then he crushed her even closer, his mouth taking everything hers had offered.

For what seemed like a thousand fabulous years, they clung to each other. Kitt's lips roved over Chloe's adoring face, even as his long, elegant hands travelled exquisitely over her body. He muttered against her neck urgent little sounds he seemed hardly aware of.

'Oh, my Chloe, you're so beautiful, so very beautiful,' he whispered.

Then, all of a sudden, and with an awful, shocking wrench, he dragged himself away from her. Denied the support of his powerful body, Chloe just flopped. She was fortunate that the settee was just behind her, otherwise

1

she might have landed in a startled heap on the floor. As it was, she stared dazedly up at him—at a man who looked like saint at the stake, in torment.

Her heart bounded inside her, and she felt a sinking sense of dread. Now she'd done it! Crossed the Rubicon, done the very thing she'd known was madness and would spoil everything.

Staring into Kitt's anguished eyes and knowing hers must be a mirror of them, she wondered just how on earth they'd come to this . . .

How had it happened?

CHAPTER ONE

Kitt's home, thought Chloe for what seemed like the hundredth time in an hour.

Kitt's home! Kitt's home! Kitt's home!

Pacing her sitting room, she felt like a fizzing bottle of over-shaken champagne. She wanted to shout out aloud, hang out of the window and howl across the garden and out into the road.

Kitt's home and I can't wait to see him!

Not that she wasn't furious with him too. He'd been home an hour—sixty-seven minutes to be exact—and he hadn't even been down to see her yet. Or called her on the internal phone. Should she get a sweeping brush and bang on the ceiling to let him know that she was home? Surely he could tell from Saint-Saens blasting from her stereo and out of the open window? The trouble was that if she started bashing on the ceiling, she'd probably get a lecture from him about damaging the paintwork—which would really put the mockers on his homecoming.

'Kitt's home,' she muttered again, 'For what *that's* worth . . . he might as well have stayed festering in Japan!' Throwing herself down on her squashy old sofa, she picked up the book she'd been trying to read—'Principles of Photographic Composition'—and began a new chapter entitled 'Capturing the Perfect Image'.

Always look with your eyes first. See the composition naturally and uninhibitedly, then use the viewfinder . . .

'Well, I would if there was anything decent to look at!' Her favourite subject was still hiding away from her, upstairs. 'And you're no good either!' she accused the other occupant of the sofa, her large black-and-white tomcat, Boy. 'You're either asleep, stuffing your face, or out murdering wildlife in the garden.' Aware that he was being disparaged, the cat lifted his handsome face, then uncoiled himself from his comfortable position. His body language as he leapt down said 'Women, who needs 'em!' Landing neatly, he sidled off, tail aloft.

'You shun me as well then! Everyone else has!' Chloe scowled and turned a page without having absorbed a single new fact. It was all fascinating stuff, but she was finding it increasingly hard to concentrate on anything. Her mind was elsewhere, and she couldn't connect with the niceties of framing and focusing. The 'perfect image' was somewhere up above her head ignoring her. 'Kitt's home,' she whispered again, feeling ticked off.

Sighing, Chloe marked her page and laid the book aside. No more studying today, might as well face it. Crossing to the open bay window, she looked out across the garden of Willow House and its short, curving drive. It was a lazy, balmy afternoon turning into a golden tranquil evening. Chloe should have felt lucky to live in such 'green' surroundings so conveniently close to London, but all she could register at the moment was disgruntled restlessness.

It's all your fault, you standoffish old misery! she thought, looking upwards again. *What on earth's the matter with you?*

An hour ago—or seventy-eight minutes ago, as it was now—she'd watched Kitt's familiar metallic-blue classic Lancia ooze up the drive like something out of a continental movie, then crunch impressively to a halt. A second or two later, the man himself stepped on to the gravel, looking travel worn, but still elegant and very sexy.

Always Mr Cool, no matter how rumpled! Chloe remembered the way Kitt had run his hand through his hair, then closed his eyes as if in relief. She couldn't think of a single male model of her acquaintance who could look as stunning as that whilst worn out by jet lag!

As Kitt had strolled around to the car's boot to get his bags, Chloe's heart had pounded so hard she'd had to hug herself. Surely it'd been loud enough for him to hear it? What if he looked up and saw her watching? With all the stealth of a master spy, she'd slid along the window seat and lurked behind the curtains, keeping Kitt under surveillance. Then, with a pang of guilt, she'd lifted up her camera.

5

You're pathetic, Chloe. Spying on him. You're like the *paparazzi.* Yet who could deny the happiness that had come from observing Kitt's lean, patrician face and his long-limbed, sombrely dressed body? Nor quash the concern at his obvious weariness. He'd been limping too—always a bad sign. He only let it happen when he was exhausted or preoccupied. At all other times, he exerted a steely self-discipline and didn't allow even his closest friends to suspect he was suffering. Chloe suspected that the long flight from Japan had really got to him.

'Poor Kitt . . .' She was mellowing now. What was it like to battle against the lingering results of injury? She hadn't any idea really, because in her own twenty-four years of life she had always been alarmingly healthy. The worst she'd ever suffered was a sprained wrist when she'd fallen out of a tree years ago. And even that'd had its compensations. Kitt, still on his crutches from his own accident, had hobbled over to make sure she was all right, then consoled her with a lopsided hug.

'My hero,' she whispered, feeling her perennial muddle of emotions. He'd been so normal with her then, despite having to fight some hideous battles. Steel pins, weeks in traction, the fear he might never walk again. He'd been on crutches for months, and had to endure gruelling physio sessions every day. Yet he'd still comfort her through the most minimal of traumas.

The crutches were long gone now, and even the hero status was problematical. The bloody-mindedness that had aided his recovery still remained, and Chloe often wondered whether it was that which made him act so weirdly towards her these days. He was always wary and serious, and she couldn't work out why, when for years they'd been such friends and laughed so easily.

'Men! I give up!' Leaving the window seat she looked around for Boy. 'Even the nice ones behave like psychotics!'

Picking up her treasured new camera, she studied the graduated and bevelled wheels that encircled the attached zoom lens. Although the thing was fairly idiot-proof in automatic mode, when set to manual it offered awesome adjustability. Buying a Nikon had been a kind of quantum leap—a real commitment to taking photography seriously—and just to handle it was both thrilling and deeply scary.

She'd just loaded the camera and had been fiddling about with the settings, when Kitt had arrived. In spite of the instant rush of nerves, it'd seemed the most natural thing in the world to train her lens on him, even though she wasn't sure whether the shots would turn out. She'd most likely get a series of fuzzy montages of light and shade, but it had certainly felt exhilarating at the time. She'd found herself peeling off frames on pure instinct, just like the fashion photographers she herself posed for. The difference was that *they* knew exactly what they were doing. Being a model gave her some insight into photographic composition, but it didn't automatically confer talent.

It might be better if they don't turn out, thought Chloe, considering making a dramatic gesture and exposing the film. Taking secret pictures of Kitt was invading his privacy. Like stealing. She got as mad as hell herself if anyone took pictures of her without paying her!

Thinking of lost income, Chloe felt a new rush of irritation. She'd turned down lucrative bookings today, just to be around when Kitt came home. She might as well have been in a studio somewhere for all the good it'd done her!

So, what *was* Kitt doing now? Suddenly, she heard the whoosh of the pipes in his part of the house, meaning that the shower was running. Knowing the layout of Kitt's bathroom, Chloe had no trouble imagining him standing beneath the teeming water, sluicing away the travel grime from his body.

'Oh, no!' cried Chloe, as her finger tightened involuntarily on the shutter release and snapped an unwanted photo of the striped Regency wallpaper and the sideboard.

You know you shouldn't do that, girl, she told herself as she switched lenses, made a few adjustments, and took another photo of the sideboard and its potted plant, utilising the low, slanting light for interest. She was using professional-quality film, and such unprofessional attention blips cost money.

'This is stupid,' she grumbled, getting fractious with her focusing. 'Why don't you just go up there now and see him, you idiot!'

Yes, why not? Saunter up, say hello, and ask about the trip. Be friendly but casual—like a normal human being, for heaven's sake.

'Friendly? Get real!'

She really ought not to talk to herself so much. One day, she'd do it when she was on a shoot and get a reputation for being loony. Switching off the camera's power, she stowed it, and the lenses, in her pristine new gadget bag, fitting in each item as if it were constructed out of eggshells.

You're skulking. Don't be a scaredy-cat, she told herself, but silently this time. You're scared because you don't know what to expect anymore. You could get warmth or indifference. Friendliness or hostility. Light or darkness . . .

And that's just *you!*

Everything's changed now, she thought, suffering a familiar hot flutter of panic. Kitt wasn't her best friend any more. It was like having a flat in a stranger's house, not that of a childhood companion who'd always loved the same bad jokes, junk food, and quirky old films that she did.

When had everything become so weird? When had Kitt stopped being her soul mate and turned into a moody, watchful tyrant?

When exactly? And more to the point, *why*?

CHAPTER TWO

'Tyrant' was an exaggeration. 'Moody' and 'watchful' were fair, where she was concerned. To everyone else he was as nice as pie, as usual.

Looking up and ignoring the kitsch-looking chandelier and the room's high ceiling, Chloe cast her mind back to the last time she'd spoken to Kitt, while he'd been packing his bags for Japan. He'd been packing and briefing her—unnecessarily, she'd thought—about how take care of herself and the house while he was away.

He'd given her a rather stern spiel about the alarm system and checking in with the Pattersons, the retired couple who lived in the other downstairs flat, but all Chloe had been able to focus on were the navy-blue silk boxer shorts he'd just slipped into his case.

'Chloe! Are you listening?' He'd picked up another pair without looking at them this time. His green eyes were stormy and worried-looking but that could have been about the journey, the project, or anything but her.

'Yeah, yeah, yeah,' said Chloe, nettled. 'Check with the Pattersons. Alarm. Floodlights. I know all this stuff. You've been on a zillion trips and I am twenty-four, Kitt, not fourteen!'

In a way, Chloe was impressed that he didn't really snap at her. In his place, she would've been giving him a jolly good ear bashing.

'As I said . . .' He was folding socks now but still regarding her steadily. 'If you're in on your own, just take the usual precautions. Even if you don't care about your own safety or your possessions, I'd like to be sure *my* stuff isn't burgled.'

'Charming!'

'I heard that,' said Kitt, having turned away to gather toiletries. 'And I was only joking. Good heavens, Chloe, your Ma would kill me if anything happened to her precious little daughter!' He looked dead straight, but Chloe thought she detected a hint of a smirk. Which might mean the return of the old, easy-going Kitt.

'If anything happened to me, she'd tear you limb from limb, or at least batter you to death with a copy of "Country Life"!' Chloe imagined her genteel parent transformed by murderous maternal fury. 'She thinks you keep a constant check on me, you know. Protecting me against the iniquities of the terrible Big

11

City. I'm not sure how she thinks you manage your own job if you're shadowing me 24/7 though.'

'Oh, I just scribble bijou little house plans for a living.' Kitt studied his open bag thoughtfully. 'I'm sure that's what everyone thinks architects do. It's easy peasy . . . I just dash them off on the backs of envelopes in my spare moments.'

'Yes, well, people think modelling is a piece of cake too.' Chloe thought of nights when she'd been too tired to see straight, and days when the perfectionist tantrums of fashion photographers and stylists made her want to scream 'It's like acting. You have to be all things to all people.'

'You have to be too thin.' Kitt's eyes narrowed. 'And if it's so easy, maybe I should take it up? I need a rest.' There was a slight smile on his face now, and not one Chloe particularly liked. He would make a fabulous male model though.

'Look, I'm not going to get into *that* again.' This was a regular dispute of theirs, the merits of fashion modelling, and Kitt was a cool and logical debater who often wrong-footed her. She knew he thought she should get a 'proper, worthwhile job', preferably involving a lot of studying. She didn't want to tell him she was already making plans though, in case it all fell through. The way he was now, he'd probably laugh at her anyway.

12

'Good. Because I don't like arguing either.' He gave her another smile; this time the lopsided, boyish one that she *did* like. She didn't see it often nowadays, but that made her cherish it all the more. When Kitt's green eyes flashed like that, and his grave, narrow face crinkled in a grin, it was impossible to believe he was thirty-five. He looked more like her contemporary than her unofficial 'guardian'.

'Let's not part on bad terms, Chloe,' he said, more gently.

'You're only going for a fortnight, Kitt.' Chloe shivered, suddenly fearing a disaster and a much longer parting. Even this prickly phase was better than not seeing him at all. 'And if you're so bothered about my welfare, you can ring me. Tokyo isn't the dark side of the moon, you know.'

'I might just do that,' Kitt had said, returning to his packing.

But you didn't ring, did you?

Chloe rubbed her neck. She'd got a crick in it from staring at the ceiling. Kitt had left a couple of brief voicemails, which to be fair was all Chloe had expected. What with her busy schedule and his, plus an eight-hour time difference, communications were bound to be tricky.

All the more reason to come and see me now!

But he hadn't done that. He'd remained alone, upstairs, in magnificent isolation.

13

Well, tough, Garbo, because I'm coming upstairs whether you like it or not!

In the bathroom, checking herself out, though, second thoughts came.

Is it my fault, Kitt? Chloe thought as she studied her reflection. I wish you'd tell me what I've done.

Her face offered no answers. It was just the image of an undeniably good-looking young woman. A pretty face that seemed to cut no ice with Kitt.

Chloe wasn't ashamed of her own vanity. She would never have been able to function in the fashion business without a healthy appreciation of her own assets. But she knew she was more than just a face and figure. It was nice to have regular features, striking blue eyes, and a slender body to go with them, but these were simply the tools of her trade. Tools she was utilising in readiness for a future that didn't particularly involve looking fabulous. A career where Kitt might respect her for her mind.

Maybe I should start looking the part? Chloe smoothed her fingertip along the arc of one immaculately groomed eyebrow. Maybe I should dress down in utilitarian grunge and a 'nothing' hairstyle? She scooped back her thick autumn brown hair into a bunch and confined it with a scrunchie—then using a lick of gel, she tamed the stray tendrils that she usually left free to look messily sexy.

But that didn't work. The severe hairstyle made her cheekbones look higher, and her eyes even larger and bluer. Frowning, she rubbed off her lip-gloss too—but that just made her curvy mouth look rosier.

'Oh, stuff it!' It was ironic really. Girls and women the length of the country would give anything to have her face, her body, and her job. Many went through agonies to get what she had been granted as a gift. She enjoyed exercise, but she'd never had to diet and her beauty regime was very simple. She couldn't imagine ever having to resort to plastic surgery.

You should be thanking your lucky stars for this, girl! she thought, drawing her fingertips in a heart shape around her face. And yet still she wondered what it would be like to be plain but blindingly academic, instead of beautiful and just reasonably intelligent.

Still, she wasn't about to wear a bag over her head, so she decided to make the most of herself, as normal.

The water upstairs had stopped flowing, so Kitt was probably towelling himself dry now. Wow, thought Chloe longingly, remembering the endless-seeming golden week-ends of her teens when she and Kitt—the man, rather than boy next door—had loafed about in her mother's garden, discussing life, the universe, and everything. He'd treated her like a child then, but it hadn't mattered because that was

15

more or less what she'd been. But at least he'd made her feel clever and capable of discussions and friendly arguments. Now he just treated her as if she was thick most of the time—or, at least, that was often how it seemed.

Oh, this is so stupid!

Her own negativity enraged her. All this soul-searching was a waste of energy. She wanted to see Kitt again—and, if he wouldn't come down, she'd have to go up. He was—according to her mother—supposed to be keeping an eye on her, wasn't he? He couldn't do that through a ceiling!

'Right then, you, get ready!' growled Chloe, psyching herself up as if for a camera or a catwalk. You're going to have to clap those gorgeous green eyes of yours on me, whether you like it or not. Lifting her chin, she tugged out the scrunchie and mussed up her hair again into an untidy topknot with trailing wisps.

Next, her face. Lip-gloss, three carefully-combed coats of mascara and a smudged line of slate grey kohl around each eye. Should she go the whole hog and change her clothes?

There was plenty of time. Judging by the sound of the pipes, Kitt was back in the shower. He must have had to answer the phone or something, although Chloe hadn't heard it.

After holding a few things against her,

Chloe decided to stick with what she was wearing—a pair of denim cut-offs and a loose, black T-shirt. She didn't want to appear to be trying too hard, and she'd probably done enough already with the hair and make-up.

'This is *me*, Kitt,' she told him as she adjusted a silky trailing tendril against her cheek. 'I can't deny what I am—why on earth should I?'

She was talking to herself again. The man was driving her mad. She did nothing these days but run pointless hypothetical scenarios and conduct imaginary conversations with *him*. Delicious self-indulgent fantasies wouldn't have been so bad, but it was mostly theoretical arguments. And lost ones, at that!

Eyeing the cold-water tap, Chloe felt like dowsing her head under it. Anything to brace herself. If she went upstairs expecting trouble, she'd probably get it. Better to be casual, neither gushing nor defensive. That way, Kitt could find no cause for irritation, and he might even be pleased to see her. After all, a change was supposed to be as good as a rest, and two weeks in Japan was a pretty big change.

As ready as she could make herself, Chloe looked around, wishing she had a calling card other than sheer desperation.

In a second, she had it.

Boy had vanished.

Which probably meant that her chunky, irresistible cat had already gone where she feared to tread.

On the upper landing, Chloe dithered. To knock or not to knock? She didn't used to have to. She and Kitt had been forever popping in and out of each other's parts of the house, and their doors had always been open to one another.

Not so now. There were invisible demarcation lines and it was all very confusing and unpleasant

Pushing open the heavy varnished door, she walked cautiously into Kitt's elegant, yet cosy, living area.

'Hello! Anyone home?' She aimed her voice at the door in the corner which led into his bedroom and *en suite* bathroom, one of the new 'no-go' areas.

'Yo, Kitt! It's me!' she called out softly, almost afraid to make herself heard.

'It's OK. Come on through!' answered his familiar, velvety voice, which for the moment sounded indistinct and muffled.

Oh, my God! Had the Iron Curtain been temporarily lifted? She pursed her lips, then immediately regretted it because she'd smeared her lip-gloss. Surreptitiously wiping her mouth, she obeyed Kitt's summons.

Once in the cream and fawn-hued bedroom, she let out her breath. Kitt wasn't there, he was still in the bathroom. Boy, however, was present. The large black-and-white cat was sleeping the sleep of the 'couldn't care less'

18

right on the centre of Kitt's previously pristine charcoal-grey suit jacket.

Chloe couldn't be angry with Boy—cats that loved humans always slept on their clothes—but she did feel furious with the owner of the suit. He was going out, the swine! Going out and leaving her when he'd only just got home. A fresh white shirt hung from the wardrobe door, and there were socks and underwear lying on the bed beside Boy and the suit.

Is this what we're reduced to nowadays, Kitt? she thought, giving the comatose Boy a gentle prod. Snatched conversations accompanied by clean socks and shirts? She felt bitter and hurt and, as if sensing this, the wily Boy remained immobile.

'Get off there, you bulbous monster!' she remonstrated, getting insolent indifference, a tail swish and a single opened eye in response.

'I beg your pardon!'

Chloe looked up, saw Kitt in the doorway and something went 'boom-bang!' in her mid-section.

Barefoot, and wearing just a towel, Kitt was breathtaking. There was no other way to describe him. Although he was a highly respected, thirty-five-year-old architect, he looked far more of an exotic wild boy than any of the male models Chloe often worked with. Somehow beyond age and convention, he looked just the same to Chloe's hungry eyes as he had done when they'd hung out together in her mother's garden, having long and ludicrous conversations about Star Trek and Doctor Who.

'Hello, little mate,' he said softly, 'have you missed me?'

It was like being released from prison. He sounded so friendly and warm. He'd called her 'little mate' . . . she could hardly believe her ears after all the weeks of prickliness, and she wanted to jump up and down and shout with relief.

To her horror though, Chloe wasn't able to answer him. She was almost in tears, and 'casual' had disintegrated. All she could do was stare—her mouth open helplessly—at the tall man who was walking slowly towards her, still rubbing his wet hair with a second towel.

Like a warrior angel, she thought numbly. A mythical hero, all dark, storm-tossed curls and smouldering deep-green eyes.

Standing about six feet in height, Kittrick Maynard wasn't a massively built man, but his body was strong and hard and tempered. He's powerful, thought Chloe, but it's only through long hours of sweat and pain. She was in awe, even now, at the amount of work Kitt had put himself through to recover his fitness. Only the thin silvery scars on his legs bore witness to what he'd gone through, although at the time it'd been touch-and-go whether he'd walk again.

But it wasn't his awesome determination

that Chloe was impressed by at the moment. She found it impossible to wrench her gaze from Kitt's bare skin, and the way his wet hair curled around his ears and at the back of his neck. In a finely-etched and ever-so-slightly haughty face, Kitt's green eyes were dangerously penetrating, and his mouth was a conundrum, determined yet tender. Chloe blushed, thinking of certain lucid dreams she'd been having lately.

'Well?'

Chloe lost it, and banished all her plans to be adult and cool like Kitt . . .

'Oh Kitt!' Darting forward, she threw her arms around him. 'I *have* missed you! Really I have!' His skin was smooth and warm and, if he'd let her, she would have clung to him until the universe guttered. Hugging him, she felt that she'd come home too, but from a far greater distance than Japan.

'Steady on! Watch the towel.'

Gently extricating himself from her grip, Kitt hitched the white terrycloth more securely around his waist and, as Chloe stepped back, she saw something chill in his eyes—and could have kicked herself! For a minute, things had been back to normal between them again . . . and then she'd blown it by throwing herself at him and grabbing him!

But, suddenly, Kitt smiled and it almost felt as if the sun had just risen, even though really it was almost time for it to set.

21

'And I'm glad to see you too, kiddo.'

There was an edgy moment as Kitt retrieved the towel he'd been using on his hair. Folding it compulsively, he seemed unhappy that Chloe was staring at his chest.

Yet why? Before the 'big freeze', she'd seen him in just as little. He'd swum and sunbathed with her wearing trunks that didn't leave much to the imagination, and even fairly recently she'd seen him shirtless. This easy familiarity had cut both ways too. Kitt had often seen her in just a bikini or a bathrobe. And, in the old days, he'd never found this at all alarming.

'I . . . I was looking for Boy,' Chloe muttered, trying to get a grip on herself. 'And unfortunately I've found him!' She glanced towards the furry black-and-white bulk reclining like a pasha on Kitt's suit.

'You certainly have!' Kitt grimaced. Chloe knew he was as soft about Boy as she was, but right now the big tom was nobody's favourite. 'Come on, you gross fool!' He swept the cat gently but firmly on to the floor. 'I've to go out in that.'

'Don't go out! You've only just got back!'

Idiot! You've done it again! Inwardly, Chloe cursed herself. 'I—I mean . . . you must be tired. All those time zones and everything.'

'I'll live,' Kitt murmured absently, holding up his jacket and flicking at the cat hairs. 'I have to go. Geraldine's picking me up. We're going out to dinner. There's something she

22

wants to discuss, and apparently it won't wait.' Abandoning the jacket, he picked up the trousers instead. Chloe frowned. He was so tense and tired, he really needed sleep.

Hell's teeth! Didn't that egocentric creature ever think of anyone but herself?

If she hadn't been so worried about Kitt, Chloe knew she would have laughed at her own special pleading. It was OK for *her* to pester Kitt when he was jet-lagged, but not his ex-wife. Geraldine was being selfish.

It's different though, thought Chloe, beginning to hunt around for Kitt's silver-backed clothes brush. I've got Kitt's welfare at heart and Geraldine only cares about herself. The horrible witch!

Don't be so childish! said the voice of inner reason as she found the brush and held her hand out to Kitt for his jacket. 'Let me do it. I'm used to getting that renegade's fur off my clothes.'

'Thanks, you're a star.' Kitt gave her the jacket but kept the trousers. 'Actually, he hasn't really decorated these. I think they'll be OK.' With a shrug, he teased a couple of stray hairs off anyway.

The reason you don't like Geraldine, Chloe told herself—brushing furiously while Kitt painstakingly scrutinised his trousers—isn't because she's horrible, but because she has access to Kitt in a way you don't. And she's been closer to him than you ever have. Or are ever likely to be.

But why *did* Kitt continue to spend so much time with his ex-wife?

Chloe beat at the jacket with brute force. Kitt and Geraldine had been divorced since not long before Chloe's move to London, but they still met regularly for dinners and drinks and who knew what else!

Suddenly, Chloe realised her inner debate must be showing, because Kitt had moved closer and was staring at her, searchingly.

'I really do have to go, Chloe,' he said, sounding uncomfortable. 'I wouldn't otherwise, but it sounds as if Lady Barbara is about to change her will again . . .' He sighed, '. . . and Geraldine probably wants to know what I know.'

'Oh, not that again,' said Chloe, setting aside the jacket out of Boy's way this time, and returning the antique silver brush to the dressing table. Avoiding Kitt's eyes, she picked up a bottle of aftershave, and took a deep sniff of his clean and manly scent. 'Yes, that again, I'm afraid,' he said from somewhere behind her. Sounding dispirited he continued, 'I wish it could be sorted out just as much as anyone. Lady Barbara needs to make a decision and be done with it. Then we could all make plans.' Chloe could hear him gathering his socks, underwear and shirt. 'I don't care if I lose claim to Arrowsmith Court. I've got this place and it suits me, and it's not as if I'm even a

24

relation.'

Was this really how he felt? Chloe knew how fond Kitt was of Lady Barbara Arrowsmith, and how much he admired the architectural beauty of her country home. He might be resisting a desire that was very understandable . . .

Chloe wasn't up to speed on the situation regarding Arrowsmith Court, but she did know that it was an unusual one. Lady Barbara Arrowsmith was a benefactress to both Kitt and Geraldine's families, through old, old friendships, and it seemed that she'd now got it into her head that the scions of those two families should be reunited in marriage. The fact that Kitt and Geraldine had divorced once for incompatibility meant nothing to the eccentric old lady.

Of course, things would have been clearer cut if Kitt and Geraldine had parted acrimoniously. But their continued friendship left Lady Barbara with grounds for hope. It was a bit like a 1920s social farce.

'But you've been kind to her,' Chloe pointed out, trying to sound disinterested. 'And you'll take the best care of the Court. With Geraldine's business record, she'd probably make it into an executive conference centre or something. She's one of the few Americans I know who doesn't go gaga over English heritage.'

'That's as may be. But we needn't worry

right at this moment, so let's drop the subject, shall we?' Kitt sounded hostile again, and Chloe knew she'd wrong-footed herself. Badmouthing Geraldine didn't say much for her own personality.

I might as well wear a sign around my neck saying 'spoiled brat!' she thought glumly. She was just about to apologise, when Kitt suddenly seemed to mellow and change tack.

'You don't really mind about me going out, do you?'

'Not in the slightest!' Chloe lied, 'I'm going out myself later anyway.' She turned away and lined up his clothes brush and matching hairbrush with military precision.

'Who with?' Kitt's vehemence pleased Chloe immensely. 'Do I know him?'

'His name's . . . um . . . Richard Brown,' Chloe extemporised furiously, avoiding Kitt's focused green gaze. 'He's in PR . . . videos and stuff.'

'Well, promise me you'll be careful. After all the horror stories you've told me about that breed, I would've thought you'd run a mile from anyone in the advertising business,' Kitt said gravely, making Chloe think of a Victorian Papa admonishing his daughter. 'We had some PR guys making a promo at Maynard-Marsham before I left, and apparently they're all either sex maniacs or alcoholics. Which didn't seem to put the typing pool off, of course.' Maynard-Marsham was the architectural consortium of which Kitt was a senior partner.

Chloe was well aware of the peccadilloes of advertising and PR men, and had her own very effective strategies for dealing with them. What she couldn't see was why any woman at Maynard-Marsham would want to waste even a passing glance on such unprincipled scumbags, when they had a gorgeous man like Kitt around every day to feast their eyes on!

Silly as it seemed, she felt almost sorry for the hastily invented 'Richard'. She couldn't summon up even the slightest bit of enthusiasm for him or, indeed, for any other man.

With Kitt around, no other man stood a chance!

CHAPTER THREE

Am I in love with him? thought Chloe, flicking through one of Kitt's architectural journals, admiring the photographs. And if I am, when did I actually *fall* in love? I don't remember it happening.

Wondering what settings had been used for a stunning shot of a futuristic shopping mall, Chloe tried hard *not* to think of Kitt getting changed in the next room. But she still kept seeing him instead of the building.

'Kitt! Don't tempt me,' she muttered. Even if she wasn't sure when she'd fallen in love with Kitt, she certainly knew that she fancied him now. And she had done so as long as she'd understood the feeling.

During her childhood, she'd had the mother of all crushes on him, and especially when he'd had his car smash and she'd been his special friend and confidante. They'd drifted apart, naturally, when he'd met and married Geraldine, but since she'd been living here in London—under what her mother fondly believed was his protection—Chloe had reclassified her crush as a harmonious grown-up friendship.

Until recently, that was.

Just as she was peering at the picture credits for the shopping mall, Kitt's voice made her jump as if she'd been stealing from him.

'So, what have you been up to while I've been in Japan?' He adjusted his tie as he crossed the room, and his dark brows lifted as he questioned her. 'Well? Surely there's been something exciting. Gallery openings. Charity bashes. Perfume launches. I thought life was just one big party for you supermodels.'

Her resentment flared. He was getting at her again. Until fairly recently, he'd viewed her modelling life with an almost amused equanimity but, all of a sudden, he seemed actively disapproving. Either that or it was *her* he didn't particularly like any more.

'Well, for one thing, I'm not a supermodel. I'm not thin enough,' she said defensively, pleased that she'd managed not to screw his magazine up and throw it at him in a temper. 'And it's both possible, and quite common, to lead a quiet, normal life as well as being a model.' Uncurling her legs, she rose to her feet. Although she wasn't a six-footer like Kitt, being tall always helped when she was arguing. 'Which you well know, Kitt, because that's the life *I* lead.' She laid her spread hand against her chest for emphasis.

Kitt gave her a look as if to say 'what about the film premiere, the book launch, and the charity tapas party, all in the week prior to my Japanese trip?' but Chloe ignored it. OK, she'd been in demand lately. But that didn't mean she espoused the whole 'party girl' ethic. She wasn't shallow. She had goals, and she knew she possessed the self-discipline to achieve them.

'OK, I've been busy,' she said, trying not to sound riled, 'I did an editorial for "Riva", a promo for "Century Woman" . . . oh, and a few sessions for next year's "Pizzazz" catalogue,' she went on. 'All indoor stuff, because it's been raining cats and dogs here . . .' Raining in my heart, she thought, because you were away . . .' And some house modelling for Rose, too. She's planning to do ready-to-wear, for catalogues and the high street.'

'Isn't your cousin Rose's stuff a bit elitist for

that sort of thing?' Kitt was at the mirror now, combing his still damp hair. Chloe adored the way his thick black curls fought the imposition of order.

'Not really.' Chloe sprang to the defence of her cousin, a talented fashion designer, known for her fairy-tale party wear. 'They all do it. It's more creative. More of a challenge.' She picked up Kitt's jacket, scrutinising it to avoid him scrutinising her. 'She hasn't sold out or anything. She's just giving more women a chance to enjoy her work.'

'Well, I bow to your superior knowledge of the fashion world.' Kitt turned elegantly, holding his arms out behind him for the jacket. Chloe grimaced. He was so sure of himself, yet she couldn't bring herself not to chuck his jacket over the chair and ask him what his last servant had died of.

'But what about your social life? What about "Richard"? Haven't you seen him?' Kitt was paying minute attention to his shirt cuffs now. His whole body seemed to be a long, wanting line and Chloe winced at the underlying criticism. His low, beautiful voice was studiously cool.

What's it to you, you monster? she wanted to screech at him. Just because *you* won't deign to look at me as a woman, it doesn't mean other men don't. Just for a second, she wished that Richard was real and she could tell Kitt she'd slept with him.

30

'Once or twice,' she muttered, 'You know . . .' Coward! You should be trying to shock him, not placate him.

'No, I don't know . . . you tell me.' Superficially, Kitt appeared to be looking around for something but Chloe knew that she finally had his full attention. When she managed to look at him, his eyes were intent, almost deadly, and that scared her. It also made her want to shout in triumph.

Ah ha! Now you're taking notice!

'He's just a friend,' she said airily, 'I like him, but it's nothing serious.'

Kitt's scrutiny didn't waver by a millimetre. 'And what exactly does that mean? In this day and age . . .'

'"In this day and age"?' she mimicked, still scared but amused too. 'Get real, Kitt, we're in the third millennium not the Dark Ages. Stop acting like a narrow-minded schoolmaster!' She stumbled there, aware that he *was* a teacher, of sorts, and certainly a mentor. 'It's insulting! I'm not some promiscuous little nitwit who's going to end up on the front page of the tabloids. I know how to behave.' She picked up the clothes brush again, then dropped it because her fingers had flexed to hit him with it. 'I—I'm sorry, but you annoy me.' There was a horrible silence.

'No. You're right. It's me who should be apologising. I didn't mean to belittle you.' Kitt's manner was so serious it made Chloe quiver all over. 'But you must realise I've a responsibility towards you.' He stopped and fiddled with a cufflink as he seemed to prepare his next words.

'Look, we both know that your mother has unrealistic ideas about the way people live their lives today . . . but I did promise her I'd look out for you, Chloe.' He gave her a small but very direct grin that made Chloe feel very hot and strange. 'And I *do* care about your welfare.'

Then do something about it, you fool! Chloe wanted to shout. One touch from you, one real touch, would do a lot more for my welfare than any amount of surveillance ever could.

'Yeah, OK, I know,' she said grudgingly, wishing she had the guts to declare herself. They'd been so close in many ways, and even the gap in their ages wasn't that enormous. Ma wasn't the only one whose opinions were unrealistic.

Yet she couldn't do it. The risk was too great. This was their best moment in weeks. She mustn't rock the boat.

'Don't worry, Kitt,' she went on, trying to sound reasonable. 'I'm more sensible than I seem, honestly. I've given a good deal of thought to relationships, and I'm certainly not serious about anyone yet.' Liar! cried the real Chloe, who'd never been more serious in her life. 'So, just trust me, will you Kitt?' She smiled, trying to appear both cheerful and adult. 'I won't let you down.'

'I know that, and I *do* trust you.' Kitt's green eyes were so intense that Chloe's good intentions were in jeopardy. 'But aren't you a bit young to make sweeping statements about relationships?' About to protest, Chloe realised that he wasn't joking, although he didn't look quite as sure of himself as he'd sounded. 'You've hardly had time for any kind of relationship. Or, at least, I hope you haven't!'

Chloe didn't know whether to laugh or cry. She hadn't made any progress with him at all it seemed, and now Kitt seemed just as entrenched as ever. His intentions were good and he did care, but he couldn't seem to credit her with even the tiniest bit of good sense.

'For heaven's sake, Kitt! I'm twenty-four, not fourteen!' she shouted. She also wanted to point out that Kitt was only thirty-five himself. Far too young to be such an 'old fogey'!

Kitt's eyes were apologetic, yet strangely bitter. 'I'm sorry, Chloe, I'm doing it again, aren't I? Doubting you.' His lips quirked and he gave a little shrug. 'It's just that you're an extraordinarily beautiful young woman in a voyeuristic, exploitative business. You could easily turn a man's head without realising it. I can't help thinking that you're in danger.' He paced a little, turning away, then returning to her. 'I don't mean to be oppressive, Chloe, but

I fear for you. I wish I *could* protect you in the way your mother thinks I do.'

'But I don't want protecting!' cried Chloe, spinning away herself, so he couldn't see that she was lying again. 'And I don't need it! I'm not an idiot, Kitt. I don't lead men on!'

'Hey! Take it easy!' Kitt caught her shoulders and made her face him. Chloe tensed, terrified she'd give herself away. 'Let's forget this subject, shall we? I'll trust you, Chloe, if you'll be careful . . . deal?'

'Deal,' agreed Chloe with a sigh. She suddenly felt much better. Was the 'big freeze' over? Her shoulders, at least, where he held her, felt warm and tingly.

But just as she was starting to enjoy herself, Kitt released her and started looking for his watch.

'And what about the photography? Have you taken any stunning pictures lately?' Watch found, he was at the window now, looking out. His face was hidden, so Chloe couldn't tell whether he was being facetious. She hoped not.

Why wouldn't anyone take her photography seriously? Kitt, most of all, should be pleased she was pursuing something creative.

He can't be pleased if you don't tell him the whole story though, thought Chloe. She was still keeping the true extent of her plans a secret, in case they came to nothing.

'Are you really interested?' Immediately

she'd spoken, Chloe regretted sounding combative. Paranoia was getting the better of her again.

'Yes, I am.' He turned from the window, his face showing that he meant it. 'How have you been doing?'

'Well, I've not had a lot of time . . .' She stalled, painfully aware that her best photographs would always be of Kitt, she realised, no matter how impromptu, or how unpromising the conditions were. But there was no future in photographing just one man, no matter how photogenic he was. 'What with one thing and another . . .' Was Kitt frowning? 'But I've got a few clear days now, so I'm going to get down to it and really give the Nikon some mileage.'

Genuine interest flared in Kitt's green eyes. 'So you got one then?'

Got one. What a way to speak of such an object of desire. Kitt and the camera had a lot in common, she thought, hiding a smile. Both were the finest in their class and, if she was to make him proud, she had to have the best equipment.

'Yes!' she said proudly, 'Do you want to see it? I could take your picture, if you like?' For a moment, she tried to see him with her artistic eye, as a structure of flesh and blood and bone, not the beloved image who haunted her day and night. 'You'd make a fabulous model. You've got the bone structure, height,

35

everything!'

She'd meant it as a compliment, but Kitt frowned, making her want to kick herself.

'It'd be a waste of good film,' he said, checking his wallet for his credit cards.

'OK then, but at least let me show you the camera?' Chloe hid her disappointment. He was hateful when he was so peremptory.

'Perhaps another day?' Kitt's tone was mellower this time, signalling that he'd noticed her annoyance. She immediately forgave him. 'When there's more time to appreciate all the refinements.' He moved to the window again, looking downwards. For Geraldine.

Why is he always so eager to see her? Chloe wondered resentfully. They're divorced. Why can't he loathe her and never want to see her again, like a normal person?

'OK. Fine. Whenever . . .' What good were new cameras and new ambitions, when he wasn't interested? She turned away, ready to leave and relinquish him to Geraldine.

'What about another of our days out in the country some time soon?' said Kitt without warning. 'We could call at your mother's maybe, or go down to the coast? That way, you'd get a whole variety of subjects. Houses and cottages. Landscapes. Boats. Holidaymakers.'

Chloe whirled again. Was there such a thing as an auditory illusion? This was the old Kitt, trying to make her feel better with a kind gesture. The man she thought she'd lost or, worse still, driven away.

'Er . . . yes.' Her heart was pounding and she wanted to hug him again. But that was what silly little girls did, so she just smiled graciously, 'That would be wonderful, Kitt. Fantastic. Just let me know when you've got a free day.' Then, knowing she was still in extreme danger, she changed the subject.

'So how was the Land of the Rising Sun?' She hesitated, hoping her enquiry didn't sounded too much like 'duty'. 'What was the "honolable client-san" like?'

Still studying the driveway, Kitt answered. 'Mr Watanabe? A tad formal, but otherwise great. He liked my sketches but he still wants me to see more traditional buildings.'

Kitt was shortly to design the new British headquarters of a major Japanese multi-national. It should have been a fairly routine project for an architect of Kitt's stature, but the client wanted a building that was both essentially Japanese in character and yet in harmony with its English surroundings. Consequently, Kitt had been on an all-expenses paid trip to Japan, to study traditional architecture. Chloe was half-expecting him to say they had decided they wanted paper walls too!

'Ah! Before I forget.'

Suddenly, Kitt produced two large, shiny-paper carrier bags and was holding them out towards Chloe. 'You get first pick. They're not the full ceremonial jobs, I'm afraid. But they're more authentic than anything you'll get in London.' He jiggled the carriers temptingly. 'Go on, have a look.'

Within the bags were two exquisite silk kimonos and, after one peek, Chloe knew which she wanted. The turquoise one with birds and willow trees was beautiful—but the ruby-red one, with fire-breathing dragons, was completely *her!* With painstaking care, she arranged the feather-light garment on Kitt's bed to examine it.

It was glorious! She picked it up and draped it against her, blinking away sudden tears. 'Oh Kitt, it's lovely! Thank you so much. I don't deserve this!'

The words sounded woefully inadequate and, clutching the exotic red treasure against her body, Chloe shivered. Forbidden images formed, and she felt confused and horrified. Surely Kitt couldn't realise how much he'd hurt her?

The kimono was a lover's gift, but Kitt didn't care for her in that way. 'Thank you, Kitt,' she repeated, feeling bleak.

A car horn blared outside and Kitt was back at the window. The recipient of the turquoise kimono had arrived, and that soured Chloe's pleasure in her own gift. Even more ominously, Kitt was showing no sign of taking Geraldine's gift with him. He left it lying on the bed—as if in readiness to be tried on later.

A crushing pain hit Chloe. If Geraldine returned to Kitt's flat after dinner—and stayed—there was every chance they'd end up getting back together again. Chloe could almost hear the explanations now. 'We can't go to the country after all, Chloe. Please try to understand. Geraldine and I have decided to . . .'

'Hey, dreamer! Wake up!' Kitt patted her gently on the shoulder. The little touch made her tremble, but she tried not to show it. 'I have to go now, and shouldn't you be getting ready to go out too?'

'Oh, yes! I'd forgotten!' Summoning fake enthusiasm for a fake boyfriend, Chloe picked up her gift and slid it into its bag, then followed Kitt downstairs, feeling lost and leaden.

Outside, Chloe was glad that the light was fading. That way, she didn't have to look too closely at Geraldine.

I shouldn't let her get to me, she thought, admiring Kitt's former wife's sleek red Porsche. Apart from Kitt, I've probably got everything she wants. I'm young, I'm pretty. For crying out loud, even Kitt thinks I'm a supermodel! Summoning the smile that made photographers sigh with ecstasy, she gave Geraldine a wave and received a token acknowledgement back. She couldn't see what her rival was wearing—Geraldine remained in

39

the car, clearly keen to be off—but no doubt it would be a big designer label. The sort of thing Chloe often modelled, but a far cry from the clothes she actually liked.

Geraldine could be a model too, thought Chloe, gritting her teeth when the horn sounded again, summoning Kitt as if he were a faithful dog.

But maybe not . . . Chloe felt a savage satisfaction in the sharpness that slightly spoiled the older woman's features.

The extremes of dewy youth were what was currently 'in' at the moment and Chloe knew that, at twenty-four, even she was pushing the envelope.

The elegant blonde gunned the engine. 'Do come on, Kittrick! We'll lose our table!' she called.

Chloe grinned awkwardly at Kitt. 'Have a nice evening.' Twisting the handles of her carrier bag around her fingers, she hoped she didn't sound grudging.

'You too.' His smooth brow crumpled. 'Don't forget what I said, will you?'

'About what?'

'Being careful.'

'Of course not!' she snapped, too upset now to even care what he thought. 'I . . .' She turned away rapidly, hiding her emotions. It was OK to seem irritated, but anything else was sad and pathetic. 'Good night, Kitt!' she called over her shoulder, already running.

She was back in her flat, sniffling and cursing, as the Porsche roared away.

CHAPTER FOUR

'But why on earth did you tell him you have a boyfriend, if you want *him* to be your boyfriend?'

Chloe suddenly couldn't remember why she'd invented the mythical Richard, and it was obvious her cousin Rose didn't understand either. Beautiful Rose frowned, and shook her mass of auburn curls.

'*Boy*friend? I thought you said this guy was thirty-five? That's not a boy.' Chloe's other cousin, Florence, was a writer and sometimes inclined to be pedantic.

'Perhaps he's young at heart?' suggested Rose.

'Sometimes he is.' Chloe fidgeted with her glass, thinking about Kitt's incessant warnings to her about 'taking care'.

'Admit it, he's a miserable old sod, isn't he?' Grinning, Florence pushing her fingers through her short elfin-cut hair. 'Lord save us from difficult men, eh, cuz?'

The three cousins were gathered at Rose's flat, which adjoined her design atelier and her shop in Chelsea, and it was a council of war, convened at Chloe's request.

41

'Why, is Jacob playing you up again?' Jacob was Florence's fiancé, another Trevelyan cousin and a temperamental actor.

Florence's sparky, intelligent face became dreamy for a moment. 'No, he's fine,' she said. 'And never mind the bane of my life, Chloe. It's your chap we're supposed to be sorting out. Why is he such a misery?'

'I'd say Kitt was a thoughtful, serious type,' chipped in Rose. 'But not a misery. No, certainly not.'

Thoughtful? Serious? But he hadn't always been, thought Chloe, remembering a rainy day during Kitt's convalescence when they'd spent an entire afternoon trading chicken jokes, and only had to stop because Kitt was laughing so hard he was making his injured legs ache.

'Kitt has a great sense of humour,' she added, 'or should I say, he used to.'

'Perhaps he's got something on his mind?' suggested Rose.

That was true. 'Yes, he has. His horrible "ex" keeps bothering him about Lady Barbara's will and all that. And he's got this tricky commission . . .' She hesitated. 'But mainly he just seems to be annoyed with me.'

'Chloe.' Florence's look was long and level. 'Maybe he has difficulty expressing emotions, and it just comes out wrong?'

'I don't know,' Chloe said doubtfully, 'I really don't know what to think.'

'Perhaps you should tell him how you feel?'

suggested Rose, who was romantic but practical.

'Let him see you in a new light,' said Florence. 'You say you used to be pals? Well, why not try and project yourself more as lover material? Nothing too obvious, just show him the potential's there.'

Chloe frowned. It would be like opening a keg of dynamite. It was too dangerous.

'Do you ever go out together? Have you ever really pulled out all the stops to impress him? My God, Chloe, you're a top model . . . you could slay him!'

'I always play it down around him. I don't like to remind him of what I do. He doesn't approve.' She pursed her lips, resigned to Kitt's preference. 'He never comes right out and says so . . . but I once pointed out a billboard of myself to him—and he gave me a look as if he thought I was the whore of Babylon!'

'But surely Kitt knows you. He must realise that you have ambitions beyond modelling . . . that you'll move on when the time's right?'

'How did you know that?' Chloe was thunderstruck. She'd never actually said anything to her cousins about her plans.

'Er, Chloe, how thick do you think we are?' Florence shook her head despairingly. 'The way you jabber on about camera angles and lighting . . . the pictures you take . . . your cameras! Most normal people tend to carry

43

nippy little compacts. You're the only person I know who bothers with the whole kit and caboodle.'

'We know you want be a photographer, Chloe,' said Rose, grinning.

'Yes, that's a given,' said Florence briskly. 'Now, what are we going to do about this cantankerous Kitt of yours?'

'Why don't you invite him to the "Right to Walk" garden party? You are going to model for me, aren't you?' said Rose, giving Chloe a look almost as steely as some of Florence's. 'Invite him along. I can wangle a spare ticket if you don't have one.'

'Right to Walk' was a new charity that aimed to give disabled children and teenagers from deprived backgrounds access to better benefits and facilities. It was currently the hot 'cause' amongst the glitterati and a big garden party was to be held in the Thames-side mansion of a notable Rock and Roll millionaire.

Chloe wasn't one for conspicuous good works, but 'Right to Walk' had struck a chord in her because of Kitt's accident. She'd agreed to model Rose's designs in the garden party's charity fashion auction.

'Right, that's settled then,' said Florence roundly, reaching for another bit of the pizza they'd been sharing. 'Chloe brings Cranky Kitt to the garden party and knocks him dead. Problem sorted!'

But it was easier said than done. Firstly, Chloe was out of town for a few days on a fashion shoot in Wales and, secondly, Kitt was virtually inaccessible. He was a busy man—as busy as she was, really, and travelling just as much—but it almost seemed that he was actively avoiding her. He was either out, or leaving too early, or out too late.

But, finally, she got her moment. On the Friday before the Saturday of the garden party.

What if I'm wasting my time? she thought. What if he and Geraldine really are getting back together? And that's why he's been giving me the run-around?

The thought of Geraldine filled Chloe with a savage possessiveness. Kitt was hers! She wouldn't let his ex-wife have him!

When she hammered on his door, Kitt called out for her to come in, his voice distracted.

He was working and the room was cool and tranquil. The Humming Chorus from 'Madam Butterfly' was playing, and Kitt was bent over his big drawing board, his face and bare arms dramatically lit by the Anglepoise lamp. He wore jeans and a blue, round-necked cotton top with the sleeves pushed up to his elbows. Obviously, he was staying in and not going out.

45

'Oh, hi Chloe.' He looked up, then frowned. 'Is everything all right? You look a bit fierce. Is something wrong?' His smile was warm, despite the fact that—Chloe realised—she was scowling. 'We keep missing each other, don't we?'

I *always* miss you.

As he swivelled his lean body towards her, Chloe noticed that he was still holding his drafting pencil. He always worked on paper fast, before switching to computer-aided design in later stages, and it looked as if she'd caught him in full creative flow. Bad timing again, she realised. He wouldn't want to talk . . .

'Did you want something?' He snapped off the music with a remote and frowned at her continuing silence. 'Chloe?' he prompted.

'Would you like to come to a garden party?' Not the casual, circuitous approach she'd planned, alas.

'What, now? Isn't it a bit dark?' Grinning, he slid off his stool, only the faint tension in his jaw indicating that he'd been working so long that his bad leg had seized up slightly. 'Or are there floodlights?' he enquired, coming towards her.

'No! At least I don't think so . . . it's tomorrow.'

I'm babbling, thought Chloe, wanting to shake herself. Where was her composure? It seemed to disappear like Scotch mist whenever Kitt was around. She saw his glance flick over her—taking in her checked shirt knotted at her midriff, and her cerise Capri pants—and she felt even more inarticulate. Kitt's face was pale and enigmatic, his expression hard to fathom, while her cheeks were nearly as pink as her trousers.

'Well, Lord knows it's a cause I'm happy to support,' Kitt said, when Chloe had finally managed to describe the event and the charity. Apparently unconsciously, he rubbed the side of his bad knee slowly with his fingertips. 'And the NHS is so under-funded that somebody's got to do something . . .' He frowned, his fingertips still slowly circling. 'But, really, a garden party? It's not "me" really, is it? Can't I just make a donation?'

There was an impasse. Chloe didn't know how to press the issue, and Kitt clearly knew she didn't like his answer.

'Would you like a drink?' he said after a moment. 'Cola? Orange juice? Perrier?' Chloe noticed that Kitt was drinking white wine and she scowled. She barely ever drank, and then only a spritzer, but it would have been nice to have been offered a grown-up drink.

'No, thanks. I've got things to do, I can't stay,' she lied, longing to stay and watch him work. She could see something vaguely pagoda-shaped forming on his drawing board, obviously the Japanese computer centre. 'Will you come to the garden party or not?' she

47

finished, more sharply than she would have wished.

Kitt looked at her. 'I don't know, Chloe.' He picked up his glass and took a sip. 'Count on me for a donation but, really, these glitzy gatherings set my teeth on edge . . . I'm sure most people only go to them just to be seen.'

'What a cynical attitude!' cried Chloe, really angry. For a moment, she hated Kitt profoundly. How could he be such a wimp about a social gathering, yet so brave about physical suffering? Clearly, he just didn't want to go with *her.*

'I hope you weren't talking about me!' she went on, 'I know I've led a charmed life so far, but that doesn't mean I don't care about things!' She looked away, gathering herself. 'I'm not clever enough to be doctor or a scientist, so I just have to do things I *can* do . . . like modelling Rose's clothes so well that women with pots of money will be falling over themselves to make huge donations!' If she'd been alone she might have stamped her foot, but Kitt obviously thought she was childish enough already. 'And I shan't feel guilty about it, either!'

Chloe was horrified. Had she sounded as if she was calling Kitt mean? That was so unjust. He had a good heart, and would do anything for anybody. And that included her, even if he didn't like her all that much any more. The shocked look on his face made her heart drop.

Kitt put down his glass. He was even paler now. 'Forgive me, Chloe. I'm sorry,' he said with quiet dignity. 'I know you'd never take up arms for anything you didn't really believe in.' His eyes held hers, but they were dark and troubled. 'Don't mind me, I'm just being bitter and twisted.'

Chloe wanted to go to him. To embrace him, tell him that he was a good man, and that he was right about all those party-going pseudos.

She wanted to go to him—but a barrier stood between them. Kitt's long elegant fingers flexed slightly, as if he too was fighting inhibition.

'It's all right.' Chloe relaxed a little. 'I went over the top. It's me who should be sorry.'

'No you didn't.' Kitt's voice was very soft, and Chloe detected a note of supplication in it. He gestured to the wine bottle—a California Chardonnay. 'Would you like a glass of wine? Come on, sit down.' Without waiting for an answer, he poured her a glass and took it, with his, towards the coffee table and the sofa that stood adjacent.

Sipping the light, fresh wine, Chloe managed to tell Kitt a little more about 'Right to Walk'.

'So, will you come to the garden party then?' she asked eventually.

Kitt looked evasive. 'I don't know . . . I have a lot of work to do. And I still don't think it's

49

really my sort of event.'

'But it's Saturday tomorrow,' Chloe pointed out. 'You should take time off. And we don't know what the party will be like yet. You might even enjoy yourself.'

'Fashion shows? Rock music? Chloe, please . . .'

'You listen to all sorts of music! I've heard it.'

'Yes, but still . . . glitterati? And me? Not really . . .'

But you've got more glamour in your little toe than the whole of the celebrity scene put together! 'All sorts of people will be there. And I'm sure there'll be loads of boring old fogies in their dotage, just like you.' She felt a giggle building up inside her. 'You'll be able to mumble away to your heart's content about pension books and the war and the state of "youff today".'

Kitt laughed, his face looking extraordinarily boyish. 'Cheeky young witch! I'm not that old!'

'Exactly!' She rushed on, 'So there's no reason for you not to come.' She rose to her feet. It was time to go now, because if she stayed she might do something silly and spoil everything.

'I'll see,' he said, 'but I can't promise.'

Chloe felt her face fall.

'But I'll buy a ticket, just in case.' He uncurled his long body and stood up alongside her. She watched him make a decision. 'And I'll buy one of your dresses or whatever too . . . one of Rose's things. Choose which one you like best and, if I'm not there, get Rose or one of your other cousins to bid for it on my behalf.'

Chloe caught her breath at the beautiful gesture. She found herself grinning again, her heart warmed by Kitt's extravagance, but knowing she had to tell him a fashion home truth.

'That's a wonderful offer, Kitt,' she said quietly, then screwed up her courage and kissed him on the cheek. 'But it's too much. Really. Do you know how much Rose's designs cost?'

'They're only frocks, for goodness sake.'

'Couture dresses. Unique and original designs that have never even been on sale in Rose's shop.' After a moment's hesitation, she took a breath and named a figure.

Kitt's jaw dropped, and Chloe was forced to smile at the incredulity on his strong, handsome face.

'Maybe I should just buy a sleeve?' He glanced quickly at his drawing board, then grinned. 'I'm in the wrong business here. I should be designing dresses instead of buildings. I could've been a millionaire by now.'

'Actually, I bet you could design clothes . . . the basics are the same. Line. Proportion.

Harmony. A sense of form and place.' The words petered out, and she became aware that Kitt was looking at her with an almost admiring glint in his eye. 'Why don't you have a go,' she finished, deeply embarrassed.

'I'll stick to concrete, I think,' he said amiably. 'And leave the silk and satin to Rose and company.'

'She *is* worth it, you know,' said Chloe stoutly. 'Her designs are exquisite. Timeless. Actually good value in the long term.'

'I'm inclined to believe you.' Kitt sounded thoughtful. 'And I did mean what I said . . . even though the price tag is a touch more than I'd anticipated.'

Chloe blushed again, guilt making her feel hot. She hadn't meant for tiffs to happen; she'd just wanted Kitt to come to the garden party with her, not to get railroaded into a huge donation.

'You don't have to do that! Buying a ticket for the party is quite enough, honestly.' Another awkward fact occurred to her. If Kitt bought her one of Rose's designs, it would be like the kimono all over again, only a thousand-fold. An inherently sexual gift in an entirely platonic relationship.

Kitt sculpted lips thinned, as if he'd seen her point. 'Let's wait and see, shall we?' Suddenly, he sounded tired. 'I'll definitely buy a ticket, but I can't make any promises about going . . . and we'll discuss the business of the dress

52

tomorrow, shall we? It's very late, Chloe.' He smiled, plainly trying to lighten up. 'And if you're to look your most fabulous for this show of yours, you'll need all your beauty sleep, won't you?'

'Yes. I suppose you're right.' She was being manoeuvred out of Kitt's part of the house by a very subtle kind of *force majeure.*

He wanted rid of her. She'd failed. He still didn't think of her as a woman, and she'd bet good money he wouldn't turn up at the party.

'Maybe I should just stick to cats, eh?' she asked Boy a while later when she was getting ready for bed and still mulling over what Kitt had said. 'They're contrary . . .' Boy looked at her in perfect understanding, '. . . but they're nowhere near as wilful and awkward as men. And at least cats show their appreciation in the nicest possible way.' Purring loudly, the tomcat rolled over to have his belly tickled.

'Will you come to the party with me, Boy?' She ran her fingers over his soft, dense fur. 'Because if you don't, it looks as if I might be going alone.'

CHAPTER FIVE

You never had any intention of going, did you Kitt? Chloe looked up at the ceiling. You were just humouring me, that's all.

53

She had no other engagements on the day of the 'Right to Walk' garden party but, even so, Chloe had risen early. The fashion auction would be a piece of cake really, an informal runway show to display the clothes, no theatricals. There were no rehearsals—the models just had to turn up in time for fairly simple hair and make-up.

Chloe had hoped this would mean that she and Kitt could arrive together but, once she was out in the entrance hall, she realised this wasn't to be. Kitt was already coming down the stairs, dressed in jeans and a sweater, and carrying a bulging briefcase and his oversized leather portfolio.

'I take it you can't make the garden party after all?' Chloe said, fiddling with the buttons on her dungarees. She'd decided to dress down as she'd be changing soon anyway, and had popped a simple, flirty slip dress in her bag for later.

'Well, not just yet. I have to go in to the office for a while.'

Is he lying? thought Chloe. And, if he is, could I tell anyway? Kitt was a master of cool. He could hide his feelings like an emotional magician when it was necessary.

'Oh, I see.'

Chloe longed to spit venom and accuse him of never having had the slightest intention of going to the garden party, but she knew that would get her precisely nowhere. 'Never mind,' she went on lightly, 'there'll be tons of other people there I know. Just come later, if you can. I'm sure you'll enjoy yourself.'

'I'm sure I will,' replied Kitt dryly, fishing in his jeans pocket. 'But look, if I don't make it, this is for the ticket.' He held out two cheques, flicking the uppermost between his finger and thumb. 'And this is a donation to the fund.' He indicated the second cheque. 'I've had second thoughts about buying a dress. I don't mind the cost . . .' He really did look uneasy now. 'But I don't think it looks good somehow. People tend to put nasty interpretations on older men buying ostentatious clothes for younger women. You know what I mean?'

Ah yes, dear, darling Geraldine, thought Chloe. Of course. She wouldn't like it if you buy me a 'Rose Trevelyan' . . . typical!

'You don't mind, do you?' Kitt was flicking the cheques and frowning.

'Of course not.' Chloe mentally crossed her fingers. 'Why should I? You only just bought me a lovely kimono. I mustn't be greedy.' She reached for the cheques, then whistled when she saw the amount he was donating. 'You don't have to give this much, you know,' she added, feeling guilty again. She'd pressured him with her arguments, hadn't she?

'It's OK. I want to.' He trade a small, self-deprecating gesture. 'I thought about what you told me, and I did a bit of ferreting around on the Internet. It seems that they're *bona fide*

55

and doing sound work for the young disabled.'

Chloe felt a dangerous prickle of emotion. Her anger had disappeared and she so admired him. Kitt was a good man, it was just this stupid mess of timing and mismatched ages that made things difficult between them.

'Anyway, I have to be off now. I might see you later but, if I can't make it, just give those to the relevant people, will you?'

She nodded. 'I'll just look out for you then,' she muttered, 'in case you turn up.'

'Yes. Right. See you later.'

'See you later.'

As Kitt disappeared, Chloe shook her head, then returned to her flat and finished stuffing her kit disconsolately into her bag.

*   *   *

Standing in front of her destination, after paying for her taxi, Chloe wondered what Kitt would think of the bizarre structure behind the elaborate wrought-iron gates.

Lionsmead was the home of a world-famous Goth rock star and a clear case of rampant self-indulgence. Built on a huge plot of prime Thames-side land, it was a modern construction masquerading as a Byzantine pleasure palace. Kitt's firm, Maynard-Marsham were a pretty conventional concern, but from the little she knew about architecture, Chloe had gathered that Kitt was an *enfant terrible.* Despite his respect for conventional form and clean lines, she suspected that he'd secretly enjoy Lionsmead's turrets and gargoyles.

The gate was manned by heavy-duty security, but Chloe was waved through with smiles when she showed her ticket. The general assumption that any pretty girl was automatically some kind of 'raver' annoyed her for a moment, but she was philosophical. It went with the territory, so she just smiled and asked directions to the fashion marquee.

'I'm going that way. I'll show you where it is,' said a confident voice beside her, making her jump.

Chloe turned and found a young man of about her own age standing beside her. A kindred spirit too, she realised. He had a camera slung around his neck and was carrying a gadget bag that bulged with photographic paraphernalia. He was medium height, dressed in what was unmistakably a Moschino jacket and blue jeans, and was rather handsome in a dark and stocky way.

'Bobby Smith, at your service.' He gave her an unashamedly admiring grin and held out his hand.

His grip was firm and his skin dry, a nice change in a business where sweaty-pawed men were a perennial hazard. Chloe rewarded him with her most brilliant and attentive smile.

'Chloe Trevelyan. Pleased to meet you,' she

said, rearranging her bags again once the formalities were over.

'Yes, I knew who you were the minute I set eyes on you,' said Bobby Smith cheerfully. 'We have your card at my agency.' He paused, frowning. 'Look, can I help you with some of that?' he went on, nodding at the capacious bag Chloe was carrying, along with her own camera equipment—both of which were proving to be a bit of a handful. This was the first time she had brought her camera with her to an event, and she was still wondering if that was wise, given its value.

'But you've got plenty of your own to carry.'

'It's OK. I'm used to lugging stuff around. It's not that long since I was promoted from gopher and general beast of burden.'

Giving in gracefully, Chloe allowed him to take her bag and they set off together towards the centre of activities. 'So, what do you do?' she asked presently.

With unabashed enthusiasm, Bobby Smith launched into a thumbnail sketch of his career to date. He worked for an advertising agency—unsurprisingly, given the camera and the general look of him—and his specialities were video and photographic images. The agency was small but they had good contacts, and he saw it as a useful springboard to greater things. At the moment, he was working mostly on bread-and-butter type jobs like promotional brochures for companies and training videos.

His ultimate goal was to become a film director, and today he was shooting a video of the fashion auction.

'I see you're a photographer too.' Bobby nodded towards Chloe's gadget bag as they reached the main marquee and the smaller tent beside it, for the models to change in.

'I just dabble,' Chloe blushed. Bringing her bag and the serious equipment it contained was a form of 'coming out', and she suddenly felt extremely naïve. Bobby was a professional photographer and might laugh at her unrealistic ambitions. He was also a stranger and she was in danger of disclosing a secret she hadn't even properly revealed to Kitt. 'But I would like to make something of it. Professionally, I mean.' She shrugged her shoulders. 'I won't be able to rely on my looks forever, so I'm making contingency plans for when I'm too old and haggish to model!'

'You'll always be beautiful.' Bobby's voice was suddenly low and more intense. 'Men will always want to look at you.'

Chloe turned and looked more closely at him. His dark-brown eyes were fiery and almost frightening somehow. He seemed about to say something else, then he changed his mind and smiled—which made his pleasant face look open and sunny once more.

The tension eased but Chloe wondered if Bobby too had unrealistic preconceptions about models. He'd get a shock if he knew what an ordinary and unrelentingly chaste life she led—and he'd probably be disappointed.

'What I mean is, you've got the right bone structure,' Bobby went on. 'You'll always photograph well.' He seemed subdued, and Chloe got the impression that a moment ago, he'd given away feelings that rather alarmed him.

'Yes,' she admitted, 'I'm lucky that way. It's a family thing. We all have good faces. But you know what fashion's like. It's all trends and fads. I'm really far too curvy to suit a lot of designers.'

Again, Bobby seemed to check himself, and Chloe could almost see his mind work. 'But surely you're getting plenty of work at the moment.' He swung her bag to the ground. 'I mean, I see your photos all over the place. And the designers showing today must like you all right, or you wouldn't *be* here.'

'It's a freebie, isn't it?' She shrugged again. 'And nepotism. I'm modelling my cousin's clothes.'

'Your cousin is a designer?' Bobby appeared genuinely surprised.

'Er, yes . . . Rose Trevelyan. Get it?'

'Oh God, yes! I never realised the two of you were related.'

'Well, we are,' said Chloe crisply, preparing to take her leave.

Bobby opened his mouth, shut it again, then blurted out, 'Look, if you want help . . .

anything at all . . . photogaphy-wise, we could get together, you know.' His smile was tentative, almost bashful somehow. 'I'm no Bailey or Helmut Newton . . . I'm not even well known. But I'd be happy to work with you, even if it was just to show you what mediocre was like—so you could avoid it!'

Chloe laughed. His modesty was laid on a bit thickly but, even so, he was refreshing. Most people in the business were only too keen to blow their own trumpets and, even though she'd only just met Bobby, she liked him very much. He had a bit of a crush on her, she realised, but that was deliciously welcome after Kitt's waywardness and frequent indifference.

'Yes, I'd like that,' she said, wanting to linger but knowing she was needed in the tent. 'We've both got things to do now, but I'll look out for you after the show and maybe we could take a few snaps, eh?' She patted the gadget bag, then reached for her other, bigger bag, which Bobby was still holding by its strap. He lifted it up for her.

'I don't know how you girls carry these things, I really don't!' he said with a laugh. 'Your agency ought to supply you with a native bearer.'

'That would be nice. Are you applying for the job?' It was such a relief to be able to flirt and not be censured for it.

'Possibly. What are the perks?'

'They're negotiable . . .'

They both smiled at each other, then Bobby said, 'Whoops, better go now, or I'll be in hot water. I'll catch you later and we'll see who can take the most saleable shots of all these celebs.' He gestured with his camera towards the sprawling gardens which were rapidly filling with designer-clad partygoers.

'OK. See you,' agreed Chloe and, with that, he gave her a last smile and disappeared towards the main tent.

'Should Kittrick Maynard be worried?' enquired a soft, laughing voice. Chloe turned and discovered that Rose had been watching her, and probably listening too, from behind the tent flap.

'Oh no, not in the slightest.' Chloe wished with all her heart that the situation were different. Kitt *ought* to be jealous! 'Bobby's just someone nice I met a few minutes ago. He's not a contender.'

'Bobby, eh?' Rose smiled as if she didn't agree.

'Yes. Bobby! Now shouldn't we be getting organised, *Madame la Couturière?*'

'Anything you say, clotheshorse,' replied Rose, still shaking her head. 'Follow me, I'll show you to our area.'

Still pondering, Chloe followed her cousin into the tent.

*　　　*　　　*

'How on earth have you managed to lose so much weight since I cut the toiles?' Rose Trevelyan bit off a thread after making a tiny adjustment to one of the outfits Chloe was going to model. 'It's not good enough, cuz,' she said, handing the dress—a sensuous tight-fitting evening gown—to her personal assistant, Connie, who was doubling as dresser and stylist.

The dressing tent was surprisingly well appointed, with better facilities than there were at some catwalk shows. Each designer had their own area, there were changing screens, and even temporary showers and loos for the models to use.

'I didn't realise I had.' Chloe scowled into the mirror, trying to see a difference. Pursing her lips, she blotted off some of the lip-gloss that the make-up artist had painted on her. Then she gave her hairstyle a tug to check that the long, sultry false waves hanging halfway down her back were securely anchored.

'Don't worry, you still look fabulous.' Rose draped an affectionate arm around her shoulders. 'But you have got skinnier. You're not pining too seriously for Kittrick, are you?'

'Of course not!' Chloe gave Rose's slender arm a quick, reassuring squeeze as she got to her feet. 'You know me . . . I'm no anorexic languishing waif. I'm more the "I'll have a bacon sandwich while I'm waiting type", aren't I?'

'True enough,' said Rose, still looking dubious as she and Connie helped Chloe into the first ensemble which was a loose, unstructured pyjama-like garment, made of overlapping layers of Italian silk. It wasn't a typical 'Rose Trevelyan', as it depended more on tucking than tailoring, but its soft jewel-like tones of lapis and ultramarine made Chloe's complexion look pearly and almost luminous. Awed as ever by her cousin's talent, Chloe smiled into the mirror, then bent down to slip on a pair of delicate sandals.

The finished effect was stunning. Realistic about her looks, Chloe usually took for granted that she was impressive when working. But this was different. These exotic blues made her look like a water nymph or a strange, alien princess. She was certainly a match for any of the top supermodels who were in attendance.

'It's amazing, Rose . . .' Her voice was hushed as she ran her fingertips over the gauze-like leaves of silk.

'*You're* amazing,' said Rose, hugging her again. 'It's just cloth until you get into it, sweetheart. I just hope that your Kittrick's in the audience to see you in it.'

'He won't be.' All Chloe's pleasure instantly dissipated. 'If he'd had any intention of coming, he'd have come *with* me. That so-called "work" was just another of his evasions.'

'Not necessarily!' said Rose brightly. 'And, even if it is, there's still Bobby Smith, isn't there?'

'Rose!' said Chloe warningly.

'Chloe!' Rose gave Chloe an encouraging biff on the shoulder, 'Now come on . . . it's Showtime! Shake that booty!'

With Rose and Connie still primping and rearranging as she walked, Chloe took a deep breath and pasted on her coolest and most regal 'thousand-yard stare'. She didn't feel like smiling her way along the catwalk today, and haughty impassivity was a safe and easy refuge.

Anything to hide the gnawing hurt inside her.

CHAPTER SIX

To Chloe's surprise, she did end up smiling. The audience liked her and it was impossible not to respond to them.

The mad mêlée in the dressing tent was fun too, and lifted her spirits. Best of all, Rose's three outfits—the layered pyjamas, a short, embroidery encrusted wind-around dress, and the slinky, asymmetrical scarlet evening gown—fetched the three highest prices at auction.

There was just one moment of panic though, and it really shook her.

Towards the end of the show, Chloe finally allowed herself to focus on something other than the first few rows of punters and, at the very back of the marquee, she glimpsed a face that made her heart leap. Familiar dark hair brushed back off strong features. And a thunderous frown. She didn't falter for even a thousandth of a second in her smooth, led from the hips, walk, but inside she started shaking like jelly.

Was Kitt here after all? There, in the back row with a face like retribution? There was no way to check because she was already on her way back up the catwalk. But having convinced herself that Kitt wouldn't come, the mystery scowler had given her a shock.

The dressing tent was a hubbub of hugs and air kisses and Chloe managed to escape and get changed without Rose and Connie noticing she'd gone white and shaky. By the time she'd got rid of the cumbersome hairpiece and was wearing her own dress and make-up, she was back to normal and showing no signs of imagining Kitt.

'I'm off to mingle now,' she said to Rose who was busy swathing the outfits in their protective dress bags. 'I'll catch you later, amongst the great and the good.' She retrieved her camera bag from Connie who had been guarding it for her.

'See you later. Look out for Florence and Jacob, won't you?' Rose called out as Chloe made her way out of the hot and muggy tent.

After a few minutes of networking, and a lot of congratulations—real and feigned—for her performance on the runway, Chloe spotted Bobby. He wasn't the one she really wanted to find but, even so, his face was welcome.

'Wow, there you are!' Bounding forward from amongst the champagne-quaffing throng, he almost skidded to a halt in front of her. 'I've been looking everywhere for you!'

'I thought you'd still be busy,' said Chloe, taken aback by his enthusiasm. Almost subconsciously, she swung her bag protectively in front of her. Then let it go again, realising she was being stupid. Models had to undress in all sorts of situations without inhibition, so why was she suddenly being so prissy? Bobby was keen, but basically harmless.

'Oh, it's OK, I can delegate a little bit now.' Bobby grinned, then pointed towards the long, white-clothed tables of the open-air bar. 'Would you like a drink? A spot of bubbly to celebrate your catwalk triumph?' His grin seemed to metamorphose and become endearingly star-struck. 'You really did look cool up there,' he said in a soft voice. 'I even felt tempted to bid for a frock myself.' Chloe's eyebrows shot up. Was he a cross-dresser? 'Only kidding,' Bobby added quickly, seeing her reaction.

'Well, that's a comfort, I suppose.' Again, she wondered if she should be worried. Maybe he was a little too keen? She knew she should act friendly yet detached, the way the agency recommended, but she'd always found that difficult, preferring to be completely up-front and open. 'But it's the clothes that you should be praising, you know. I'd be nothing if it wasn't for designers like my cousin.'

Bobby expressed denial with a choice, pithy epithet, then apologised, blushing profusely.

'No sweat,' Chloe laughed. It was hard not to warm to Bobby, really. 'I hear far worse in studios every day—and that's just me!'

They laughed together and approached the bar.

Mindful that the party was a long one, Chloe accepted a glass of champagne from Bobby, but resolved to make it last. She always resisted the ever-present bubbly backstage at fashion shows too. The effects of alcohol weren't worth doing a nosedive on the catwalk!

'Let's go over there.' Bobby touched her elbow and pointed towards a more formal area of the gardens, where an elaborate arrangement of hedges formed a series of cosy arbours containing wrought-iron benches. 'We can compare kit.' He nodded first to his camera, still slung around his neck, then to Chloe's camera bag.

Relieved that his intentions seemed businesslike, Chloe nodded and fell into step beside him.

It turned out that Bobby, too, had a Nikon. 'May I take a photo of you?' he asked. 'I know it's total cliché, but . . . well, we don't get models like you for most of the jobs we do.' He held the camera poised for her answer.

'It's OK. Go ahead.' Chloe scooted to the end of the bench, then relaxed, allowing her subconscious to take over and shape her pose. Bobby refocused and reeled off a few shots, quickly and confidently, and in the space of only seconds he finished the roll. Turning to shield the camera from the light, he'd reloaded in an instant and started snapping again, making minute adjustments without even appearing to think about it.

'A photo?' Chloe queried when he finally lowered the Nikon.

'Sorry, I couldn't resist.' His fingers tightened on his camera as if she might confiscate it. 'As I said, it's not often that one gets a chance to photograph a supermodel.'

Chloe frowned. 'Oh, not you as well! Everybody says that and I'm not a supermodel by a long chalk.' Struggling with her own camera, she was embarrassed that she couldn't whip it out as assuredly as Bobby had his. 'I'm just a jobbing girl, Bobby. Nothing spectacular. Today was a rare event for me. I mostly do advertising, with just the occasional editorial.'

Bobby's quizzical expression made him look younger somehow. 'You're underestimating yourself. I hear everybody, but everybody,

69

talking about you. You're in all the top mags. Don't you even look at your own tear-outs?'

It was Chloe's turn to be puzzled. Had she actually become a supermodel without realising? Was that possible without the party going and turning up at glitzy events? She never thought about fame and, although she always kept copies of her own editorials and advertising spreads, she only perused magazines for the latest fashion looks. She couldn't be bothered with gossip pages and tittle-tattle, when there was never enough time to read all the photography articles she wanted to. Or the good books and general non-fiction titles. Kitt Maynard might think she was a badly-educated bimbo, but that didn't stop her wanting to improve her mind.

And there she was, back to Kitt again even while she was in Bobby's company. She frowned and then, as if Kitt's name was a form of black magic, she looked up and actually saw him striding along towards her.

Subliminally, she noticed he was limping quite pronouncedly but, apart from that, all she could was wait for the bomb to drop. Beside her, she sensed Bobby looking at her in puzzlement.

Chloe rose to her feet. 'I didn't think you'd come,' she said, unable to think of a better greeting. Seeing Kitt in this unusual setting was tantamount to discovering him all over again. He looked exceptionally handsome in a

70

stone-coloured suit Chloe had never seen before, but that didn't mitigate his scowl or his patently obvious displeasure with her. He looked angelic but he was plainly mad as hell.

'That's obvious,' he said, his green eyes savaging both her and Bobby. Chloe opened her mouth to make introductions, but Bobby got there first.

'Hello, Mr Maynard. I didn't expect to see you here. How are you?' .

Reluctant to tear her gaze from Kitt, Chloe swivelled towards Bobby. What on earth was wrong with him? He sounded like a nervous schoolboy and, what was more, he clearly knew who Kitt was.

'Have you two met?' She glanced from one to the other. From confident, angry Kitt to Bobby, who seemed to have regressed to adolescence. Not that she could blame him. She suddenly felt furious with Kitt for his patent hostility. What on earth had got into him? Why was he acting like Attila the Hun when he was usually so easy-going in social situations?

'We have indeed, my dear,' Kitt said coolly. 'I believe I mentioned Maynard-Marsham's training video?' She nodded, recalling not only the mention but also the homily that had gone with it. 'Mr Smith is part of the team who're making it.' He nodded grudgingly at Bobby. 'Hello, Smith.'

Ah, I get it, thought Chloe. According to

Kitt's code, Bobby's one of those ad men with loose morals and I shouldn't go within fifty feet of him. Now she understood the frigid atmosphere.

'Well, Bobby's just been letting me in on a few photographic trade secrets,' she lied, feeling a mad urge to push Kitt even further. 'And we were just going to try out a few of them. Can I take your picture, Kitt?'

Kitt looked horrified. 'I don't think so, if you don't mind,' he said quietly. 'But don't let me interrupt the lesson.' He gave Bobby a narrow-eyed look. 'I'll be circulating if you need me, Chloe. I've seen one or two people I know. I'll catch you later.' With that, and another curt nod to Bobby, he turned and left.

Chloe suddenly realised her heart was pounding. Oh why had everything gone so gruesomely wrong in the space of a few seconds? The whole idea of inviting Kitt to this party was to get him to see her in a new, more desirable light, but now she seemed to have alienated him completely.

'Hell!' she muttered, then heard Bobby let out his breath as if he'd been holding it for five minutes.

'Well, now it's my turn . . .' He touched his gelled hair as if he was about to rub his head perplexedly. 'Have you two met?'

'I'll say!' Chloe fidgeted with the straps of her camera bag, 'That particular old misery is my landlord, worse luck!'

'He's not that old,' said Bobby glumly.

Chloe looked at him for a second, and then the penny dropped. It was male competitiveness again. She had a sudden vision of a pair of stags clashing antlers over a doe.

But if Bobby was feeling threatened, was that also the reason for Kitt's unreasonable behaviour? If that was the case, then maybe she'd made some progress after all.

'No, he's only thirty-five' she said, giving Bobby a conspiratorial smile. 'He just acts as if he's ninety-three because my stupid mother asked him to "keep an eye on me".' She raised her eyes to heaven. 'That means we're back in the Dark Ages, and he's a sort of cross between Prince Albert, a guardian uncle, and a prison warder. It's really embarrassing.'

'And you're mad about him, aren't you?'

Chloe's heart leapt like a beached fish in a net. She stared at Bobby, aghast, and he stared back.

'Don't worry, it's nothing to be ashamed of.' He sighed. 'I've been there myself . . . well, to a similar place.' The sad little quirk of the lips was nearly a smile. 'It's no fun loving someone when they're blind to it, is it?'

In that instant, the hairs on the back of Chloe's neck stood up. Was there more to Bobby than she realised? More to him being here with her now? But when she looked at him again, he seemed to be just a kind person

73

who empathised with her problem.

'It's a pain,' she said succinctly. She felt the need to confide, but kindness could only stretch so far. She didn't want to bore Bobby to death.

'Go on, tell me all the gory details,' he urged however, settling back on the seat, his face all attention.

Reluctantly at first, and then with a blissful sense of unburdening, Chloe recounted the pathetic history of her obsession with Kittrick Maynard—from its early, barely understood, flickerings in her girlhood, right up to the stupid state of affairs that currently prevailed.

'I feel such an idiot,' she finished. 'If I had any sense at all, I'd accept the fact that he'll never really think of me in that way, and cut my losses. There are plenty of other men around.' She looked to Bobby for a reaction shot, and saw he was deep in thought. 'And I should also sort out this "guardian" business with my mother. Then I could get a new flat somewhere and make a clean break.' Bobby was still cogitating. 'What do you think?'

'You're probably right,' her companion replied slowly. 'It'd be the logical thing to do.' He hesitated, as if unsure about what to say next. 'But you're not ready to give up on him, are you?' He didn't wait for a reply and went on, 'So you *could* try more of the same tactics advised by your cousins . . . only take them a bit further.'

'How do you mean?'

'Keep trying to make him jealous. If there is a spark there . . .' He hesitated again, '. . . and I think there is, it would really stir him up to see you with another man. Or men. You know . . . boyfriends.'

Chloe thought of Kitt's reaction to the fictitious 'Richard' and the way he'd glowered at Bobby a few minutes ago.

'It might work. He did get pretty steamed when I told him that fib about having a date.'

'Well then,' said Bobby, spreading his hands. 'Take the step. There must be scores of men panting to take you out but, if you need someone quickly, I'd be honoured. No strings attached, of course. And we could even get to grips with some photography at the same time,' he finished quickly.

Chloe had been asked out many times during her career, but had only accepted the most innocent of 'cup of coffee' type invitations. This was the first time that the man asking had implied that he was doing her a favour. If she hadn't known that Bobby meant well, she might have felt insulted. As it was, she knew she could do a damn sight worse. Bobby was intelligent, presentable, and good company—the answer to most girls' prayers. She should be flattered that he'd put himself forward to help her out.

'Look, I only met you today Bobby and, according to Kitt, you and your kind are all unprincipled swines who should be horsewhipped, but I really think that you and I could have a good time together,' she said smiling. 'It'd be great to go out. If you don't mind, of course.'

'Not a bit! It's a deal!' He looked so happy that Chloe felt a pang of guilt at 'using' him. 'Why don't we start right now?' he suggested. 'I've shown you mine, so you show me yours!'

'I beg your pardon?'

'Cameras, silly,' he replied, nodding to her still-unopened camera bag.

'In a minute,' said Chloe then, before she could think twice or stop herself, she leant over and gave Bobby a swift kiss on the cheek. 'There, that seals it. As far as Kitt Maynard's concerned, you're officially my new boyfriend!'

CHAPTER SEVEN

As the afternoon wore on into a golden, blowsy evening, Chloe found herself on the dance-floor. She'd managed to get an obliging security man to lock her camera in a safe place, and now she was gyrating wildly to techno 'house' beats in an attempt to exorcise all the frustration of loving Kitt but not being loved in return. Bobby had been called away to deal with some crisis over the fashion video, and Chloe had only seen Kitt himself once since their earlier confrontation. Depressingly, he'd been in the company of a stunning brunette at the time, and the sight of that had put a damper on all her optimism.

Now she was left with her cousins, Rose and Florence. They weren't dancing round handbags, but they might just as well have been.

'May I cut in?' shouted a familiar voice over the rhythmic din of the dance music, and Florence and Rose moved to make a space for Bobby. He grinned at her as they jigged about and she smiled back at him.

There wasn't much scope amongst the crush of bodies for artistic expression, but Chloe was impressed. Bobby was surprisingly graceful and seemed to thoroughly enjoy his dancing. They all flung themselves about to a dozen or so numbers which all sounded more or less the same, and it was only when a slow romantic tune came on that Chloe realised she was now alone with Bobby. Florence had found her fiancé and Rose must have gone to get a drink.

Now this was a dilemma. Bobby had an expectant look on his face, even if he was too subtle to hold out his arms to her. She ought to slow-dance with him.

Sadly, though, it was only Kitt she wanted to slow-dance with. It was his tall body that she wanted to be enfolded against, supported by, moving with. It was Kitt's shoulder she wanted to lay her head on.

Her skin itched with awareness. He wasn't far away, she could tell, and he was probably waiting, just like Bobby, to see what she would do. The seconds ticked on and she saw Bobby start to look less hopeful. She felt so sorry for him, that she stepped forward and let him put his arms around her.

They didn't speak at first, and Chloe was glad of that. She felt uncoordinated, and it was only her natural poise that saved her from massacring Bobby's toes as they slowly swayed together. She was with him, yet not with him, and her sixth sense was becoming increasingly aware of Kitt.

He was here somewhere, she knew that. Yet she couldn't look for him because that would give her away, and it was insulting to Bobby.

But she couldn't stop her mind forming a picture. Kitt dancing with his brunette friend, their bodies dovetailed together in exactly the closeness she was trying to avoid with Bobby. She seemed to see Kitt's mouth brushing the woman's ear, whispering sweet nothings, then stealing a secret kiss. It all looked so unbearably real that Chloe shuddered.

'Whoops, sorry about that.' Bobby's voice was a sudden shock in her ear. What on earth was he talking about? Then, just as suddenly, she knew. And she didn't know which was more worrying—the fact that now they were closer and their pelvises were grazing, it was obvious he was aroused by her, or the fact that until he'd mentioned it, she hadn't even noticed. Dear heaven, she was so obsessed by Kitt getting excited over his notional partner, that she hadn't even been aware that the man who held her was turned on!

'Don't worry. Just ignore it,' Bobby said, gently easing himself away from her with admirable *sangfroid*. 'It's just the novelty of smooching with the most beautiful woman here tonight. Just think of it as a compliment.'

Chloe grinned awkwardly, then allowed herself to relax. There was nothing she could do really, except be grateful that Bobby was a gentleman. As their steps meshed again, he made a little 'umm' sound of appreciation.

A moment later he was tense again. 'He's over there, at the other end of the floor, near to the pillars.' As Bobby spun her round so she could see, Chloe had no doubt whom he was talking about. 'Don't worry though, he's dancing with the host's girlfriend.'

Chloe felt instant relief. Kitt and his partner were dancing slowly but rather decorously to the music, holding each other at arm's length, and obviously chatting. No clinch and, with any luck, not even a hint of arousal.

'See, nothing to worry about.' Skilfully, Bobby manoeuvred her so she had a better view of her quarry. 'He's not "with" anyone.' Chloe felt him grip her harder. 'Although why he should even *want* to be when he could have you, I can't imagine. The guy must be brain dead!'

'Flatterer,' murmured Chloe, trying to keep things casual and worrying that Bobby sounded as if he were getting heavy. 'Do you think he's seen us?' she added, even though her inner radar was already on red alert. Kitt's apparent disinterest was almost certainly a total fiction.

Then, as if he'd read her mind, he suddenly looked straight at her. It was just for an instant, because he was speaking to his partner at the time but, even from a distance, his brilliant green eyes flashed like emeralds.

Chloe was transfixed.

Kitt was furious and he was jealous! Elation rushed through her and she had a mad urge to thumb her nose at him. But instead she just edged a little closer to Bobby—who groaned softly but immediately got the message. Pausing to brush aside her hair, he nuzzled his face against her neck.

'OK?' he whispered.

'Perfect!' answered Chloe, 'his face is like thunder! I only hope he doesn't come across and punch you.'

'I hope so too!' Bobby sounded as if he meant it. 'Shall I kiss you properly? Or shall we just leave it at that?' He turned her again, and she felt his tension. 'He already looks insanely jealous to me.'

Or insanely righteous, Chloe thought, wondering if she'd actually misread Kitt. He might just be angry and disgusted with her. If there had been any element of possessiveness there, he would already have prized her from Bobby and been shouting the odds. Instead of which, he was still nattering to his beautiful partner as if he didn't have a care in the world.

Damn him!

Winding her arms around Bobby's neck, she drew him to her and kissed him. She felt him start in surprise, then almost immediately respond, matching her gentle pressure with his own. His arms tightened against her back, and his mouth began to move seductively on hers.

It was a surprisingly accomplished kiss, given the circumstances, yet Chloe felt completely detached, as if she were watching herself. If she'd been watching herself being kissed by Kitt, she would've been totally involved in the scene, but in Bobby's arms, she felt nothing. No spark. Not even a sense of revulsion. The kiss wasn't unpleasant, it simply didn't move her.

And it didn't have any affect on her target either. Several moments sped by, but still no Kitt arrived to split them up. Bobby drew back, his eyes questioning. 'No dice, eh?' he said with a shrug, and Chloe wasn't quite sure whether he was referring to the non-appearance of fire-breathing censure, or to Chloe's lack of response to him.

'Not at this time,' she whispered, choosing to believe he meant the former. A few steps brought her around so that she could see Kitt again but, by now, he had moved to the edge of the dance floor and was talking to one the security people—coincidentally, the one who had stowed Chloe's camera away.

'Don't worry, it'll happen,' hissed Bobby. 'Either that or, like I said, the man's mad.' Pulling her closer, he repeated the kiss with all the expertise of before—and Chloe experienced the same fat zero excitement. In despair, she had a horrid premonition. Was this all she'd ever feel if the man wasn't Kitt?

Disengaging her lips from Bobby's, she murmured, 'Let's just dance, eh?' and, compliant as ever, he acceded to her wishes.

Lost in gloomy contemplation, Chloe lost track of time. She had just decided that if she was doomed to live without love, or a sex life, she might as well become the world's greatest female photographer ever, when she finally regained an awareness of the party around her. Mainly because Bobby had shuffled to a wooden halt, and let go of her. Without having to ask, she knew what had happened. Using every bit of her carefully schooled composure, she counted to five, winked at Bobby, then turned around.

'Hello, Kitt!' Facing a cold, threatening expression she countered with a brilliant smile. 'Isn't it a great party? Are you enjoying yourself? We're having a wonderful time.'

Unfazed by the people dancing all around

them, Kitt seemed to have enclosed himself and Chloe and Bobby in a column of silent tension, separating their private drama from the mass of swaying partygoers. Even so, one or two interested faces were already turning . . .

'Yes, it's a wonderful party.' His urbane voice seemed at odds with his dark expression. Then, entirely without warning, Kitt reached toward Chloe and took a firm grip on her arm. 'But it's time you and I made tracks for home. I've got a taxi waiting and I think we'd better share it.'

His tone was low and measured, but it still carried clearly over the music. There wasn't the slightest element of question in what he'd said. It was a command, pure and simple. Seething with defiance, Chloe opened her mouth to tell him where to get off, but then something implacable and deeply exciting in his gaze made her voice seize. Everyone else on the dance floor seemed to speed away from them, as if on rails. She'd been right all along, he *was* jealous.

'Of course. You're quite right.' She fought to sound cool even though she was a mess of fear and triumph. 'But I'll need to get my camera. One of the security men put it somewhere safe for me.'

'That's all taken care of.' Kitt nodded towards the side of the dance floor where the security guard in question was standing with her bags in his arms.

'How efficient of you, Kitt,' she said. It was weird, but she felt strangely exhilarated by this confrontation. 'Would you excuse me a moment?' Without waiting for an answer, she turned towards Bobby and held out her hand. 'Make it look good!' she mimed, pulling him towards her.

As they kissed, she counted out beats as she sometimes did on the catwalk. She calculated, too, how long she dared stay in the clinch before Kitt went ballistic. When there was no reaction, she drew back and raised her eyebrows at Bobby.

'Let's get together really soon,' she said. Bobby looked totally sideswiped, but she couldn't tell whether it was from the kiss or fear of Kitt. 'Do you have a card?' Visibly shaking, Bobby pulled out a business card and handed it to her. 'Do you have my number too?' He nodded. 'Give me a ring then. And don't wait too long! *Ciao*, Bobby!' Blowing a kiss, she smiled at him luminously, then turned back towards Kitt.

'OK. Let's go.' Meeting his baleful eyes for a second, she swept forward off the dance-floor, walking tall. She heard the men exchange a curt leave-taking behind her, but she didn't look back or falter. She also took only her camera bag from the security guard, and left Kitt to bring her heavier model bag. That would teach him to be such a high-handed monster!

The journey home was a nightmare. After quick farewells to the host and to Rose, Florence and Jacob, she and Kitt didn't speak in the taxi. The tension was agonising but she, for one, had had enough for one day.

When they reached Willow House, Kitt still didn't say anything as they went inside, and didn't even object when Chloe grabbed both her bags and shot off as fast as she could towards her flat.

'You little fool!'

Chloe whirled, alarmed by the sound of her flat door closing. She hadn't heard Kitt following her, and hadn't expected him to. She'd assumed she'd get more of the silent treatment, and that his punishment would be to ignore her—as he'd often done lately—not indulge in a slanging match.

'I beg your pardon?' Steeling herself, she put aside her bags. She was quaking but Kitt mustn't see that.

'What on earth do you think you were doing with Robert Smith?'

Kitt wasn't cool, contemptuous, or impassive now. His eyes were ablaze and the very air around him seemed to scintillate.

Chloe trembled harder. Oh God, why had she goaded him? This was much more than Kitt's usual Mister Moody act.

And yet, what right did he really have to be angry? He was the one that had been vague about his plans, then spent virtually no time at all with her at the party. And when he had deigned to pay her some attention, he'd behaved like a domineering dictator and dragged her away when everybody else was still enjoying themselves. If there was justice to be had, it was she who should be angry!

'I was dancing with him! So what?'

'It was a damn sight more than dancing!'

'I might have kissed him a couple of times. It was just smooching, there's no harm in that, is there?'

'Of course there's harm in it, you idiot!' Kitt stepped towards her. 'Haven't you been listening to me? I've seen Robert Smith in action. That Nice Guy act of his probably gets him into any bed he fancies—and, judging by the way he was mauling you, your bed is the next one he's set his sights on!'

Chloe gasped. Before her now stood a new Kitt, one she had never seen before. His calm persona was a thing of the past, he'd never blown up quite like this in all the time she'd known him. The subtle barrier between them stood in ruins now and, in the space, stood a dark, avenging angel—who didn't mince his words!

'Don't be disgusting, Kittrick!' Chloe drawled. 'And, anyway, what does it matter if Bobby *is* a stud? He's a "nice" stud . . . better to be one of those than a sanctimonious, overbearing Fascist!'

Even as the words left her lips, Chloe darted backwards. How could a human being move so fast? She braced herself for the unthinkable, a slap, but instead Kitt grabbed her roughly by the upper arms as if preparing to shake her. His fingers scorched her skin and he suddenly seemed in shock and lost for words.

'Y . . . you've got it all wrong, Kitt,' Chloe stuttered, scared witless by this livid stranger whose fingers were really hurting her. 'The kisses . . . there was nothing happening . . . really!'

'What do you mean . . . nothing happening?' Kitt's voice was tight and angry.

'Just what I said. I wasn't in danger.'

'For pity's sake, Chloe!' His fingers pinched harder. 'You're so naive, you wouldn't know danger if it jumped up and bit you!'

But she did know danger. It was here right now and she *wanted* it to bite her!

'Well, show me then!' she flung back. 'What am I supposed to be so scared of?'

'*This*, you little half-wit!' Then suddenly he was kissing her—and it was the kiss she'd always yearned for.

Kitt's lips were hard and demanding and they conquered hers in a way Bobby's never had, and never could, filling her with exactly the forbidden magic quality she'd dreamed of and hungered for. She responded to him, opening her mouth on instinct, knowing that with this man there would be no hesitation or

87

doubt. Her arms slid around him, embracing the taboo, making him want her, pushing him onwards. She heard him groan like a dying man, then felt him give in to her.

She didn't know how long the kiss lasted, but she didn't want it to end.

'Oh, my Chloe, you're so beautiful, so very beautiful,' she heard him whisper and, a second later, he pulled away from her, visibly shaken.

Chloe fell back, landing on the sofa, and just stared up at him, still in a haze.

'Oh Chloe, I'm sorry!' he gasped, running his fingers through his raven-black curls. 'That shouldn't have happened . . . no, not at all . . . it's exactly what I said I'd keep you safe from.'

'But I don't want keeping safe from you, Kitt!' cried Chloe, bereft. Their angry, passionate intimacy had dissolved. Completely. 'I *am* safe with you. I lo . . .'

'Chloe! Shut up!'

Kitt sounded as if he were being twisted up inside, just as she was. 'You're probably far safer with Bobby Smith than you are with me!'

Chloe started to protest, but he silenced her with a short chopping gesture and moved to stand in front of her—with a safe two-pace distance between them.

'Listen,' he said quietly, his voice back under control now. 'We're going to forget what just happened . . . no! Don't look at me like that! It's for the best, Chloe. Just pretend I never came in here, and I never touched you.'

Chloe bit her lip. How she could deny something so exquisite?

'Chloe!' he snapped when she remained silent. She nodded glumly, unable to speak yet knowing she'd have to answer somehow.

'All right,' he said flatly, seeming to accept the nod. 'I'll say goodnight then. You just go to bed, get some sleep and forget all this. Promise?'

And you don't treat me like a half-baked child! Chloe raged inside, grudgingly nodding again.

'Goodnight then,' said Kitt and, when she wouldn't answer him, he sighed then turned and walked out of the room, closing the door behind him.

'Well, that was a complete disaster, wasn't it?' observed Chloe to Boy who, having clearly hidden behind the sofa during the shouting, had now come forward, his long tail swishing, looking for some affection.

Thank goodness for uncomplicated males who were just happy if you tickled their ears and fed them twice a day, she thought, sinking down amongst the cushions and letting Boy jump on to her lap. She sighed. Even the purring comfort of her cat couldn't negate the desolation she was feeling.

It had happened. The wonderful, forbidden kiss she'd spent so much time and emotional energy anticipating. Kitt had kissed her, and it had been every bit as beautiful as she'd hoped, and then they'd spoiled it by arguing. Well, not exactly arguing . . . Kitt had snarled and she had sulked—the damage was done.

'Ow! You fool!' Boy too had decided to inflict damage, kneading her bare knee with his claws. Very gently she prised him off and adjusted his position.

'I hate this!' she muttered, not to Boy but to the man in the rooms above her.

They had been so close and, even if he didn't actually love her, Kitt had wanted her. She'd felt him hard against her, and that contact had been thrilling.

So why didn't you *continue* to want me, Kitt? She leant back, staring at the ceiling. It was amazing that she didn't have neck problems the amount of time she spent craning upwards!

Surely he couldn't turn it off, just like that? She couldn't do it herself—she still wanted him, even though she was inexperienced and wasn't precisely sure what it was she wanted. Oh, she understood the theory all right, but her practical knowledge was vestigial. Something that would have caused her fellow models to howl with amusement and disbelief.

Eroticism, in photographs, was pure theatre to Chloe. Art but a fabrication. She'd never done nude shots but, like all models, she'd frequently appeared in diaphanous clothing and always changed for shows in the semi-public conditions behind the scenes. It didn't embarrass her, because she was always conscious of somehow keeping the best of herself back. Hidden. Locked away.

'Oh Kitt, what have you done to me?' she demanded, hugging soft, furry Boy as a tear trickled down her cheek.

She'd been saving herself all these years for a man who didn't want her.

CHAPTER EIGHT

Never a great believer in the value of crying and sulking, Chloe made a conscious effort not to do either.

The Sunday after the garden party was difficult though, and she could do nothing but think of Kitt and listen for him up above her. She kept fantasising that he'd come down and apologise. After that, the dream went soft-focus, and involved more kisses, then the natural progression from kisses . . . and, after that, Kitt said he loved her and life was lollipops and roses from that day forward.

Chloe's sensible side said, 'Get real. It'll never happen. Move on.'

Fortunately, she quickly became too busy to brood much, faced with wall-to-wall work, and some of it with some pretty demanding photographers. The very slave drivers who taught her the most about how to use a camera.

Bobby Smith cheered her up too, phoning her several times during the week for casual chats and suggesting that they might meet at the weekend.

Chloe's cousins were not so easy to talk to, both demanding, in their different ways, to know what was happening with her and Kitt.

'Did Kittrick find you?' asked Rose. 'He came by the dressing tent asking after you.'

'Oh, he found me all right,' said Chloe, 'but he was in a foul mood and he behaved abominably to both Bobby Smith and me. I've decided I hate him.' She heard her cousin sigh before Rose tactfully changed the subject.

Florence was less easily distracted. 'You've got a bit of handful there, kiddo,' the journalist said crisply. 'He looked as mad as a hornet when he dragged you off the dance floor. I hope all that delicious smouldering was suitably redirected later?'

'Fat chance,' lied Chloe. 'We had a big tiff, Kitt treated me as if I'm eight-years-old, and then gave me a boring lecture about kissing Bobby Smith.'

'A clear case of jealousy!' proclaimed Florence.

'No way, just being a narrow-minded pain in the butt,' said Chloe, feeling weary.

'Maybe not . . .' Florence was unswayed. 'The stubborn ones just take longer.'

Chloe sighed and, though she listened to her cousin's reasoning for a good while longer out of politeness, she knew that Flo was wrong.

Each night, when she came trudging in, weary and longing for a cup of tea, she listened intently to try and work out if Kitt was at home. It was hard to work out which worried her most—knowing he was out, or knowing he was in!

If he was out, he could be with Geraldine or some other woman. If he was in, he was obviously still mad with her because he didn't come down or ring her.

Ah, what a dissolute life I lead, Kittrick, she reflected bitterly on Thursday night when she was sitting up in bed in a very modest nightie, sipping hot milk. It's all sex and drugs and rock and roll for us models, she thought, turning over a page of 'Principles of Photographic Composition', then sighing as she caught the faint sound of music playing above her.

It was Rachmaninov tonight—passionate, but very softly played. Kitt was clearly avoiding even the slightest possibility of encountering her, so he was giving her no reason to complain about noise. Maybe she ought to put on some tempestuous Wagner or Berlioz and force him to come down and complain at her?

A horrifying notion occurred to her. What if the Rachmaninov really meant passion and Kitt had Geraldine up there right now, and was wooing her? Oh God, what if the music was a cover? So that she couldn't hear the inevitable sounds of their love-making?

Chloe wished that her milk were either hemlock or a truly enormous brandy. That was it. He and Geraldine—or even some other female—were in bed together and the music was masking the ecstatic gymnastics!

As if by alchemy, she seemed to feel Kitt's lips on hers again. That's the nearest I'm ever likely to get to being Kitt's lover, she thought, mortally envying the fortunate woman who was with him now. Being taken to heaven, no doubt, by his strength and grace and power. Feeling the touch and caress of his lips, not only on her mouth but all over her naked body . . .

Enough!

The pain of knowing she was so close to what she wanted but not a part of it was agonising, but there was nothing to be gained by whining and cringing like a drama queen. She took a deep breath and tried to concentrate on her book again. She'd just managed to find her place when she almost jumped out of her skin when the bedroom phone rang.

'Hello. This is Chloe,' she said, her spirits soaring as she anticipated Kitt's voice.

'Hello, it's Bobby.' Chloe's spirits plummeted again. 'I'm sorry to ring you so late, but I wondered if you fancied dinner tomorrow?'

'Oh . . . yes. That would be lovely.'

For pity's sake, sound a bit more enthusiastic! She hoped Bobby wasn't disappointed by her lifeless reaction.

'Are you sure?'

'Yes, I'd love dinner!' she proclaimed, then found herself struck dumb at a sudden sound, other than music, from the direction of upstairs.

'Chloe? Are you all right?' Bobby sounded anxious.

'Yes, I'm fine. I'm great. It's just been a long day and I'm a bit tired.' She paused. 'But if I get a good night's sleep, I'll be at my stunning best tomorrow!' To her surprise, she managed to summon the semblance of a chuckle.

'Where would you like to eat?' asked Bobby, naming a clutch of top restaurants.

'Oh, nothing so posh,' said Chloe, not wanting anything too lavish. 'We have a lovely little Italian place in our local high street. Fab food, cosy atmosphere, decent wine list and, even if they're full, they'll find a table for me, I promise you!'

Bobby seemed to like the sound of that, but just as he seemed about to launch into further conversation, the music upstairs ended abruptly. 'Look, I'm desperately tired now and I really need to sleep,' Chloe said quickly. 'Why don't you come here and pick me up at seven-thirty.' She gave him a set of sketchy instructions on how to get to Willow House, then rang off as soon as she could without being rude.

A dense silence fell the moment she put the phone down. Even without the music, Chloe could hear nothing. She stared up at the ceiling, wishing she had some kind of spying device and at the same time knowing that was horrible.

She stood up shakily, then wavered and tumbled down again when she did actually hear sounds. As she leapt lightly from her bed, she tracked footsteps moving above her.

Geraldine getting dressed? No, it couldn't be, the limp said it was Kitt himself on the move. Perhaps he was going to get champagne so he could bring it back to bed to share? Worse still, maybe it was only half-time refreshments?

Stop it, Chloe! she ordered herself then, finding her mug empty, decided on more milk for its soporific qualities.

She'd just removed her mug from the microwave, when she nearly spilt the whole lot.

There had been a soft knock at her door— which meant someone from *inside* the house had come to visit her.

Hampered by her slip-on mules, Chloe flip-flapped to the door that led to the hall, then stood for several seconds, afraid to open it. The knock came again, accompanied by a call of 'Chloe?'

It *was* Kitt.

Chloe paused to draw a deep breath and, in the few seconds before the door swung open, she seemed to see Kitt's face, granite-like with anger as he'd looked the last time she'd seen him.

But Kitt was smiling. A cautious, half-shamefaced smile, almost as if he expected her to tell him to take a running jump, but at least his stunning green eyes were warm.

'Er . . . what is it?'

What an erudite opening!

'I wondered if we could have a talk?' said Kitt quietly. 'I know it's late, but I didn't think you would have gone to bed yet.' In his dressing gown and with wet hair, Kitt was obviously ready for bed himself, but Chloe didn't think he'd leave a lover alone upstairs to come down and talk to her.

'Well?' He rocked from side-to-side as he stood waiting, his hands thrust into the pockets of his thick burgundy towelling robe. His legs were bare beneath the knee length robe, showing his strong, lightly tanned shins and calves. His feet were also bare and Chloe could see some of his scars but, in an odd way, they only added to his beauty. At that moment, Boy suddenly appeared from around the corner and began to wind his furry body around Kitt's exposed ankles. Immediately the man whipped his hands out of his pockets and swooped down to pick up the purring cat.

97

'Can we come in?' Kitt gave Boy a chin tickle, then bobbed down to kiss the fat tom's butting head.

Something leapt inside Chloe at the sight of such easy but genuine affection. Boy was a loveable animal, but most men were too image-conscious to kiss cats, even if they adored them. Kitt had no such qualms and proceeded to rub his cheek against Boy's soft and silky coat.

Why can't you love *me* like that? Chloe wanted to howl but, instead, she managed a smile and said 'Come in.'

Chloe led the way into the kitchen and Kitt followed, setting Boy gently down in front of his food dish.

'That looks good,' he said as Chloe stirred her milk.

'It's only milk. Would you like some? I've plenty.'

'Yes, please. We can sit and drink it in front of the fire while we talk.'

Very cosy, thought Chloe, but she didn't think, somehow, that flame effects would calm her.

'What do you want to talk about, Kitt?' She watched him warily as he took a sip of milk, then put it aside.

'That I'm sorry for snapping at you the other night. And for other things. I've been a bit of a pig lately, I know.' His well-shaped shoulders rose and fell expressively. 'I've

98

either been working too hard or the male menopause is making me cranky.'

Chloe had to laugh. 'Don't be an idiot, Kitt! You're only in your thirties!' She felt a strong urge to slide down and kneel at his feet then cradle his hands. Were men really concerned about the loss of youth? The way some women were . . . Was that why he so stubbornly resisted any kind of adult interaction? Because her relative youth triggered primal fears?

'I feel ancient sometimes,' he said with a smile. 'Ancient and bad-tempered and narrow-minded. I know I should lighten up.'

For me? thought Chloe. Or for Geraldine, or some other woman? A sudden shadow fell across the moment. Why couldn't she stop being so jealous? If she really cared about him, she should want him to be happy—with anybody.

'Yeah, you're right there,' she couldn't resist observing dryly, 'and it'd be nice if you credited me with a bit of common sense now and again too.'

'I know, I know, I know.' Kitt stared into the fire. 'I'm sorry for being a heavy. But, believe me, it's only because I worry about you.'

But not because you love me or desire me. Chloe fought her growing disappointment. Here they were in their robes and there wasn't the slightest sexual frisson between them. At least, not on Kitt's part. Her own hormones were firing on all cylinders, whipped to a frenzy by the proximity of his powerful male body and its smell of lemon soap.

But I should be grateful, she thought suddenly. Glad that he's here at all.

'And I appreciate that, Kitt, I really do,' she said, reaching out to pat his towelling-clad arm.

Touching him, Chloe saw an image of a match head dropping into a powder keg—and Kitt flinched as the resulting flames raced up his forearm. Complex and fleeting emotions flickered across his marvellous face and her head went light with a pure mix of joy and recognition.

He does care! Or at least, he wants me!

But for some accursed reason, he was fighting her, and fighting hard. Chloe snatched back her hand, hating the sudden awkwardness.

'You're a kind man,' she said.

Kitt made a vague shrugging gesture. He seemed as shaken as she was, but there was no comfort in the way he pulled away from her. The distance was minimal, but it felt like miles.

'Anyway, I've had some good news this week,' she said, changing the subject. 'Apparently, the garden party was a huge success and they've raised an absolute fortune for "Right to Walk"!' She took a quick sip of milk, pleased that Kitt looked interested. 'They want to create a multi-purpose centre— for new therapies, and also as a sort of country holiday environment too. So it's informal, not like a hospital . . . better for the kids!'

'Are they purpose building or are they planning to convert a property?' He was the professional Kitt now, asking relevant questions. 'I read some of their literature at the party, and it seemed to me they'd need some architectural guidance.' Chloe looked at him closely. Was he blushing? Whatever for? 'So I . . . I offered my services. I've done plenty of conversion design in my time and it would save the charity approaching a consultancy formally and getting stung. It's something I could easily do in my spare time. I've co-designed a new hospital wing for a retirement home, so I know what's required.'

Chloe was awe-struck. Such a huge investment of Kitt's time and talent made her own stroll up and down a catwalk seem puny. She barely knew what to say to him, but thought how many people would ultimately benefit from his kindness.

'That's fabulous, Kitt,' she said eventually, longing to touch his arm again but holding back.

'So, have you any photographs to show me?'

It was Kitt's turn to change the subject now and Chloe went along with it. Not that she felt like showing him her latest photographs. Apart from a few at the party, most were stolen images of *him*.

They were clandestine shots—when he'd

101

just arrived home from Japan—and though far from technically perfect, each had a strange, forbidden charm to it. The moving, striding Kitt was informed with a haunted quality. The motion of his body vigorous, while his face—in each instance—was vulnerable and painted with a fatigue and preoccupation that only enhanced his allure. They were private moments, and Chloe knew that to reveal them would destroy his fragile trust in her.

The garden party shots would displease him too. Mainly because a lot of them were either of Bobby, when they'd been experimenting with her camera, or of her, clearly taken by Bobby.

'I haven't had anything developed this week,' she fibbed. 'I've been rushing around all over the place and I haven't had a chance to go into the shop.'

'Well, whenever . . .' Kitt sounded uncomfortable now. 'I may not be quite the photographer your friend Smith is, but I do know my fair share about form and line.'

Uh oh! We're back to that again, are we? Chloe challenged silently, doubly glad now that she'd withheld the garden party photos.

'As soon as I have some new shots developed, you'll be the first to see them,' she said quickly, feeling oddly cheered at the thought that he might actually be jealous of Bobby.

'Good!' he said. 'That's good . . .' He

hesitated, picking up the end of his dressing gown sash and fiddling with it. 'I've been thinking . . . now we're, well, OK again, how do you feel about going out to dinner tomorrow? We could go to "Lucci" . . . have a mountain of spaghetti or linguini? Something evil for dessert?'

Chloe felt as if she were flying, soaring, ascending to heaven almost—then suddenly she was plunging back down again, her wings in tatters.

She'd already agreed to go out tomorrow night with Bobby, the very man Kitt so despised. 'I can't make tomorrow, Kitt. I'm sorry.'

Kitt's face shuttered immediately and Chloe had a horrible feeling he knew why she'd refused.

'I see,' he said tightly. 'No problem. Some other time.'

Chloe longed to grovel and to regain the rapport of a few moments ago. For Kitt, she'd reject Bobby Smith out of hand and tell Kitt that the younger man was history.

But even though it hurt, she couldn't do that. She had her pride, and she had to be independent. She was no simpering doll who leapt to obey every time Kitt tweaked her string. Because that just wasn't the sort of woman Kitt wanted anyway.

And it was unkind to Bobby to ditch him like that. He'd been kind to her, so she

103

couldn't hurt him.

'Yes. That would be great.' She watched in despair as Kitt retrieved his mug and rose gracefully to his feet.

'I'd better go now. It's getting late.' His smile seemed to cost him something but, to his credit, he was still trying to be conciliatory. Chloe wished to goodness that she'd had the answerphone on tonight. That way, when Bobby had called, she could have kept her options open.

'It certainly is. Shall I take that?' She put out her hand for the mug, and felt crushed when Kitt passed it to her with such scrupulous care that it was perfectly clear he was avoiding contact with her.

'Thanks for the milk,' he said politely when Chloe saw him to the door. 'Goodnight, Chloe. Sleep tight. I'll see you soon.'

Good night, my only love, thought Chloe as she stared at the space where he'd stood. She yearned to throw the door open, follow him, and beg him to let her cancel her date with Bobby. She knew she'd cancel every plan, every commitment, every facet of her career if it would please him.

But it was too late. The moment for mad, passionate avowals had gone and, made now, such a gesture would only seem ludicrous.

Yet a part of her couldn't help but wonder if it would have worked.

CHAPTER NINE

'Does he know you're out with me?'

Chloe looked carefully at Bobby. Was he gloating? Or was she imagining things?

Yes, it seemed so. The only expression on Bobby's face was concern. What was more, he seemed to respect Kitt rather than resent him, even though he knew Chloe cared for Kitt. She wondered how forgiving Kitt would be in his place.

'He knows I'm out, but I didn't say who with.' She closed her menu without looking at it. 'Not that it's any business of his.' A pang of sadness speared her heart, but she shaped her lips into a carefree smile.

They were in 'Lucci', waiting in the small bar, deciding what to eat. Chloe wished she'd made plain to Bobby what a relaxed place it was. He was dressed in a sharp, fashionable suit and she was wearing jeans and a little camisole top Rose had given her.

Casual or not, it was clear that Bobby appreciated the way she looked. His eyes were very bright as he laughed. 'Well, Kittrick Maynard's loss is my gain. He must be mad not to fall on you like a wolf on a Sunday roast. It's strange, because around Maynard-Marsham he seems to be quite a force to be reckoned with where the ladies are concerned.'

Chloe stared at Bobby, thunderstruck. It was one thing to torture oneself with fantasies about Kitt's sex life, but to hear this really knocked the wind out of her. How did Bobby know about Kitt and other women?

Bobby clearly sensed her question. 'I've been there this week, remember? I've probably seen more of him than you have and, believe me, there isn't a single woman on the staff who isn't besotted with him.'

Chloe forced a grin. 'Funny . . . *he* said there wasn't a woman there who hadn't been come on to by you and your team!'

Closing his own menu, Bobby shrugged. 'Foul lies.' He waggled his eyebrows fiendishly. 'We were just being friendly.'

In spite of her qualms, Chloe was still smiling when the waiter came over with his notepad.

As soon as they'd ordered, Chloe said, 'OK, I've been patient long enough . . . what's in the portfolio?' She nodded to the slim, black document case that Bobby had brought with him. She suspected it contained photographs because she'd brought some too.

Bobby shrugged and looked pointedly at the manilla wallet in question. 'As if you didn't know. Come on, let's compare notes.'

Bobby Smith had a talent that made Chloe's efforts look raw. His black-and-white shots were particularly dramatic, especially the ones of her. Chloe had seen hundreds of pictures of herself, and she knew quality when she saw it.

'Wonderful,' she said, 'and I mean the photography, of course.'

'Thanks,' he replied, blushing. 'But I couldn't fail, given the subject matter.' He made an odd, tentative little gesture, as if he wanted to reach out and touch the face that had inspired him, yet dared not.

Chloe gave a heavy sigh. 'Come on! I'll start thinking you're just softening me up for the bad news.' She tapped the folder containing her own photographs.

'No, don't worry.' Bobby reached for the folder and flipped it open. 'If they stink, I'll tell you.'

Chloe really doubted that but, even so, she felt nervous. She'd been pleased with her work when she'd first looked at it, but after seeing Bobby's professionalism, she felt far less satisfied. There was obviously a long way to go yet.

Bobby didn't say anything as he studied the pictures, but presently a little smile started to play around his lips. As Chloe sipped her spritzer, he flicked back and forth through the photos, and picked out specific ones. His lips thinned as he studied the 'stolen' pictures she'd taken of Kitt but, despite that, he consigned them to the 'chosen' pile.

'Well?' Chloe demanded

'There's hope for you.' He smiled flippantly.

'Oh thanks! Thanks a bunch! How much

hope?'

Bobby's pleasant face grew more serious. 'A lot, actually.' He gestured that she should look at the selected shots. 'You could be a pro eventually. Especially if you specialise.'

'In what? This lot are hardly more than happy snaps. I can't see how you can make any kind of judgement from them and every time I pick up a camera, I completely forget my theory.'

'Theory's useless if you don't have the "eye",' said Bobby seriously, 'and you've got it. The eye, I mean . . . it just needs a bit of refining. Look at these.' He redirected her attention to her photos. 'Look closely. What do they all have in common?'

To Chloe they seemed a random selection, though mainly of Kitt. 'I don't know,' she said at last, frowning and reaching for her drink again—only to find it empty.

'They're all of men, Chloe. There's nothing wrong with your views and your groups and your women—and the cat studies are sweet— but it's the men that you really have a knack for!'

'Oh my,' murmured Chloe.

Bobby was right though. Her photographs of men were different. There was a discreet, hard-to-define quality that set them apart from ordinary snapshots, but for the life of her, she couldn't pinpoint or define it.

'Why do you think it is?' she asked the

smiling Bobby. A second later, her spirits sank again. 'You don't think it's . . . it's because I'm "me", do you?' She frowned. 'That because I'm a so-called good-looking woman, they light up for me somehow. Because they fancy me . . .'

'You're forgetting one thing,' said Bobby seriously. He lifted up one of the photos of Kitt. '*He* had no idea whatsoever that he was being photographed . . . and I bet he still doesn't know, does he?'

Chloe nodded.

'And neither did most of these others.'

She had no idea how she'd done it.

'So, what now?' she said, gathering up the photographs as the waiter arrived to escort them to their table. 'What do I do with this "thing" I can do?'

'Anything you want, Chloe!' Bobby sounded exultant. 'I can't wait to get you started.'

As they ate their pasta, they discussed ideas. Chloe hooted with laughter when he suggested fashion photography. She'd never be taken seriously in that arena and that was a fact, but Bobby was adamant. He told her to begin a portfolio now and just shoot and shoot and shoot and not be put off when the professionals who were photographing her tried to mock her.

'Get anyone and everyone to pose for you,' urged Bobby. 'Even his nibs, the King of Cool . . . he's the obvious subject for you. If you could get him to pose in a studio situation, you could do incredible things.'

'Kitt would never pose for me,' said Chloe. 'He'd sooner have his arm eaten off by wild dogs?'

'What? Not even to further your new career?' Bobby looked sceptical. 'Surely he wants you to move on from modelling?'

As she considered the remote possibility of getting Kitt in front of a camera, a prickle of awareness lifted the hairs at the back of her neck. She'd been rearranging the last of her pasta on her plate, but suddenly she felt compelled to look up towards the open doorway to the cocktail bar.

Oh, no!

Kitt was just being ushered towards a nearby table by the waiter. Worse still, Geraldine was with him and had fixed a beady eye on Chloe and Bobby. It was too late for lowered heads and avoided glances.

'Good evening, Chloe. Fancy meeting you here,' said Kitt's ex-wife pleasantly, while Kitt stood behind her, his face like marble.

'Hi, Geraldine,' Chloe said just as breezily, wishing that Kitt wasn't looking daggers at her. 'This is our . . . my local. I often come here.'

'Yes, it does seem nice.' Geraldine's tone suggested 'quaint' was the appropriate adjective. Behind her Kitt maintained his silence. 'Who's this then, Chloe?' continued Geraldine, giving Bobby a look of undisguised interest. Chloe cringed, half-expecting the older woman to call Bobby 'your little friend'.

Bobby leapt to his feet, smiled and held out his hand and, as the introductions were made, Kitt finally deigned to speak.

'I didn't know you were dining here, Chloe,' he said suavely. 'You should have mentioned it, we could have booked a table for four.'

You what? thought Chloe at such a grotesque prospect. Geraldine's fleeting look of horror said that she didn't like the idea either. His wild card, however, made Kitt suddenly seem more cordial. He nodded a swift greeting towards Bobby, and gave a contained smile.

'Perhaps we could all have a drink together afterwards?' suggested Geraldine, poise clearly regained. To Chloe's astonishment, Kitt affirmed this with a nod.

'So that's the ex-wife then,' observed Bobby when Kitt and Geraldine were gone.

'Now you see what I'm up against.'

Chloe couldn't see the couple from where she was sitting, but she remembered the solicitous way Kitt had guided his ex-wife forward. A light touch at her waist, all proprietorial and easy. No edging around like a pair of electric eels, the way she and Kitt did these days. Lucky Geraldine could have physical contact whenever she liked and, judging by the look of things, she liked it pretty often.

Who could blame her? Kitt looked as stunning as ever tonight, even more so if that were possible.

Chloe pictured the contrast between the designer-clad Geraldine and Kitt, dressed down in casual style. With a pair of light chinos, he wore a deep olive-coloured collarless shirt—open at the throat—that brought a hot light to his vivid green eyes. His look was effortless, continental, and vaguely roguish. Chloe had never seen it done better, not even on the Italian catwalks. No wonder all the women in the place were staring.

Bobby poured more wine into Chloe's glass and urged it towards her. 'OK, so Geraldine's a looker, but she's no contender where you're concerned. And if you ask me, Kitt knows that. Maybe he's brought her here to make you jealous? Are you sure he didn't know we were going to be here tonight?'

Chloe couldn't be sure. There were ways Kitt could have found out easily enough. But why would he?

'Kitt's not like that. It's only juvenile creatures like me who play those games . . .' She looked up at Bobby, grateful for his niceness and hating herself for wishing he was Kitt. '. . . And exploit smashing men like you for their own nasty purposes.'

'Exploit away!' said Bobby stoutly, 'I'm not complaining. How fabulous it is for me to be seen out with a gorgeous model? And one who's going to be a top photographer too!' He raised his glass, tipped it to Chloe's and said, 'Cheers, Chloe! Here's to new beginnings!'

CHAPTER TEN

The after-dinner drinks encounter had been terrible. A nightmare. Even a couple of weeks later, it made Chloe shudder. She couldn't stop seeing Kitt's face, pale and watchful, full of anger.

An all-out shouting match would probably have been more bearable, but instead they'd all been excruciatingly polite to one other—so the torment had just dragged on and on and on.

Acting her socks off, Chloe had tried to make bland but interesting conversation but, even to her own ears, her voice had sounded strained and silly. Playful banter with fashion people was second nature to her, but having to talk to Kitt and Geraldine and Bobby, all at the same time, had been like having her fingernails and toenails pulled out.

So, she'd been nervous and giggly, Geraldine had been silkily civil, and Kitt had just been weird. Chloe guessed he was trying to act normally, the way she was, but it was obviously an uphill struggle. His voice had been almost frighteningly flat and lifeless and, if he hadn't looked so wonderful, she'd have been worried that he was ill.

Only heroic Bobby had kept the evening and the conversation afloat, and Chloe could have kissed him in gratitude. She felt guilty that she'd exploited him, and later on the guilt expanded when he'd kissed her. She knew she owed him a coffee, but she just hadn't been able to invite him in. And when his lips met hers, she couldn't summon any excitement. Which was a pity because he was a good kisser and more and more he deserved her affection, far more than contrary, mercurial Kitt did. He'd even arranged for a gallery owner to look at her photographs.

'You've got to be joking!' she'd said when Bobby had phoned her the next day and had made his startling proposition. 'I'm a rank amateur, Bobby. Who on earth in their right mind would want *my* photographs in an exhibition?'

But it seemed that someone did, and in the midst of a spectacularly hectic week, including a daylong test shoot in Paris for a major perfume and cosmetics campaign, she'd managed to fit in a trip with Bobby to the Hagan Gallery in Soho.

'I don't think Kitt would approve,' Chloe said to Bobby as they were waiting in the gallery to meet Simon Hagan, the owner. The images currently on show weren't exactly pornographic, but they were slightly disturbing. Elegant and classy, but sexually graphic in the extreme. 'In fact, he'd go bananas. He thinks that shots of Boy unclothed are about as far as I should go.'

'But Chloe, remember it's not you that'll be taking the photographs,' Bobby observed calmly as they mounted the stairs that led to Hagan's office. 'It's Chloe Brown, the photographer—not Chloe Trevelyan, the supermodel. He need never even know you've exhibited.' Chloe had insisted on using a pseudonym, not only in case any fashionistas she knew should happen to scan the art listings, but also on the off chance that Kitt should see them.

After a short wait, they entered Simon Hagan's sanctum.

As Bobby began the introductions, Chloe hung back and looked around her. There were more photographs lining the walls, all just as risqué as the ones outside in the gallery, and all fearsomely well composed.

'And this is Chloe Brown, the fabulous newcomer I was telling you about.' Bobby's face shone with proprietary pride as he gestured Chloe forward.

'Pleased to meet you.' She held out a hand and waited what seemed like an age for Simon Hagan's response. He was a surprisingly ordinary character for someone with photos of naked men and women on every wall, but he looked her up and down, then raised her

115

fingers to his lips and kissed them, continental-style.

'Ah, the glorious Chloe.' His voice was husky but strangely plummy. 'I'm privileged, not to say rather turned-on to meet you. You're a famous beauty!'

Chloe gave Bobby a stony look, but Simon Hagan intercepted it 'Don't be angry with Robert. He was perfectly discreet.' Hagan gave her a winning smile. 'It's just that you're instantly recognisable, my dear, even dressed for an assault course!'

Chloe looked down at her clothes. She'd hoped that the grungy ex-army look would make her seem like just another 'arty' type. But, clearly, not even a 'Che Guevara' style beret and mock horn-rimmed spectacles from her prop collection had worked

'I didn't realise I was so well-known.' She pulled off her hat and released her hair from its scrunchie. As she was beginning to realise, she must be more famous than she'd thought

She soon found it easy to relax with Hagan and Bobby, and even felt much better about her work once she'd heard the gallery owner's comments.

'Yes, this is just the sort of thing I want for the "New Sensuality" exhibition,' he said, rifling through the prints. 'I see you very much at the softer end of the spectrum obviously . . . but I'm getting a bit tired of "in-your-face" erotic stuff.' He made a vague gesture to

116

indicate the photos on the wall. 'I want "New Sensuality" to express a gentler, more accessible palette. Your style is perfect for the romantic image. Sort of sensual mainstream with a twist.' He continued to shuffle her photos like playing cards. 'Who is *this*, Chloe?' he said, selecting a sheaf of about five photographs. 'He's a stunner. Absolutely gorgeous! Is he your muse?'

Kitt, a 'stunner'? Well, he was to her, but it sounded odd to hear someone else describe him that way. And she wasn't surprised that Hagan had chosen the shots of him as her best.

'He's a friend,' she said, lifting her gaze and catching a quick glance flashing between the two men.

'I see,' said Hagan, rifling again. 'Well, he really pushes the button obviously. I'd like to see several more shots of him in the "story" you do for me.'

Chloe noted the use of the fashion term 'story'—meaning a small, self-contained group of themed items—and felt her heart thud. How many photographs did Hagan want? She'd thought one, perhaps two at the most.

'Er . . . how many photographs would you want from me?' She kept her voice dead level.

'Oh, six or eight. Maybe more. But definitely more of *him*!' He tapped the glossy image of Kitt again.

'He won't pose,' she said to Bobby as they left the gallery. 'He'll just laugh in my face—or worse—if I ask him!'

'You don't know that,' replied Bobby, sounding confident. 'And, anyway, you can always try and catch Kitt while he's sunbathing or something? Unposed shots are often the best, you know.'

But, afterwards, alone, Chloe knew that she was right. Kitt would not pose for her, and if she took clandestine photographs of him, he'd be livid.

Which meant for the sake of the man she loved, she was going to have to give up the best break she'd ever had, high-profile cosmetics campaigns notwithstanding. It was such a bitter piece of irony that he didn't love her.

*   *   *

Oh lor! Why did a knock on that door always mean trouble nowadays?

Chloe paused as she swept her arms down to touch her toes. Even on a free day, she still did her exercise routine to keep her body toned.

The knock came again, but softer this time. Chloe flinched and rose from her mat, knowing it was very probably Kitt out there, but almost wishing that it wasn't. A confrontation had been on the cards ever since that gruesome night at 'Lucci', a couple of weeks ago.

Oh, what the heck! Steeling herself, Chloe

flung open the door with a flourish, grateful that she was working out in a T-shirt and jogging pants, and not an abbreviated leotard.

'Good morning. Lovely day, isn't it? May I come in?'

Chloe felt like shaking her head to wake herself up. Who was this cheerful, smiling stranger who'd come to her wearing Kitt Maynard's handsome face? Where was the scowling thunder? The cold disapproval? Was this a changeling?

'Yes . . . do . . .' Bemused, she led the way into her sitting room. It wasn't actually a different Kitt at all, she realised, just the good friend she'd always had, suddenly returned to her. If she hadn't known it would spoil things, she would have leapt at him and hugged him.

Instead, she asked, 'Would you like a coffee? I was just about to have some.'

'No thanks.' Standing beside the table, Kitt looked down at some of the photos she'd left there. 'I hope I didn't disturb your exercise routine.'

'No, I'd just finished,' lied Chloe, wondering which prints she'd been looking at last. She hoped there weren't any of Kitt, or Bobby . . .

But Kitt seemed only mildly interested in the shiny black-and-white rectangles that littered the table. 'I just came down to see if you had any assignments today.' He turned from the table, a print in his hand, and a curiously tentative look on his face.

119

'Nope! I'm free as a bird.' Chloe's spirits clamoured and leapt like a demented inner cheerleader, 'My booker's having hysterics. She thinks I should work 24/7, of course, but I don't care. I deserve a day off!'

It was partly a lie. She'd planned to do some prep for the 'New Sensuality' exhibition today, and she was supposed to be seeing Bobby for a lesson in darkroom technique. But none of that mattered now that Kitt was here, asking about her time.

'That's great!' Kitt dropped the photo back onto the pile. 'I'm going to the coast today to see a client, but I thought I might make it a round trip and call in at Arrowsmith Court, then swing by Bramlington and see the parents.' His almost-shy smile melted her heart and dissolved away all doubts. 'Do you want to come with me? I'd love some company.'

One of the doubts resurfaced. He'd said 'some', not 'your' company. Did that mean Geraldine had already turned him down? But the offer was too choice to nit-pick at. She answered his smile and said, 'Yes! I'd love to go!'

For a moment, Kitt looked vaguely uncomfortable. Was he already regretting the offer, Chloe wondered? She'd just have to curb these shows of overt emotion because it was plain that Kitt just wanted friendship and easy, relaxing company and not her behaving like a love-lorn groupie.

'When do you want to set off?' she asked quietly. 'I can be changed in two ticks.'

'We'll need to get on the road as soon as possible, really.' Kitt was already crossing to the door. 'There's a lot to fit in if we want to have some free time too.'

'Fifteen minutes! Tops!' promised Chloe and, as he gave her a little wave, then disappeared, she was already planning. How useful it was to be a quick-change artist . . .

*   *   *

It was exactly twenty minutes later when Chloe opened her door again in answer to Kitt's knock. She'd just finished putting out food to last Boy for the day.

'When I said a day out, I didn't mean on manoeuvres,' Kitt said, looking her up and down and grinning in amusement.

Chloe had on her 'ex-army' look again—although without the glasses and the beret this time. She'd decided that asexual clothing was probably the safest bet whilst around Kitt—it was less problematical. 'It's comfy,' she said, following him out of the building. 'And practical too. While you're busy chatting up your business colleagues, I can just blend into the background.'

Kitt raised his dark eyebrows. 'Well, actually, we'll be having our discussions in a modern site office, not in the undergrowth.' He smiled again and took her gadget bag from her to put safely on the Lancia's tiny back seat. 'Although I must admit the outfit does have a certain industrial charm . . . And, at least, you're not wearing hobnailed boots with it.' He was laughing outright as he stepped back to let her climb into the car.

'My hobnailed boots are at the menders,' Chloe laughed back at him as she settled into old, but deliciously comfortable, upholstery.

'You know, I half believe you, young lady,' said Kitt, shutting the passenger door.

Young lady? Oh, not that again! Chloe watched covertly as he slid into the driver's seat beside her. What was he thinking? Had he really so conveniently forgotten everything she knew he'd felt when he'd kissed her?

But she wouldn't get into that debate again. It was safer for the moment to let him nurse his strange notions. That way, they'd both have a good day together.

As Kitt engaged the engine and set the Lancia rolling down the drive like some sultry mechanical predator, Chloe looked up into a sky that was brilliantly blue and full of promise. Then she smiled and sneaked another look at her chauffeur.

She was in a beautiful car, with a beautiful man, on what now seemed likely to be a beautifully sunny day. What more could she ask for?

CHAPTER ELEVEN

The journey down to Westbourne on Sea was idyllic. Having Kitt to herself, and having back the old, easy companionship they'd always had was like a dream come true, and Chloe had no idea what she'd done to deserve it. There was only one infinitesimal niggle in her perfect happiness, and that was the fact that she'd summarily abandoned her plans to meet Bobby, but she consoled herself that, while Kitt was busy, she'd be able give Bobby a call from her mobile and explain matters. She was being selfish, she supposed, but hopefully she'd find a way to make things up to him.

When, eventually, they fell into a companionable silence, Chloe watched the passing scenery for a while, then stole a sly glance sideways at Kitt.

To offset the glare of the sun, Kitt had put on his sunglasses, hiding his magnificent green eyes—but everything else was on show for Chloe to feast on. His strong, freshly shaven jaw line, his black hair, endearingly tousled by the wind from the wound-down window, his powerful body, simply dressed in the plainest of white shirts and close-fitting jeans. It was all Chloe could do not to sigh aloud with pleasure and when Kitt turned to her suddenly and she jumped in surprise, she almost wondered if she had actually made a sound.

'Are you all right?' He looked at her for a split second, then back at the road.

'Yes! Fine!' she replied, straightening in her seat. She'd have to watch herself or he'd think she'd really gone mad!

But it was hard not to dream, to revel in his presence, and Chloe spent most of the rest of the journey in an elaborate soft focus fantasy of herself and Kitt picnicking beside a river somewhere. They were both wearing pastels, and there was a lot of running through meadows and herself looking very fetching in a wide straw picture hat. It was all very Calvin Klein, without much dialogue, but a great deal of touching and kissing.

Of course, it ended deep in the long grass, on a blanket, with them making love . . .

Half in and half out of her dream world, Chloe turned to watch Kitt drive for a moment. His hands were strong yet light on the steering wheel, and his wrists supple. He did everything without seeming to exert any effort, and she wondered if he'd employ the same adroit simplicity if he ever made love to her.

What would his touch feel like? she wondered, drifting back to the soft-focus riverside. What would it feel like to have those narrow, artistic fingertips seeking out the most intimate and sensitive zones of her body? What would it feel like to have him naked and glorious inside her?

Enough already! Feeling strangely short of breath, Chloe gave herself a strong inner shake. That way lay madness, and it would be better not to go there if she wanted to hold on to her sanity.

'Do you want to take your stuff with you?' asked Kitt when they'd arrived and he was parking the Lancia in a secured parking area adjacent to the project site.

'Yes, definitely.' She wanted to take some photographs of the soaring building and its exo-skeleton of scaffolding, and she also wanted to make that sneaky call to Bobby. 'If that's all right?'

'Sure.' Kitt opened his door and swung his long legs out, stretching them. With a grimace, he grasped his right calf and drew the whole leg upwards, bringing his knee almost up to his chest to loosen the seized muscle. 'You can be my official photographer for the day—if you think you're up to it?'

'Of course,' said Chloe, trying not to show that she was nettled. When, oh when, would he ever take her photography seriously? Her irritation faded, though, when she saw that Kitt's eyes were closed as if he were mastering considerable pain.

It was her turn to say 'Are you all right?' now.

With some of his knots apparently loosened, Kitt turned towards her. 'Yes, I think so. It's nothing that a good trek around a building site won't sort out.' He rose lightly to his feet beside the car. 'I think I need to do more swimming,' he went on, stretching his shoulders now. 'I've been getting too tense lately. Spending too much time at the board and not enough time relaxing.'

I could help you with that, thought Chloe, as she reached for her gadget bag, then began setting up her camera. She was loaded and ready and needed only a few final adjustments.

'Can I take your picture,' she said when they were both out of the car and Kitt was fishing his jacket out of the boot. She thought it was unlikely he'd agree, but there was no harm in seizing the moment.

Kitt shook his head, and turned away. 'Not now . . . I'm not ready,' he said, laughing.

'Later then,' insisted Chloe, her hopes of fulfilling Simon Hagan's mandate sinking.

'Maybe,' he demurred.

Kitt's jacket was casual and loosely styled, but even so it seemed to imbue him with additional elegance. In her khaki fatigues, Chloe felt like a scruff beside him. 'I'll make myself scarce for a while, and you just go and do your thing.' She looked across at the half-constructed edifice, a dramatic, rather futuristic, sports centre. 'It already looks pretty stunning, even though it isn't finished.'

'Thank you,' said Kitt, giving her a self-mocking grin. Despite that, he looked pleased that she'd praised his work. 'You will take care, though, won't you? It *is* a building site.'

'Nag, nag, nag!' said Chloe lightly, determined not to get rattled again by his protectiveness.

'Seriously, though, take care. And you'd better wear one of these.' He reached into the boot again and retrieved a safety helmet.

Chloe knew that even she would look vile in the ugly white plastic headgear but, for peace and quiet's sake, she decided not to quibble. She crammed it on her head, then adjusted the angle to something jauntier.

'I'll see you in about an hour,' said Kitt, donning his own helmet, which didn't look nearly as silly on him as Chloe imagined hers did on her. 'And if I'm finished sooner than that, I'll come and find you. I'll just follow the wolf whistles.'

'I might not get any,' said Chloe, still fiddling with her helmet, and finding that when she lifted the camera to her eye, she had to tilt the hard hat backwards. 'They might not fancy me as GI Jane.'

'Oh, they will,' said Kitt as he left her, his smile ironic.

The first thing Chloe did once she was on her own was make her call to Bobby. Unfortunately, his mobile was off so she was forced to leave a message. Feeling acutely conscious-ridden, she left a suitably vague voicemail, then tried to put her thoughtlessness behind her.

Returning her attention to the burgeoning sports centre and its artistic possibilities, Chloe soon discovered that Kitt had been right. She got plenty of catcalls and barracking as she made her way around the perimeter of the site in search of good angles—but the shouts were good-natured, and extravagantly complimentary rather than offensive.

It wasn't the first time Chloe had seen or visited buildings designed by Kitt, but now she had new eyes to see his work. Maybe because she was beginning to be more creative herself, she felt better able to appreciate his genius, and it felt wonderful just to be associated with someone so gifted.

It was a curvaceous structure, reflecting the natural arcs of sport itself—the flex of a longbow, the high swing of a tennis racket—and, as such, it was a heavenly subject for the composition-seeking eye. Chloe's found herself peeling off shot after shot, experimenting with different depths of field and exposure, and several times reloading with film without even thinking. She knew she was doing good work, and it was only a shame that Simon Hagan's exhibition wasn't of architectural photography.

But what about taking some candid shots of the bare-chested builders themselves? They were men after all, her supposed speciality.

The first ten minutes was taken up in much

saucy banter and very little photography, but soon she was able to take photographs while they just got on, quite unselfconsciously, with their work. They were all young and fit, and had better bodies than many of those that Chloe encountered in the studio. It wasn't very long before she was convinced she had some pictures to be proud of, and she was just taking down some of the men's names, so she could send them prints, when she heard her name being called.

It was Kitt. He was coming towards her down the unmade road that swept around the side of the building.

'All done now,' said Kitt as he drew close. 'Are you ready to go?' He cast a dubious look at the builders who, seeing 'management' bearing down on them, were already returning to work.

'Yes, I think so,' Chloe replied, fiddling with her hard hat again. 'I thought it would be nice to have a few bodies along with the building.'

Kitt was quiet as they walked back to the car.

'What's wrong?' Chloe demanded when they were stowing her gear, the hat, and Kitt's jacket in the boot. 'Is something wrong with the building? Or are you annoyed with me for hob-nobbing with workmen?'

'There's nothing wrong. Construction workers have a reputation to live up to, but basically they're harmless.'

'Well, what it is then? The building? It looks amazing from where I'm standing.'

'There are one or two little snags. Nothing major,' said Kitt indistinctly. Nevertheless, Chloe had a gut feeling that he was lying, and not about the sports centre.

No, Kitt was fibbing about his attitude to her. He really hadn't liked the way she'd been so friendly with the workmen.

'Oh, that's all right then.' She glanced at her watch. 'Flipping heck! It's midday already. What're we going to do? Have lunch here? Or get on our way?'

Kitt seemed to sigh—but so faintly that it was little more than just a breath. He looked down at his own watch, his eyes thoughtful.

'Let's have lunch here, shall we?' He shrugged his shoulders as if he were consciously trying to shake off his own ill humour. 'I fancy something hideously greasy down on the sea front . . . how about you?'

'Super. Bring on the grease,' said Chloe. She would have agreed to eat nails to salvage the moment. 'I'll bring the camera. Maybe I'll catch a shot of you scoffing candy floss or ice-cream?'

'Fat chance of that,' said Kitt equably. 'There's junk food and there's junk food.'

'Whatever,' said Chloe, with a shrug of her own as Kitt locked the car and they set off downhill towards the sea front.

She was frowning though, as she matched

130

her long stride to his. Candy floss or no, she was determined to get some pictures of Kitt soon, whether he liked it or not.

CHAPTER TWELVE

In the end, they had fresh crab sandwiches and mineral water for lunch, which was positively saintly, and it was after this impromptu meal that Chloe finally got the chance to photograph Kitt.

Returning from the Ladies on the promenade, she saw Kitt waiting for her by the sea wall, completely absorbed in the comings and goings of the yachts and other boats in the harbour. Hardly daring to breath, lest somehow he should realise she was watching him, she flipped off the lens cap, made a couple of quick adjustments, then drew a bead on her beloved's pensive profile. Kitt was so wrapped up in the harbour activities that she was able to take several shots without him becoming aware of her.

They wouldn't be what Simon Hagan really wanted, she realised. There was too much background and not enough actual Kitt on show. But, despite that, Chloe knew the images would still be sensual. Kitt looked preoccupied and almost yearning, almost mystical, as if somehow he was seeing more than the sleek lines of the tall-masted sailing boats. Her heart twisted as she slowly lowered her camera.

What was he thinking about? Was he thinking about her? She hardly dare speculate. There was every chance that it was Geraldine on his mind, or even someone else. Whoever it was, Chloe had never seen him look so passionate—or so young, with his black curls ruffled by the breeze.

She could have stood for hours just admiring him, but they had to move on. They were already well behind schedule.

'Watch the birdie!' she called once she was within Kitt's earshot. This time, she aimed the camera without any subterfuge.

Caught unawares, Kitt looked uncomfortable and vaguely embarrassed. Chloe felt guilty until he suddenly smiled. 'OK, I give in!' he said, visibly loosening up and laughing as he swept the hair out of his eyes. He raised his hands in surrender. 'It's a fair cop! I knew I couldn't really get away with it.'

'Wonderful! Hold that!' Quickly, Chloe reframed him and took another sequence of shots as fast as the motor drive would let her. 'Now, look scared. Surprised. As if you really were surrendering . . . that's it! Perfect! Hands higher!' Realising how she must sound, she started laughing—and couldn't stop. She had to lower the camera. She'd actually become a snappie without ever realising it.

Kitt was laughing too. 'You sound just like a pro,' he said as she reached his side.

Chloe recapped the lens, then they set off, heading back towards the sports centre.

'With luck I will be one eventually,' she said without really thinking. 'A pro photographer, that is . . .'

Chloe almost stopped in her tracks. Oh God, she'd gone and told him! She waited for the laughter and the gentle scorn.

Kitt continued to walk and, at first, Chloe thought that that was the end of the matter. Maybe he wasn't really all that interested in her plans? But then he spoke again, thoughtfully. 'Yes, I had a feeling that's what you were planning. It would be a natural progression.'

Again he fell silent as they walked, and Chloe seethed to know what he was thinking. This was such a big deal to her, and he seemed quite calm about it.

'Is that all you can say?' she demanded eventually. 'I thought you'd be pleased. You've always made it blindingly obvious that you hate me being a model.'

They were climbing a hill, and there was a bench set in a lookout point, surveying the bay. Kitt took Chloe's hand, led her to the seat, and made her sit.

'I don't hate your modelling career.' His beautiful green eyes. were level and serious. 'I just worry about you. I can't help myself.'

133

Chloe's spirits bubbled, he was still holding her hand. 'And I worry about you going into photography too, I suppose.' He looked out to sea for a moment, pursing his finely moulded lips before he spoke again. 'I know you're a good photographer, perhaps even a great one. Heaven knows, you've always taken pictures, and you probably know more about the craft than most of the posers who photograph you.' He paused again, weighing his words. 'But it's a really tough business—possibly tougher than modelling even—and I don't want you to be hurt if you don't succeed.'

He gave her strange, wistful, half-sad smile. Chloe's heart melted and, momentarily, she experienced a finer, more complex feeling for him than her usual confused hodgepodge of love, lust, and deeply-frustrated resentment. She was so touched by his concern that she almost forgot that he was holding her hand. That his thumb was travelling gently to and fro across her knuckles.

'I still have to try,' she said quietly.

'I know that.' The sad smile warmed. 'And I'd expect nothing less of you.' His fingers tightened around hers, exerting a gentle pressure. It was only for emphasis, but it thrilled her. 'Just be prepared for some hiccups, Chloe. There could be snags that have nothing to do with lack of talent.'

'I know that,' said Chloe, struggling to sound and to be rational. 'And I'm prepared.

You'd be surprised how realistic my expectations are. I'm aiming high . . . but I'll still be happy if I just achieve the middle ground. I'll still enjoy myself.' She looked down at their linked hands. If only her expectations about Kitt could be so realistic. If only she could accept his friendship without yearning for the stars.

When she looked up again, Kitt's expression was indecipherable. But then, she saw something she recognised but hadn't dared hope for.

Respect. After months in the wilderness, finally, professional respect.

'You're a wise girl, Chloe,' he said, releasing her hand but somehow not their connection. 'And I'm a blind fool sometimes, for not crediting that wisdom.' He grinned. 'Do you think that you can ever forgive me?'

'I'll consider it,' she replied, trying to sound pert, but really hardly able to think straight for happiness. 'I'll put you on probation.'

'Fair enough.' Kitt rose and flexed his weaker leg after the immobility. Chloe felt a pang of sympathy. 'Shall we get on? We've got a good few miles ahead of us.'

But as they left Westbourne behind and struck out into the beautiful English countryside, Kitt continued to ask questions.

Chloe was thrilled by his interest, even if the more seriously he took her, the faster her stress levels rose. She stole sly glances at his profile as they drove along, and flashing slices of sunlight created a strobe effect, making Kitt's male beauty seem unearthly and surreal. He looked fierce and dark and war-like, even though his voice was friendly. She mustn't spoil things by mentioning Bobby and the Hagan Gallery.

They discussed all kinds of photography and what Chloe's preferences were and, after a while, Kitt asked after the pictures she'd taken at the 'Right to Walk' garden party.

Uh oh! Chloe's emotional radar pinged. Had she detected a note of tension there? They both knew she'd spent most of her time at the garden party with Bobby.

'I only just got them back. I'll show them to you when we get home,' she said as unconcerned as she could, making a mental note to take out some of the shots beforehand.

The rest of the way to the Court was spent in relative silence. Chloe was mulling over whether she should tell Kitt about the photographic exhibition, but she couldn't tell what he was thinking at all.

'Beautiful, isn't it?' said Kitt, eventually drawing the Lancia to a halt at the roadside. They had just crested a hill and, below them, nestling in formal gardens and woodland and in its own shadow-gilded valley, lay Arrowsmith Court.

'Glorious,' agreed Chloe. She'd been to the Court a number of times, and she loved it for its beauty and its inimitable character. Now it seemed more inspiring than ever, and its honey-gold stone sent her fishing in her bag for colour film.

'Hard to believe it was built in the middle of this century, isn't it?' observed Kitt, as Chloe joined him, camera ready. 'If I didn't know otherwise, even *I'd* swear it was genuine Georgian. The weathering of the stone, the layout . . . Maybrick took the best of classical style, and made it completely functional for modern living.'

Dragging her eyes away from the lovely house, Chloe looked at Kitt. His animated face was full of pleasure and admiration. He loved Arrowsmith Court both as a piece of art, and for its own sake. She wondered if he would like to live there some day—that was, if Geraldine gave him the chance. Lady Barbara had no potential heirs other than Kitt and his ex-wife, and Chloe didn't think that Geraldine would cede the Court to Kitt completely, just like that.

'Just look at the *port-cochère*! It's so authentic. That lovely pediment.' Kitt grabbed Chloe's arm, pointing out architectural features, but all she could do was tremble at the contact. Then he turned to her, laughing.

Chloe laughed back. It was always the same where this house and other buildings were concerned. Kitt would start talking nineteen to the dozen, entranced by both the art and the craftmanship and trying to help her see what he saw, which was the mind of its architect.

'I'm rabbiting, aren't I?' He gave her a boyish, self-deprecating look that dangerously undermined her.

'Ah, but it's interesting,' she countered, wishing she could just kiss him and be done with it. With every minute of this day that passed, the more she loved him. How much more could she take and not make a fool of herself?

'Well, yes, it *is* to me,' he said solemnly, 'but I know you've heard all this before from me about the Court. You must be getting fed up of it.'

'I don't mind.' Chloe raised her camera and framed the perfect proportions of the Court within a border of its elegant gardens. 'It's a jewel of a house,' she murmured, reverently squeezing the shutter.

'Shall we go on down then?' Kitt said when Chloe finally lowered the camera. He didn't seem impatient though, somehow. If anything, the opposite.

'How is Lady Barbara?' Once they were in the car again, Chloe sensed the source of his sudden disquiet.

'Not good. When I rang, the nurse said she's rather poorly at the moment, but she still insists on seeing people.'

Chloe said nothing. It didn't require a mastermind to work out why Lady Barbara craved visitors, but she wondered if she would really be welcome. The old lady wanted to see Kitt with Geraldine, not other people.

'Do you think Lady Barbara would mind me taking some photographs inside?' she asked when they'd nearly reached the house. 'It's so gorgeous in there . . . but, of course, if you think she'll think it's an invasion of her privacy?'

'I don't think Barbara would see it that way.' Kitt seemed relieved to be off the subject of mortality. 'She's very proud of the Court, and it was quite a society gathering place in its heyday.' His eyes brightened as if he'd suddenly had a very good idea. 'You know . . . she'd love a photo spread of the place in one of the glossies. That would be right up her alley.' He gave Chloe a quick, sharp glance. 'Do you have any contacts? The journals I contribute to are a bit too dry and serious . . . but if *you* could take some pictures and show them to the right people?'

Chloe thought about it. She *did* know people, and so did Florence. Not to mention Bobby . . .

'I can't make any promises,' she said cautiously, 'but I can try. I doubt if they'd accept my photographs though. Those mags usually use their own people.'

'Good girl!' Kitt gave her a smile of surpassing brilliance as he drew the Lancia to a standstill, and Chloe basked in it, ignoring

139

the fact he'd called her a 'girl'.

Lady Barbara's housekeeper, who seemed both delighted and relieved to see Kitt, met them at the door and escorted him upstairs to see Lady Barbara. Chloe was left to her own devices to explore the house.

Cruising the downstairs rooms, Chloe marvelled at how welcoming the Court was. Lovely though the place was, there was an air of warmth and informality about it. There was nothing to intimidate the casual visitor, and the very eclecticism in the mix of art and furnishings seemed to invite familiarity, rather than signalling 'do not touch'. Genuine treasures rubbed shoulders with objects that gave simple pleasure but had little intrinsic value, in a captivating jumble.

Aware of the pitfalls of interior lighting, Chloe decided to photograph some of these smaller items and arrangements. Her flash unit was first rate, but it couldn't illuminate an entire room successfully, even in addition to ambient daylight. So she chose cameo shots that she hoped would capture the flavour of the Court in microcosm. She laughed at the sight of a jolly, polished stone Buddha, sitting on a small table by one of the big, French windows, and she only hoped that her choice of lens had done it justice.

So absorbed in her work did she become that she completely lost track of the passing time. When she looked at her watch, Chloe realised that over three-quarters of an hour had passed since Kitt had gone upstairs. What on earth could they be talking about all this time? She popped yet another exposed roll of film into her bag, then reloaded. Maybe Lady Barbara wasn't quite as fragile as Kitt had feared, and was enjoying a good chinwag.

Deciding to go outside and photograph some more exteriors, Chloe found herself pondering the Court's future.

What if Geraldine did get sole control of it? Would she actually live here, or would she use it for something? Chloe shuddered, imagining the Court as a business convention centre, or something completely soulless like that. She couldn't imagine even Geraldine being so mercenary, and it would certainly be an unmitigated disaster in Kitt's eyes.

Chloe was just walking backwards to try and frame the ivy-clad frontage when she lost concentration again because Kitt suddenly appeared in the viewfinder. He was coming around the corner of the house, obviously from the rear entrance. His stride was brisk, showing no sign of his limp and, though he looked thoughtful, his expression wasn't particularly gloomy. Chloe felt relief that Lady Barbara obviously wasn't too poorly.

'How is she?' Chloe enquired when Kitt reached her.

'Better, actually.' Kitt's relief was clear upon his face now. 'She perked up quite a bit while

141

we were talking, and seemed really interested in things.' He frowned. 'I should visit her more often. I should make a real effort . . . work isn't everything.'

'You do the best you can,' said Chloe firmly. 'I'm sure she appreciates your visits.' She hesitated, wondering if she was going to seem pushy. 'Do you think she'd like it if I went up and said hello too? That is, if she remembers me?'

'I'm sure she'd like that,' said Kitt, smiling again. 'In fact, she's having a little nap at the moment, but then she's going to get up and dressed and, after that, she's going to hold a little tea party.'

'Really?'

'Really,' he confirmed. 'And, in the meantime, why don't we have a stroll in the grounds? You could take some nature photographs.' He touched her lightly on the back, prompting her towards the outer gardens. 'What about doing a modern version of "The Edwardian Lady"? There might be a market for a photographic nature notebook by a millennial woman . . . it's worth considering.'

Chloe laughed. 'Sounds a bit on the scholarly side. I'd need a botanist as co-author.'

'Just a thought,' said Kitt mildly as they walked on.

The formal gardens of Arrowsmith Court were girdled by an expanse of open green parkland where sheep from the nearby home farm grazed. Beyond that lay mature woodlands, bisected to the south by a meandering tributary of a river. It was in this direction that Chloe and Kitt meandered too, soon reaching the division between the sun and the shady copse.

'Fancy a paddle?' said Kitt, casting a glance at Chloe over his shoulder as he led the way.

'Sure! Why not?' The afternoon was just getting more and more blissful!

This is just too good to be true, she thought, staring at Kitt's broad back as he took point along a roughly defined track. Any moment now, something had to go wrong. She'd say something stupid. Kitt would take issue with it. And suddenly they'd be back to square one, all prickly and on tenterhooks.

And yet peace continued to reign as they pioneered along the path.

'Here?' asked Kitt, as they broke out of the tangle into clearer ground along the riverside.

'Fine,' said Chloe. Moving ahead of him, she selected a shady area in deference to her complexion, then slid down to sit with her back against a tree trunk. She needed a chance to sort through her bag and see what film was left.

In times gone by, they might have ended up having a water fight in a place like this, and playing the sort of mad games two old, old friends played. But, somehow, Chloe couldn't see that happening today. They'd crossed a watershed some time in the last few weeks, and Chloe still wasn't too sure about the state that lay beyond it. She couldn't forget how Kitt had kissed her and, whenever she looked at him now, her thoughts always seemed to sidle back to it.

I want you, Kitt! she thought, stifling an inner cry of longing. I want you and I can't deny it, even if you don't want me!

At that moment, Chloe nearly dropped her camera. Almost as if he'd heard her voiceless declaration, Kitt had turned towards her, his green eyes shadowed and questioning. The expression only lingered an instant, but it was enough to fill Chloe with depression.

It'd been quite clear, in those dark, haunted eyes, that he didn't share her lust.

CHAPTER THIRTEEN

'Can I take another picture of you?' said Chloe a while later, when they were sitting on the bank in companionable silence. She didn't hold out much hope for a 'yes' but she couldn't stop herself from trying. She'd been watching Kitt skim stones, but suddenly the urge to take pictures had overcome her.

To her surprise, he said, 'All right then,' even though he sounded dubious. 'But just one

144

or two, eh? I'm not really model material.'

'OK. And thanks!' Chloe's voice was crisp and professional as she moved closer and did more fidgeting with her camera's focusing ring.

There was no magic way to make him relax when she knew he was unhappy in front of the camera, but Chloe worked as quickly as she could to get the best of the unexpected opportunity.

Surprisingly though, the shots felt good as she was taking them. Kitt might not have been comfortable in front of the camera, but he didn't show it. He looked at her challengingly, without inhibition, and seemed to command the lens.

Eventually, she lowered the camera, and said, 'Enough, I think.' It was no use pushing it too far, she'd been lucky enough already. She gave him a grateful smile, as she returned the camera to the safety of its bag. 'I can tell you're getting twitchy . . . and the moment a model tenses up, you might as well cut your losses and call it a day.'

Kitt nodded. 'It didn't hurt too much,' he said gazing absently out across the water.

'It's gorgeous here,' Chloe observed, looking up into the dappled canopy of trees that shaded them. 'Like a secret hideaway. I half expect to see fairies peeping out from amongst the reeds.' She glanced quickly at Kitt, to see if he thought she was talking nonsense, but he was still staring at the surface of the river. 'Do you think anyone else comes here?' What was this? What was she saying? 'What I mean is . . . I fancy a swim, and I wondered if anyone was likely to come by and tell me that I shouldn't.'

'Well, it's Barbara's stretch of river, and I know she wouldn't mind.'

Chloe almost did a double take. She'd expected a sharp instruction not to be ridiculous, but he seemed to be encouraging her. What was the matter with him?

'I think I'll join you. I fancy a swim myself.'

Chloe's jaw dropped and she was glad Kitt wasn't looking at her. She could hardly believe her ears. It was almost as if a different Kitt, the Kitt of her dreams, had suddenly stolen into the clearing and replaced the cautious, sensible one. She watched in wonder as he began to unbutton his cuffs.

Shock interfered with the way her own fingers worked, but as Chloe glanced cautiously across at Kitt, he already had his shirt off. Everything had changed in a blink of an eye. For weeks, she and Kitt had been on tenterhooks with each other, and now he was calmly preparing to go skinny-dipping with her. It was as incomprehensible as she'd been demented to even suggest it.

Kitt's white shirt was on the grass now, and so were his shoes and socks. Any moment now, his jeans and underwear would follow.

If I say anything now, he'll change his mind,

Chloe thought. Or maybe I'll wake up and find I've been dreaming. Moving as neatly and unobtrusively as she could, she began tugging off her trainers and socks, trying not to look at Kitt in case she moaned out loud.

Thinking laterally, she worked off her trousers before her vest, because she was wearing no bra beneath it, because everything could capsize if Kitt bottled out before she bared her breasts. With her long, slim thighs on show, but still technically decent, she raised her eyes and stole a split-second look at Kitt.

He was still undressing, just as she was, with the minimum amount of fuss. But Kitt had started first, and was miles ahead . . .

It wasn't as if she hadn't seen Kitt without clothes before, Chloe owned, gripping the hem of her vest as if she were clinging onto a precipice. Only the other week, she'd seen him in his flat in just a towel, and there had been rare occasions, in the past, when she'd seen him in less. During impromptu swims like this one, when she'd once or twice seen rather more of Kitt than she'd been meant to do.

But she'd never seen him naked—and been so *aware* of him. Truth be known, as Kitt stepped elegantly out of his grey Calvins, she had never been more aware of anything in her life than she was now of his unclothed body and its vivid maleness. When he tossed his underwear on top of his other clothing, Chloe snapped her jaw shut because it dawned on her that she'd been watching him with her mouth wide open, like a drooling dog!

Kitt had every reason to be proud of his body, and all the more so for having rebuilt his physique through hours of gruelling exercise after his accident. Not one of her male model colleagues was anywhere near as beautiful as Kitt was, and he would have been flawlessly perfect if it wasn't for those long, telling scars.

Aware of being watched, Kitt turned suddenly, making Chloe blush and mangle her already-crumpled vest. She didn't know what she expected him to say, but his small, shy smile was strangely touching. 'Are you joining me then?' he asked, then seemed to hesitate, bashfully unsure of himself, rooted to the spot.

'Yes! Um . . . yes, of course,' she jabbered, as pink in the face as if she'd never stripped off without a thought behind the scenes at fashion shows. Her model friends would laugh themselves silly to see her cringing and shrinking away so, as nonchalantly as she could, she whipped her vest off over her head, then tugged off her knickers with an equal lack of ceremony.

Once she was naked, she couldn't meet Kitt's eyes, and she sensed that he didn't know quite where to look either. If the moment hadn't been so fraught with tension, it would have been hilarious. It was difficult to tell which one of them was more embarrassed.

This is ridiculous! thought Chloe. We're

both adults. We've both been naked in front of the opposite sex before. 'Last one in's a sissy!' she cried, striding forward into the water.

The river was cool, but not freezing, and the second after she hit the water, Chloe felt the wash of Kitt plunging in beside her. A few feet away from the bank, the depth of the stream increased sharply and they were able to start swimming. Chloe applied herself to breaststroke with a vengeance. It seemed the easiest way not to think about Kitt naked just feet away.

They swam for about a quarter-of-an-hour without speaking. The river was wide, and though fairly sluggish, the water level was high due to recent rain and pleasantly clear.

'That's better,' said Kitt after a while, as he glided up to her, then floated beside her, mid-stream. 'I didn't realise how knackered I was feeling.' Treading water, he raised his hands and slicked his hair back out of his eyes.

'You don't look knackered.' Chloe feathered her legs slowly to hold station at his side. You always look wonderful to me, Kitt, she thought helplessly, wishing she dared say it.

Kitt rubbed his wet face, then swept his arms back down into the water and gave her a grin. Chloe avoided following the motion with her eyes. The river water was like glass.

'I've used a ton of film,' she said, changing the subject and nodding to her bag, where it

149

lay on the bank, beside her clothes.

'You could do a book,' said Kitt, closing his eyes and fanning his arms lazily so he floated on his back. Chloe glanced away, feeling warm despite the coolness all around her. 'You could call it "A Day out with Chloe".' He sounded quite serious.

'It's an idea,' she said, fighting the urge to stare at his naked body, perfectly revealed by the transparency of the water. 'I wonder if it would sell? I suppose with the right sort of marketing.'

Kitt's eyes flicked open. Fortunately, Chloe was looking at his face, not his groin! 'It'd sell . . . you're a famous model.' His gaze bored into her for a moment, very intense, very green. 'But you don't want to trade on that, do you?' he said, beginning to smile.

'No, I don't,' said Chloe. At last! At last! He was finally understanding what drove her. 'I want to succeed purely on merit, not because I've had my face in glossy magazines.'

'It'll happen, Chloe,' Kitt said quietly. The conviction in his voice made her heart sing. With Kitt on her side, anything was possible!

There was a long moment of silence. Chloe wanted to propel herself through the water and draw Kitt lovingly into her arms, but there was a pleasure almost as great in the simple fact of his presence—and his approval.

'We'd better get out of here and get dry somehow,' Kitt said at length, smiling, but somehow also reluctant, as if he'd been enjoying their quiet moment too. 'I don't know what Barbara will say when we turn up looking like pair of drowned rats!'

'We could say we fell in the river,' suggested Chloe. 'That it was an accident.' Yes, it would be difficult to explain why two sensible adults in a supposedly platonic relationship would suddenly tear off their clothes and go swimming together. Only lovers did that.

'Come on, we'd better get out,' said Kitt. If he was worried about revealing himself, he wasn't letting on.

'Yes, you're right,' she concurred, striking out for the side, but not sure how they were going to get dry again. Climbing out of the water with as much grace as her nerves would allow, she considered shaking herself as a cat or a dog would, then immediately dismissed the idea. She didn't want Kitt to think she was deliberately provoking him. She supposed she could mop herself all over with her vest—but it wasn't exactly big, and the moisture she removed from herself would only be transferred to the material.

'I think we should let our skin dry off naturally,' she said. Without thinking, she turned towards Kitt as she spoke.

The sight of him emerging from the river took her breath away. With arms raised, as he smoothed the excess water from his curly hair, he was a classic picture of the alluring, supremely fit male. She couldn't imagine even the naked athletes of the original Olympics being more imposing. He was gorgeous. He was exciting. He made her hot. She almost giggled, thinking that if she blushed again, her skin would dry faster.

'Good idea,' he said, rubbing moisture from his face. 'But you won't dry off very fast if you stay in the shade.'

Chloe hadn't noticed Kitt look at her—she had a feeling he was actively avoiding doing so—but clearly he had done. 'Ah, my complexion, remember?' she said, 'I can't afford to burn or tan . . . I've got a shoot on Monday where I'm supposed to look ethereal.'

'Well, you'll look ethereal *if* you catch pneumonia,' replied Kitt. 'But I suppose you're right.' He cast around for a suitable, partly shaded spot for himself, even though he was blessed with the sort of complexion that never burned.

'I'll be all right.' Feeling as if they were suddenly losing their rapport, Chloe found a place of her own to sit, in deeper shade, then sat down carefully. Then suppressed a yelp when some stiff grass stalks stuck into her bottom. Kitt didn't seem to be having the same problems—yet he was laying face down—which put even more tender areas at risk!

For a while, she just watched him, admiring his beautiful body, and wondering how he could possibly lie there so calmly when they were both naked and it was obvious they were both sexually aware of each other?

Or were they?

Chloe knew she was. She could almost feel the texture of his skin against her fingertips—from several yards away. But Kitt, she quickly realised, was so unconcerned by her that he'd fallen asleep!

Unbelievable! All those looks. All that edgy atmosphere. Obviously, it was all purely on *her* side, and that made her furious.

You utter pig! she thought. You don't care two pins. You're just tolerating me! Unable to look at him any more for fear that she might march across and yell at him to wake up, she glanced around the clearing.

And saw her camera bag.

Oh no, Chloe, don't do this, she told herself, reaching for the bag, bringing out the Nikon, and slowly and surreptitiously setting it up. He'll kill you if he finds out. And even if he doesn't, you'll never be able to show them to anyone. But despite these objections, she couldn't seem to stop herself.

Switching off the noisy motor drive, Chloe engaged the camera's 'stealth' mode. She knew this meant truly silent running, as she'd tried it when photographing Boy.

Don't do this, she said silently, using an old model's breathing trick to still herself before raising the camera. Then, still damp and naked, she crept soundlessly forward, and

153

focused her all-seeing photographic eye on Kitt.

Even as she took it, she knew the first frame would be a dud. She'd almost jumped out of her bare skin as she'd pressed the shutter—even though the camera was whisper-quiet.

The next frame, she sensed, would be better and, still seeking improvement, she then crept closer and silently arranged Kitt's white shirt alongside him as a rudimentary reflector—filling for the stray shadows that lined his gleaming skin.

Working as fast as she could without making any noise, Chloe took a series of shots from slightly different angles and with various settings. As she worked, she felt as if there were two Chloes circling around Kitt's sleeping form—one the photographer, on a roll with a fantastic subject, and the other, the woman who loved him, who longed to forget the camera and just touch him. Thankfully, the former seemed to be in control for the moment.

Kitt was a marvellous life model, and Chloe wished she could draw as well as take pictures. The contours of his body seemed to embrace the light and turn it into a new and magical substance, and his strength and masculinity were the very essence of his gender. Even the silvery scars that tracked along his legs were a subtle enhancement. They transformed the image into that of a man who'd lived and suffered, and who had a history.

The window of stolen opportunity didn't last long. Through the viewfinder, she saw a minute twitch disturb the silky surface of Kitt's left shoulder, then a slight movement of his darkly curled head. Her heart pounding with more than just desire, Chloe skittered back to her previous location. It took enormous self-control to put her camera away carefully and not just cram it haphazardly out of sight but, by the time Kitt slowly shook himself and started to sit up, every item was safely packed and shrouded in chamois.

'I'm dry now, how about you?' Kitt frowned as he reached for his shirt, then looked towards the place where he'd dropped it. Chloe panicked for a second but, instead of asking questions, Kitt merely shrugged and began to pull the garment on.

'Yeah, I'm OK,' she replied. Her skin had dried in the warm air while she'd been creeping nefariously around taking photographs. With a mixture of reluctance and relief, she reached for her clothes.

The day was still bright—although it was already teatime—but as Chloe wriggled into her knickers and jeans, she felt despondent. The afternoon had promised so much, but all she had to show for it was a clutch of illicit negatives that just made her feel guilty. Nevertheless, when they were both dressed and she'd slathered more sunscreen on her exposed bits, she shouldered her gadget bag and gave Kitt a cheery smile.

'I hope we won't be too late for tea,' she said, falling into step behind him as they made their way back along the track.

Kitt checked his watch. 'Well, we'll be fine for tea at the Court, but we'll have to give Bramlington a miss.' He looked back over his shoulder. 'Perhaps we could visit your mother next week instead?' His green eyes were intent, and Chloe realised that he meant it. Her spirits took an upswing. 'If you're not flying off to foreign parts, that is?'

'I don't think so.' Mentally, she crossed her fingers. 'I'll have to check with my booker.'

'Do that,' said Kitt briskly, moving forward.

Yes! Result! thought Chloe. Maybe they'd made more progress than she'd realised?

Energised, she pushed forward once they were out in the open parkland and strode along beside Kitt, matching his stride. That was the beauty of being tall, you could keep pace with the man you loved. She quashed the urge to whistle merrily.

As they trekked across the grass towards Arrowsmith Court, Chloe tried out a few pleasant mental scenarios. Kitt and herself driving down to her mother's home, herself taking photographs of him in the orchard, a moment when he tenderly asked her to put aside her camera, so that he could take her in his arms and kiss her.

This delightful scene was progressing beautifully, with a much more intimate love scene imminent, when a gasp from Kitt made them grind to a halt.

'What on earth is *she* doing here?' His voice was harsh with anger.

Blinking away her fantasies and focusing on the broad sweep of the drive at the front of the house, Chloe saw a stylish red car parked beside the *porte-cochère*, defiantly askew.

Unmistakably, it was Geraldine's crimson Porsche.

CHAPTER FOURTEEN

Kitt was silent and set-faced all the way back to London—and given the argument she'd witnessed, Chloe couldn't blame him.

Not that she'd overheard much. While Kitt and Geraldine had faced up to each other, beneath the *porte-cochère*, Chloe had lurked around the front gardens taking more photographs. But in the tranquil air, a sense of conflict, if not actual words, had carried clearly.

As had Geraldine's occasional hard glance in Chloe's direction. Once or twice, Chloe had the distinct impression that she was being discussed, and she didn't think that Geraldine had been singing her praises.

157

After about fifteen minutes of confrontation, Kitt had suddenly turned on his heel and walked quickly away from Geraldine, his limp quite noticeable.

'Let's go!' he'd said, taking Chloe firmly by the arm and propelling her, if not dragging her, to the Lancia.

'I thought we were having tea?' she asked cautiously. Judging by Kitt's body language and the way he'd abused the gear change as they pulled away, she sensed she was sitting beside a powder keg. 'Isn't Lady Barbara well after all?'

'No, not now,' Kitt's lips were tight. 'Someone has upset her. Worked her up into a state of agitation with their protests and accusations and stupid ideas. The nurse has given her a sedative, and she can't see anybody.'

Chloe hesitated. 'But Geraldine's still there,' she pointed out. Kitt's ex had flounced back into the house as they were leaving.

'She's probably trying to wheedle another ten minutes with Barbara. Telling the nurse what an unreasonable swine I am.' Kitt's tone was caustic.

'Why would she do that?'

'Please . . . let's leave it, shall we?' Kitt's hands were tense on the steering wheel, where usually he drove with the lightest touch. 'I don't want to talk about it.'

'OK,' Chloe had said and, for the rest of the

journey, neither one of them had said a word.

Chloe was relieved when they finally pulled up outside Willow House. It wasn't as grand and beautiful as Arrowsmith Court, but at that moment it projected peace and normality. As she stepped out of the car, Boy came gliding out from amongst the shrubs and, ignoring the silent Kitt, she bent down and swept the purring tom up into her arms.

'Hello, my darling,' she cooed, her nerves settling as she absorbed her cat's tranquillity. 'Have you missed me? Not to worry . . . Mummy's here.' Boy replied by rubbing her cheek with his furry face. Chloe reciprocated, hearing footsteps just behind her as Kitt joined them.

When she had given Boy one last kiss and set him down on the gravel, she slowly gathered herself and turned around to face Kitt. She was surprised to find him smiling. Had the sight of her cuddling Boy touched his gentler feelings?

'Look, I'm sorry if I've been a creep all the way home.' He looked down for a moment, as if ashamed. 'I'd no right to take things out on you . . .' He hesitated, making Chloe wonder if he was going to explain his row with Geraldine, but then gave her a winning, boyish smile. 'Will you let me make it up to you by taking you to dinner? Somewhere a bit smarter than "Lucci" . . . you deserve a treat for putting up with me.'

159

Careful! Chloe told herself, realising she was on the point of going all mushy. She was *entitled* to an apology, and a special dinner was only what she deserved.

'Yes! Please! That'd be lovely,' she said, more enthusiastically than she'd intended. 'But we don't have to go anywhere elaborate. "Lucci" will be fine, and we're bound to get a table there,' she finished, feeling hungry now that she was happy.

'Are you sure?' said Kitt.

'Positive.'

'Well, in that case, we'll have a decent bottle of wine then, shall we?'

'Fabulous!' Chloe felt her heart flurry.

'OK then.' Kin retrieved her bag from the Lancia and handed it to her. 'After wallowing in all that dubious river water, I think we both need a nice long bath. So what if I meet you in the hall in about an hour? Then we'll go out and make total pigs of ourselves, eh?'

'Right on!' cried Chloe, before darting up the steps into the house. Kitt followed her, but she didn't dare look back at him—in case he saw how wide and silly her grin was!

*　　　*　　　*

Accustomed to changing in a matter of minutes, with an hour ahead, Chloe had time on her hands. Choosing her clothes didn't take long, because a flirty little lavender silk top

160

and skirt almost leapt out at her, demanding that she wear them. With her hair hanging loose and minimum make-up, it would be a perfect look—not too sexy and not too safe.

Almost insane with anticipation, she couldn't even abandon herself to a scented soak. She was soaped, rinsed, hair washed, and out of the bath in a little over fifteen minutes. Dressing and doing her face and hair would only take another five or ten minutes—which still left her with ages to get wound up.

I ought to try and meditate, she thought. That would make me serene.

Emotional regeneration, however, wasn't easy. The minute Chloe lay down—wearing just her red kimono so she wouldn't crush her outfit—she heard Kitt moving around upstairs, and she suddenly felt guilty about the photographs she'd taken. She'd only really taken them out of pique with him, but now she realised her annoyance had been unfounded.

If I had any scruples at all, I'd expose that film straight away and be done with it. Turning over, she tugged at the silken panels of the kimono as it got caught beneath her and gaped open. Still pulling at it, she sat up, willing herself to go and do the right thing immediately.

But you want to see how they've turned out, don't you?

Rolling on to her side and beating her pillow, she imagined the shots printed up to super-size and placed in an album that she could look at whenever she wanted. It would be far easier than having to deal with the real man sometimes, but it did seem a bit kinky.

I'm obsessed, she admitted. But, all the same, those photographs might be the nearest I ever get to my fantasies.

Blow it, I'm keeping them!

Now all she had to do was to find someone to develop them. It wouldn't have been a problem if she had her own darkroom, but she'd been too busy to explore that avenue so far. Simon Hagan would probably laugh in her face if she'd told him she was still taking her film into a local camera shop.

So, she had a dilemma. Taking the negatives to her usual place was out of the question, because Kitt used the same shop whenever he took photographs, and he'd be recognised before the prints left the tray.

The only other alternatives were to wait until she had her own darkroom—which could be ages—or take them into some other photography shop and risk an unknown service with her most precious negatives ever. Or, she could ask Bobby to let her develop them in his darkroom! She'd need a tutorial on the finer points of developing and printing, but she was sure he'd help her out.

That was if he was still speaking to her. She still hadn't managed to contact him, and she knew she should do something about it now but just couldn't make herself. This was a 'Kitt' day. If she spoke to Bobby now, she'd break the spell somehow, and only give him second best anyway.

Managing to relax at last, she felt strangely fatalistic. She couldn't go on pinning all her hopes for an adult relationship on Kitt, and spoiling the friendship they did have. If tonight he said nothing, did nothing, and made no serious indication of any kind, she would stop torturing herself There would be no more of this 'yearning for the forbidden' nonsense, and no more grey areas to mangle her soul with . . .

All or nothing, she thought, finally closing her eyes.

*   *   *

Floating up out of an extraordinarily deep sleep she'd never expected to fall into, Chloe realised that something in the room was different. Cataclysmically different. The thing that was forbidden and longed for in vain and in a hopeless way was right here, right now, and within her reach.

Opening her eyes, she didn't say a word, in case it was all a dream. She just waited, hoped, and tried to believe.

'Oh, Chloe,' Kitt whispered, sounding as if he was having trouble with reality too. Chloe had no idea how and why he was here, but she knew he needed encouragement. Even though

163

he was reaching for her, he was afraid of both her and himself. Smiling a welcome, she lifted her arms and drew him to her.

Their lips made contact, tentatively at first, as did their bodies. Chloe could feel the crisp smoothness of Kitt's shirt against the bare skin of her chest, and against her nipples where her robe had slid open while she slept. The material was cool and still carried the imprint of laundering, but through it burned the fever of Kitt's hot skin. Which became hotter as the kiss grew wild and deep.

'If you want me to stop, just tell me.' Kitt's voice sounded strange, new, and very young as his mouth tracked over her face, exploring it. 'But please tell me soon, or it'll be too late.' His hands were travelling now too, but still avoiding any danger zones. He caressed her back, his fingers curved, almost pummelling.

'Don't stop, Kitt. Why would I want you to stop?' she demanded, unable to keep herself from shimmying with excitement and need.

With her desire for Kitt Maynard unresolved, Chloe had never wanted another man, and not once been remotely near the situation she was in now. But that didn't mean she wasn't familiar with wanting. Her body seemed to twist within itself somehow, to tie itself into a knot of anticipation that only he could unravel—and not with words, nor with forbearance and gentle reasoning. Her body craved his in the most basic way. She needed him to touch her and be inside her—that was the only way she could honestly describe it. Throughout all her dreams and fantasies, she'd fooled herself with notions of lofty romance and extended sensitive foreplay. Now she knew she was wrong. She was going to scream if he wasn't inside her soon.

Kitt said no more, but he drew back and, again, his eyes questioned her. Chloe gave a little gasp of frustration, took his hand and placed it on her breast, then arched her back to press her flesh more firmly against his palm. When he began to delicately caress her, the impulse to squirm grew almost painful. Barely aware of her actions, she rolled against him and rocked her hips.

Kin's reaction to this was a low, inarticulate sound that could have been either desire or surprise, and the instant she heard it, Chloe drew back, feeling the cold touch of fear. Had she repelled him by displaying so blatantly what she wanted?

A second later, it was plain she hadn't. Almost growling, Kitt abandoned her breast with a last, gentle squeeze, then put both his arms around her to mould her closer to him. Half rolling on top of her, he cradled her head with one hand, to give force and precision to his kisses and, with the other, he clasped her bottom so that their pelvises were brought together in a tight, unbroken contact.

And what Chloe felt there made her want to

growl and moan every bit as fiercely as Kitt. All her doubts were banished. He too craved, but somehow it was no longer 'basic'. What they felt was complex and perfect, it was exactly what it should be.

For a while, they lay against each other, kissing, moving restlessly, breathing heavily, their hands traversing without inhibition over each other's bodies, now that they both knew what they wanted. Chloe still felt an intense need to have Kitt possess her—it was stronger than ever now, although a few moments ago she couldn't have imagined it greater—but there was a magic too in this high plateau of frantic anticipation. Her kimono was so totally awry that she was as good as naked and, when Kitt took advantage of that, she laughed aloud with nervous triumph. She didn't truly know what she'd expected to feel when her lover finally touched her right at her centre, but the reality of it left imagination far behind. She squealed aloud when a quite exquisite sensation pierced her.

Clinging to Kitt like a castaway, Chloe remained in a state of stupefaction for several long, trance-like moments. Even though she was a virgin, she hadn't been entirely unaware of her own body's sensual potential but, despite this knowledge, what Kitt had done to her left her senses reeling. She squeezed her eyes tight shut, feeling physically dizzy, but in a way that was so delicious she longed for more of it. Thinking dreamily of the description 'mind-blowing', she laughed with joy at its glorious, amazing aptness.

'Are you all right, my darling?' whispered Kitt, still holding her, still gently touching her in a way that rekindled the gorgeous fires.

Relishing the endearment every bit as much as the sensations, Chloe didn't growl this time, but found herself making a throaty sound she could only describe as a purr. 'Oh yes, oh yes,' she said, laughing at herself, laughing at the wanton female animal she'd just discovered herself to be. 'I've never been more right than I am at this moment in my life!'

'Good,' said Kitt gruffly, kissing her neck.

'But . . .'

He came up on his elbow, looking down upon her, his whole adorable face a question.

'I'd like to feel even more right . . . I'd like us *both* to feel even more right.'

'Oh dear heaven!' Kitt's voice was indistinct as he wrenched first at his shirt, then finding that intractable, began to scrabble at the belt and the waistband of his cotton chino trousers. Chloe realised that somewhere along the line he'd already kicked off his shoes.

Kitt cursed furiously as his clothes defied him, and Chloe was forced to hide a sly womanly smile.

'Here, let me,' she said, then demonstrated her superior mastery of fastenings. There were never enough dressers to get models in and out of outfits, so she knew how to handle every kind of button, zip or popper known to man. Or woman . . . Within seconds, she had parted his shirt and his trousers and she was touching him—and he was groaning.

My man. The man I love, thought Chloe, beginning to caress Kitt with a surety that seemed to come purely from instinct. To her great joy, she suddenly knew exactly what to do, even though she'd never done it before. She knew exactly what to do to please her lover.

'Oh Chloe, oh Chloe,' Kitt gasped, moving restlessly, his body arching, his warm flesh growing even harder, 'That's so wonderful . . . yes! Yes! Oh, how I want you!'

And I want you Kitt, thought Chloe, her hand stilling. She was reluctant to release him, but at the same time she wanted to progress. Sliding close to him, she set him free, then grabbed at his shirt to pull him over her. Kitt made motions as if to undress completely but Chloe stopped him. She'd waited too long already, and she couldn't wait any longer.

'Please! It's all right!' she urged him, still flexing her body to push it closer against his own.

Kitt hesitated a heartbeat more, then capitulated, reaching down briefly to slip his fingers between her thighs, then positioning his body for the resolution they both desired.

Oh my darling, my darling, go on! thought

Chloe, too consumed with emotion to speak out loud. She used her stroking hands on Kitt's strong back to indicate her need. It was now or never, and she was afraid, but she loved him madly.

For just a second, Kitt was against her, demanding possession of her, then his hips jerked and he was pushing, pressing, entering. Chloe felt a jag of sharp pain that made her hiss and gasp and, for a brief time, she was extremely uncomfortable. Then, as suddenly as the pain had begun, it was gone again, and she was able to relax, her body yielding to let Kitt in.

Although she'd hardly realised it, her eyes had been tight shut for a few moments, but when she opened them again, she saw a look on Kitt's face of shock and wonder, combined with a tension that seemed peculiarly sensual and male. He looked sideswiped, as if he'd been hit with the greatest of surprises, but happily it didn't affect his sexual vitality. Deep inside her, he remained steadfastly hard and hungry.

'You're a virgin,' he breathed, awe in every syllable.

'I *was* one,' she said, emphasising the participle by moving slightly beneath him. Which evoked another intake of breath, both from him and from her. The inner feelings she experienced were as volcanic as they were voluptuous. As silky as the pain before had been ragged. Kitt seemed about to say something else, but Chloe felt so momentarily afraid of what it might be that she swirled her hips, moaned at the pleasure of it, then pulled Kitt's contorting face down to hers so she could kiss him.

Every movement, every undulation of her pelvis, every clasp and stroke and flex of her fingers came naturally. Even as she was being swept high and away by the power of Kitt's thrusts, there was a dispassionate monitor within Chloe's consciousness that was amazed at her own wantonness. Her own aptitude for the art of love. This cool observer was just about to pose the question of what Kitt might be thinking of this erotic virtuosity, when the degree of pleasure became so great that observation was completely lost in participation. Chloe could only feel and feel and feel, her cries of rapture soaring up like a bird's as she writhed and tossed and twisted.

CHAPTER FIFTEEN

Oh my God, what on earth have I done?

Very carefully, so she wouldn't rock the bed, Chloe sat up in the moonlight and looked down at the man sleeping beside her.

You know what you've done, you idiot, answered a cool inner voice. You've let things

170

get out of hand and you've seduced Kitt!

She tried to work out the 'how' and 'why'.

The 'how' was that she'd fallen asleep when she should have stayed awake and been ready and waiting when Kitt arrived, instead of sprawled on the bed half-naked. The 'why' was because she'd offered him a temptation that not even the most monkish of men could resist—precisely when he was most vulnerable. That stormy argument with his ex-wife—whom he obviously still had feelings for—had fired him up. Built up a sexual tension that was like lightening and had to dissipate somehow. Through the path of least resistance . . .

But would you change things?

Gazing down at Kitt's relaxed, oblivious face, she knew she wouldn't change a single second. Not even if she could go back and choreograph the event to another place and time of her choosing. There was no need for bowers of roses, magnums of champagne, and perfumed moonlight. Being with Kitt was romance by definition, and nothing else was needed.

Sex had been a revelation and, even if she hadn't already been in love with Kitt, she would certainly have fallen deep and hard by now. After their frantic first joining, they'd rested a while, then begun again more slowly and thoughtfully. Kitt had been gentle, graceful and kind, yet so strong that he'd almost literally taken Chloe's breath away.

The adroitness of his touch had made her gasp time and time again and writhe against him.

Oh, Kitt, I love you so much!

She hadn't said it while he was caressing her, she had been too stunned. This was Kitt! The man she'd yearned for as long as she'd known how to. Kitt, whose warm, male body she finally had all to herself.

Despite the fact that she loved Kitt to distraction, Chloe had been realistic in her expectations of sex. From raunchy talk amongst fellow models, she'd gathered that sex sometimes wasn't all it was cracked up to be, and sometimes it took time and patience to get it right.

But Kitt hadn't disappointed her.

'Oh, what have I done?' said a soft, dark voice in the night. Chloe swivelled around, watching anxiously as Kitt's long black lashes flickered, and his eyes opened.

'Are you OK?' she whispered, horrified by the telling note of self-recrimination in his voice. He regrets what happened, Chloe thought, feeling her happiness slip away. He wishes it *hadn't* happened.

And it was all her fault. Subconsciously she'd offered herself to him on a plate, been easy. 'It's my fault, isn't it,' she said, keeping her voice emotionless. It was either that or start sobbing and wailing and beating her breast the way tragic heroines were supposed to.

172

'Hey! What's this?' Kitt was obviously cleverer than she was at reading emotion. He put his arm around her. 'I'm the one who's at fault. It's me who should be sorry.' His fingers tightened gently on her shoulders. 'I took advantage of you.'

'Don't be an idiot, Kitt. Of course you didn't "take advantage of me"!' Chloe said, feeling suddenly frazzled. She tried to squirm out of his grip. 'This is a new millennium, remember. I wanted you, so I encouraged you. Demand creates supply.' She met his eyes, which looked almost black in the shadows, the green barely apparent, 'And I bet if I'd changed my mind, you'd have stopped, wouldn't you?' she challenged.

'Yes.' His fingers moved against the back of her neck, as if to soothe her. 'It would have been difficult, but yes, I would've stopped if you'd asked me to.'

'So what happens now?' she asked as Kitt took her hand and cradled it in his. Chloe looked down at his tanned fingers and her pale ones—and shuddered.

'Are you cold?' Releasing her, he hauled at the tangled duvet.

Chloe shook her head, and snuggled a little closer to him. His body was as warm as toast, and he couldn't begrudge her a little heat. Living heat, not from bedclothes. 'So?' she persisted, hardly daring to look at him.

'I don't know what to do really.' He ran his

fingers through his tousled hair and frowned. 'We could get married,' he said. 'Yes, we could definitely get married,' he repeated very evenly. 'It shouldn't be too much of a problem to get a special license.'

'Married?'

Chloe shuddered. Part of her wanted to leap up and down, shouting and cheering, but the rest of her was chilled by how pragmatic his voice sounded. It sounded more like a case of problem solving than anything else.

'Yes, Chloe. Married,' he replied, with a touch of impatience.

'No need to snap!'

'Sorry. But you would like to get married wouldn't you?'

Well, thought Chloe, even if my first sexual experience was blissful, being proposed to leaves a lot to be desired so far!

'Yes.' She tried to sound as rational and self-possessed as Kitt was. 'Of course, I would . . . but you don't *have* to marry me, you know. I'm not "dishonoured" because I've been to bed with a man I lo . . .' Steady, Chloe! Don't make things even worse. 'Because I've slept with a man I like,' she finished, studying the duvet cover so she didn't have to look at Kitt.

'I don't think of you as "dishonoured", Chloe. Of course, I don't.' Kitt's voice was tight. 'But I can't help thinking of certain things. Certain considerations . . .' He appeared to be studying the same bit of quilt

174

she was. 'I *will* want to make love to you again. That's a given.' Chloe's heart began a rapid thaw. 'But I don't take sex lightly and I don't go in for casual affairs. Relationships are important to me, and . . .' He was still staring intently at the polycotton, '. . . and our relationship may well *have* to be a marriage.'

'But . . .'

'But what, Chloe? I thought you said wanted to get married?'

'I do.'

'Well, I do too,' Kitt went on. 'I miss having someone to share things with. Someone to wake up with. Someone to reach for at night.'

Feeling a curious mix of elation and despair, Chloe leaned forward a little and buried her face in his warm chest. She must not look at him right now or she couldn't be responsible for her actions.

'Don't worry, Chloe.' Soothingly, he stroked her hair. 'Everything will work out . . . and the sooner we get the process in motion, the better!'

His voice sounded very intent, almost vehement.

'What's the big rush?' Chloe pulled away and looked at him. What was this sudden preoccupation with hurry? A few moments ago, he'd been regretful and cautious, now it was full steam ahead. If he wasn't sure what he wanted, things could end in disaster. 'There's no need for a special license, at least . . .

perhaps we could just live together for a while and see how it goes?'

'No, Chloe, I told you.' Kitt's tone was as unswerving as his intentions obviously were. 'I *want* to be married as soon as possible . . . and you might *need* to be!'

Chloe stiffened her shoulders. 'What on earth do you mean?'

Kitt gave her a long look, his black brows raised in exasperation. 'For pity's sake, girl,' he said, 'don't be so obtuse! Consider cause and effect for once.'

Chloe began to get an inkling. 'Spell it out to me!' she commanded.

'All right.' Kitt sat up straight and the quilt slid away to reveal his smooth, lightly muscled torso. Chloe dug her nails in her palm, determined not to be distracted.

'I got a bit of a surprise when I discovered you were a virgin,' he went on. 'But . . .'

'But what?' she mocked him. 'I don't see why you're surprised. You watch me like a hawk and give me the third degree . . . if I'd had sex, you'd probably know about it before I did!'

'Don't be stupid, Chloe, I've never interfered with your life. You must have had hundreds of opportunities to sleep with men!'

'I'm choosy,' she muttered. 'But even so, why does being a virgin mean we have to rush to the altar?'

Kitt rubbed his hand wearily across his face.

'Because *I* didn't take any precautions and, if you were a virgin, it's unlikely that *you* did!'

'So?'

Kitt sighed and seemed about to tear his hair. 'Chloe, you might be pregnant! And, if you are, I don't want your Ma doing her arithmetic and coming after me with a pair of secateurs because the months don't add up!'

'Pregnant!' Chloe was genuinely thunderstruck. Good grief, why hadn't it occurred to her?

'Yes, pregnant,' he said more gently. 'You're in a sexy, up-front business, Chloe, but you're really quite innocent, aren't you?' He reached for her, his arms folding possessively around her. 'I should have remembered that . . . At least one of us should have been thinking about the consequences.'

'Don't patronise me, Kitt,' said Chloe, her mind a carousel of conflicting emotions as she tensed in his hold. 'I know that one and one can make three. But I wanted you and I had a slight brain fade, that's all. You should be flattered that I find you so intoxicating!'

Kitt was quiet for a moment, and Chloe sensed that he might be feeling chastened.

'You're the one who's intoxicating, Chloe,' he said, touching her face to make her look at him.

'OK, so we're both fabulous.' She allowed a smile to emerge. 'But don't you think it's a bit drastic to insist we get married straight away?

I'm probably *not* pregnant . . . and, anyway, babies are born out of wedlock all the time nowadays. It's quite the vogue.' What am I doing, she thought, I should be dragging him to the altar, not discouraging him.

Suddenly Kitt frowned, took Chloe by the shoulders, and made her sit up and face him. She quailed. What now?

'Give me a straight answer, Chloe.' He looked her hard in the eyes. 'Do you want to get married?'

'Yes, I do.' She loved him. What was the point of lying?

'In that case, we get married. And soon.' His fingers loosened a little, but his gaze was just as determined. 'If you're pregnant, we've done the best thing for the baby and, if you're not, you can still go on modelling and taking photographs . . . I'll support you in whatever you choose.'

'I don't suppose it really makes any difference,' said Chloe, thinking how much difference it *did* make to know Kitt would always be there for her.

'Thank God that's settled!' Kitt smiled, then leant forward to place a frustratingly sexless kiss upon her forehead. 'Now, do you think we could get up and make some toast or something? I was starving before we came to bed, but now—for some unknown reason . . .' His green eyes flashed. '. . . I'm absolutely ravenous!'

178

So am I, thought Chloe, watching him rise gracefully from the bed and search for his clothes. But not for anything as mundane as buttered toast . . .

But toast turned out to be the most delicious meal on earth. They'd missed a meal and used a lot of energy. The slices disappeared as fast as they leapt out of the toaster.

But it was while she was digging around in her small freezer compartment for another loaf that something dawned on her that suddenly ruined her appetite.

She'd been to bed with Kitt at last and, sooner or later, they were going to be married. She might even—although she doubted it—be having his baby. She was about to get everything she'd always wanted from a man she had always loved.

But not once had he said that *he* loved *her*.

*   *   *

The more Chloe tried to ignore it, the more she thought about it. The omission seemed like a dark barrier standing in the way of her future. It took all her reserves of optimism not to let it vanquish her.

Kitt's strange, though no-doubt well meaning, actions didn't help much either.

After supper, he had quietly suggested that they'd both get a better night's sleep if he went back off to his own bed. Chloe had been too flabbergasted to protest, and just accepted his goodnight kiss and the strangely guarded look that had gone with it.

He's being deliberately contrary, she thought, chasing in vain after the sleep he'd interrupted. He makes love to me, asks me to marry him, even tells me I'm intoxicating . . . then what does he do? He clears off to sleep alone!

What if I'd told him I love him? Would that have made a difference?

Dawn was rising and, ironically, Chloe wasn't getting any sleep at all. Was it possible, she wondered, that he needed a spur to get him to admit his feelings? She knew some men were like that. Kitt was what she would've classed as a relatively 'new' man but, even so, he might still have unreconstructed instincts lurking.

Should she give him that nudge? Admit her own feelings? With a failed marriage behind him, Kitt was probably deeply cynical about 'love'. Goodness, she'd once even heard him categorically deny its existence! That had been a few days after his divorce had come through, of course, but still . . .

Oh, stupid Geraldine again! Always screwing things up for me! Immediately, Chloe felt guilty. Geraldine had loved Kitt too—and lost him. To her, that would've been the greatest disaster.

But where does that leave me? Chloe pondered, listening to the birds singing cheerfully outside.

I should be completely happy! she thought, wishing she had a brick to lob at the infuriating chorus, or that Boy would suddenly come hurtling out of the bushes like an Exocet. But I'm still whingeing and wanting more!

It was all such a muddle. For different reasons, both she and Kitt were trapped in something that wasn't ideal for either of them. What could she do?

Suddenly, Chloe made a calm decision.

I'll tell him 'no'. Simple as that.

I'll sit him down and talk to him. Face him as an adult, and explain that it's highly unlikely that I'm pregnant and he doesn't *have* to marry me. Then I'll let him decide. It's better to take that risk than to tie him down under false pretences.

And I might even tell him that I love him too!

*   *   *

When Chloe next woke up, there were no birds singing. They were probably sunbathing! It must be nearly midday! Eventually, she'd slept far more deeply than usual.

Did I dream it all?

Chloe tried to piece together the events of last night, and her cheeks flamed when she

181

remembered things she couldn't have imagined.

So that's it, I've done it now. She ran her fingers across the bed sheet where the momentous acts had occurred. And I'm engaged too. Well, sort of . . .

Reaching for her kimono, she wondered what would have happened if she'd fallen asleep wearing a thick chenille dressing gown, winceyette pyjamas and woolly bed socks. Would everything have been normal this morning, and she and Kitt just friends who'd shared a pleasant meal?

But the lingering smell of Kitt's cologne reminded her that it was all real and, wondering why he hadn't wakened her, she shuffled into the sunlit kitchen.

Where there was evidence of Kitt, if not the man himself.

Boy was back from his nocturnal ramblings and looked up only briefly from a full dish of cat food and a saucer of milk placed thoughtfully beside it. Clearly her fiancé had been down and fed her cat.

Suddenly wide-awake, Chloe noticed more innovations. Her stay-warm cafetière was on the table and a rich, delicious coffee smell filled the room. Beside the coffee, the table was neatly set for one, with what looked like croissants keeping warm in a table napkin and, as a final touch, there was a posy of garden flowers in her best white china vase.

As she moved closer, Chloe saw an envelope propped up against a jar of the very expensive, imported black cherry preserve that Kitt always bought for himself. The envelope had 'Chloe' written on it in his bold, angular handwriting.

As she hefted the envelope between her fingers, she was almost afraid to open it.

He's changed his mind! He's thought things through and decided he doesn't really want to marry me after all!

Even though she'd had her own second thoughts, the possibility of Kitt doing an about turn was acutely painful. Shaking violently, Chloe flipped open the hateful envelope.

Good morning Chloe, the note began, the script forceful and distinctive.

You were fast asleep when I came down and it seemed a crime to wake you. I'm working on some stuff upstairs, so just come upstairs when you're ready. Enjoy your breakfast.

It was signed, without any kind of endearment, *Kitt*. To Chloe's horror, there was an added P.S.

I phoned your mother this morning and she's absolutely thrilled about our news.

'For crying out loud, Kitt, what on earth did you do that for?' she snarled, causing Boy to lift his head briefly from his food and look at her.

Oh God, there's no backing out now! She sat down, her legs having suddenly turned to

183

water. What on earth has Kitt told Ma? Not the whole truth, surely? Obviously not, or Ma wouldn't have been 'absolutely thrilled' and there would have been some apoplectic phone calls already.

Still, Chloe wondered about the conversation. Obviously, Kitt had been tactful and couched things in the conventional, romantic terms that would please Ma. He'd hardly have told her the bald truth . . . 'Oh by the way, Mrs Trevelyan, I'm marrying your daughter because I might have got her pregnant.'

Chloe sipped her delicious coffee. Kitt, bless him, had made it strong, just as she liked it, and the nutty flavour helped her to think. Buttering a croissant, she began to formulate a plan.

She would have to phone a few people first, principally her mother, who was probably camped out beside her own phone waiting to hear from her.

Then there was Rose and Florence, who would probably be as astounded as she was given the state of play with Kitt last time she'd spoken to them.

And Bobby. Oh poor Bobby . . .

Chloe laid down her knife and stared at the tablecloth. How was she going to tell Bobby about the momentous changes that had taken place? For a minute, she couldn't even remember what he looked like, and then she remembered and saw his face all shocked and hurt.

Thinking of Bobby, reminded her of another complication. The photographs. *The* photographs. She really did ought to expose the film now, but the thought was heart wrenching. She knew they would be beautiful and she had to see them at least once before she destroyed them.

And for that she needed Bobby's help and his darkroom. Although, for the life of her, she didn't know how she was going to ask him.

Oh, I'm such a selfish witch! She took up her knife and plunged it into the conserve. I've treated Bobby abominably, and I'm probably going to do even worse to him before I've finished.

And she still hadn't explained about yesterday either. She would have to ring him soon, no putting it off and being a coward. At least it would be more honourable to take the initiative, than to wait until he rang her.

Glancing down at her empty plate, Chloe realised she'd eaten three croissants with butter and preserve and not tasted a single crumb.

That was it! As soon as her breakfast had settled, she'd go for a run to clear her head, then she'd start making calls.

A while later, after a brisk but sensible jog and a bracing shower, Chloe found her mother a little tearful on the phone, but only in jubilation.

'Oh Chloe, it's just what I've always hoped for! Kitt's perfect for you . . . I'm so happy!'

'I thought you wanted Kitt to be my guardian angel, not my husband,' said Chloe, smiling. She'd foreseen her mother's pleasure at her engagement, but hadn't realised Ma had been harbouring ideas of Kitt as a son-in-law.

'Oh, that was just part of my master plan, sweetheart,' said her mother knowingly.

'Mother!'

'But it's what you want too, isn't it, Chloe?'

'Yes, it is,' Chloe admitted, just as she'd done to Kitt.

You wouldn't be quite so chuffed if you knew the whole story, thought Chloe wryly as her mother rushed on to the subject of wedding plans. Anxious not to tarnish Ma's euphoria, Chloe said 'yes' and 'no' and 'maybe' in the appropriate places, but didn't commit herself to anything. There would have to be some degree of compromise on both sides eventually but, for now, it was harmless enough to let her mother spend some happy hours poring over bridal magazines. They could start wrangling in earnest nearer the time.

Well, at least someone's happy, Chloe thought, dialling the next number.

'When on earth did all this happen?' Rose sounded almost as ecstatic as Chloe's mother. 'You were with Bobby Smith at the party, and it was all doom and gloom on the Kitt front . . . something drastic must have happened.'

Chloe gave her cousin an edited account of events, but Rose's 'hmm' now and again suggested she could read a lot between the lines.

'We must get together as soon as possible,' said Rose when Chloe had finished. 'I want to hear the *unabridged* version of all that, and also we've got to make a start on your wedding dress. When's the big day likely to be? It would be marvellous to have your dress as the finale of a show—but only if that fits with your plans, of course.'

'Aren't we getting a teeny bit ahead of ourselves here?' said Chloe quickly. Between Rose and Ma she was going to end up with the society wedding of the decade. 'It might not be a big "do".'

'Never mind, I still want to know all the delicious details about you and Kitt,' said Rose.

'I'll give you a bell in the next few days, Rose,' said Chloe, trying to reconnect her brain to the real world and her work commitments. 'I've got quite a bit on next week and some foreign things coming up, but as soon as I've checked with my booker, I'll get back to you and we'll fix something up, eh? And I'll ring Flo too.'

Chloe punched in Florence Trevelyan's number next, but all she got was her cousin's answerphone, so she left a brief message.

Her last call was to Bobby. She half-expected to get his answerphone too—because he didn't want to speak to her—but he picked up after just a couple of rings.

'OK, lay it on me!' he said good-naturedly after Chloe's grovelling apologies for standing him up. 'Judging by that worried voice, something bad has happened, hasn't it? Between you and the formidable Mr Maynard, I presume?'

'You could say that,' Chloe paused, gathering her nerves. 'He's asked me to marry him.'

'Jeepers Creepers!'

Chloe didn't have to be able to see Bobby to know he was hurt, his voice was evidence enough.

'I know,' she said, feeling as if she were treading on eggshells, or perhaps on Bobby's heart. 'It came as a bit of a shock to me too.'

'Good Lord.' Bobby sounded shaky, but he was clearly trying to rally. 'How did all this happen? The last time I saw him he was dining with Geraldine, and you weren't all that optimistic . . .'

'Oh, Bobby, I'm sorry . . . I . . .' Chloe was upset. Bobby was great—he didn't deserve this. He was probably furiously angry, but trying to hide it. At a loss, she stared dumbly at the receiver.

'Don't worry, Chloe,' Bobby said, sounding

as if he'd pulled himself together again. 'I knew the score. I'm just surprised by the speed of it all!'

Once again, Chloe gave out a judiciously censored account of events—which Bobby seemed to accept without demur.

'Congratulations, Chloe, you deserve to be happy,' he said when she was finished. It made her feel worse than ever.

'We can still be friends,' she said firmly, 'and we can still work together for the exhibition. I'm not going to turn into a "little drudge wifey" overnight, you know. Kitt accepts that I have my own career and interests. And besides . . .' she laughed, acknowledging her own self-interest as well as her genuine fondness for Bobby. '. . .You know far too much about photography and far too many useful people for me to just dump you!'

'Too true!' said Bobby, also laughing. 'And talking of photographs, have you got anything else for the exhibition? It's almost upon us, and we've really got to give Hagan something impressive.'

'Well, I have got one or two shots,' said Chloe, trying to think back. She had some photographs she'd taken of the builders at Westbourne, and one or two of Kitt on the sea front. Any others, she had to dismiss from her mind entirely.

After a few minutes chat, Chloe made the same promise to Bobby that she'd made to

Rose. That she'd get in touch once she knew her commitments.

But even as she put down the phone on Bobby Smith, it was those images of Kitt —those other images—that she was thinking of . . .

CHAPTER SIXTEEN

'So, how did it happen? What's it like being engaged?'

Bobby's face looked almost satanic in the red safety light, and Chloe hesitated.

What *was* it like being engaged? She'd only been engaged a day, and she didn't think her experience was typical.

She was already keeping secrets from her fiancé. She'd said nothing about having a shoot cancelled at the last minute, and she'd said nothing about spending the subsequent free time with Bobby, learning about developing and printing.

They were in Bobby's North London apartment now, working in his own small, but well-equipped, darkroom.

'Sorry, shouldn't have asked . . .' Carefully, Bobby transferred a set of contact prints from speed wash to dryer. They were using Chloe's own photographs as a tutorial, processing some of the many rolls of film she'd used on the trip to Westbourne. She hadn't mentioned their content, especially not the roll they'd just printed. She'd kept that one until last, and she still wondered if she should have printed it at all.

'There, that'll just take a few minutes.' Bobby screwed a loupe into his eye and studied some of the dried sheets. 'Flip that light-switch will you. We're safe now.'

Chloe obeyed, then picked up a magnifying glass to study another sheet. 'I don't feel engaged really . . .' She kept her eyes firmly on the images—pictures of the builders—which had turned out brilliantly.

'How do you mean?' Bobby appeared just as intent on his prints as Chloe was on hers. 'Is he still treating you like a kid?'

Chloe went as red as the darkroom light. There were times when Kitt treated her in a very grown-up way indeed. Like yesterday, later on, after she had finally plucked up the courage to go up to Kitt's apartment and interrupt him. But she couldn't tell Bobby about that, both for his sake and out of respect for Kitt himself.

'Well, I think he's just about admitted I'm twenty-four now.' In fact, Kitt had been wonderful yesterday. Kind, good-natured and funny. They'd gone out for a pub lunch, then spent several passionate hours in bed. Infuriatingly, he'd insisted on going back to his own flat at night, but Chloe supposed that

191

made sense—because he had an early start the next morning, visiting a northern client. He'd also been under the impression that she had a hectic day ahead of her too.

'He's great, in fact. Just how I hoped he would be,' she said, using a red marker to tick the best frames.

'But how come it happened so fast?' Bobby sounded genuinely mystified, but Chloe detected a hint of anger too.

'No idea,' she said, trying to analyse it for the hundredth time. What *had* brought Kitt to her bedroom? She couldn't believe it was only his incendiary row with Geraldine that had propelled him there, not with such consequences. But maybe it was just that? A series of random nudges that had pushed them both far further than they'd ever planned to go. It was a chastening thought—she was probably engaged by accident!

'Chloe? Are you OK?' Bobby's concerned voice made Chloe jump and realise she'd been daydreaming.

'Yeah, fine,' she said, picking up another sheet of contact proofs. 'I'm still a bit sideswiped by what's happened . . . I just can't believe that I've got what I wanted.'

'Lucky you.'

Chloe looked sharply at Bobby but, to her surprise, his expression wasn't all that grim. He gave a little shrug and turned his attention back to his study of her efforts.

'Some of these are very good, you know,' he said, making ticks of his own on one or two shots, 'These of Kitt by the boats . . . amazingly clever . . . to disguise the artistry in the format of a holiday snap. Even the lighting is conventional.'

'Bobby, they *are* holiday snaps!' Chloe laughed and felt tension release. 'I'm not that good yet. I just point and press most of the time. It's the posh camera that does all the work.'

Bobby laughed too. 'Well, don't tell anyone that, will you?' He reached for the next print sheet from the dryer and Chloe's nerves jangled again. He had no idea of the surprise that lay ahead of him.

'Jesus Christ!' he hissed, 'I *see* how it all happened now.'

'No, it didn't! Nothing happened then.' Chloe almost knocked him out of the way, and ran her magnifying glass over the contact sheet. She'd known of course more or less what she would see—but, even so, she felt a rush of awe and shock.

The photographs were beautiful. Kitt was beautiful. He was a sleeping god caught unawares in a magical grove, and she found herself rubbing tears out of her eyes in an attempt to see better and with more detachment.

'Oh wow,' she said after several fragile moments. She turned and looked at Bobby and saw jealousy, confusion, and a muddle of emotions in his face. But strangely enough, he also looked proud of her.

'Let's have another look,' he said tightly.

Bobby studied the photographs for a long, long time. 'We need enlargements of these,' he said eventually, his tone brisk and professional. 'Yes, we definitely need to see these.' He was already reaching for the negatives. 'Hit the safety light. Let's do it.'

Chloe learnt nothing more about developing and printing. She couldn't hear Bobby's quiet, instructive commentary for her own pounding heart, and it was a battle not to grab the finished prints from the dryer before they were ready. But when she finally had them in her hands, she could hardly believe what she was seeing. The tiny contact prints had been nothing in comparison . . .

'These are the exhibition shots, of course,' said Bobby quietly, as they stood over bench where they'd laid out all the enlargements.

Chloe tore her gaze away from the elegance and vulnerability of Kitt's prone body, and looked at Bobby in pure horror.

'No way! No way on earth! He doesn't even know these were taken.' She felt an illogical urge to gather up the pictures immediately and protect Kitt's modesty.

'But they're your best work!' Bobby protested. 'They could make your name! If the right people saw these, you could really be on your way, don't you want that?'

'Of course I do,' said Chloe, shocked by Bobby's high opinion of the pictures. A lesser man would have taken against them immediately.

'But I don't want to launch my photography career by embarrassing Kitt! He's my fiancé ... I love him!'

'I know you do.' Bobby sounded tired, dispirited. 'But don't you think he'd be prepared for that? To help you? Because he loves you?'

But would he? Chloe sighed and studied the photographs. Kitt hadn't said he loved her, not even once.

*   *   *

'They're very good,' said Kitt, studying a large glossy of one of her 'builders' pictures. 'You should use them somehow. In a book or a magazine maybe.'

Chloe let out the breath she'd been holding. Unwittingly, Kitt had made things easier for her.

'Well, actually, I've been offered a space in an exhibition at the Hagan Gallery. I don't know whether you've heard of it. It's in a few weeks and I'll be showing a selection of these ... and possibly some others.' She indicated the rest of the prints, which were spread out on Kitt's worktable. She'd had to screw up her nerve to show them to him, and she'd waited until they'd had dinner and a glass of wine or two to mellow him.

Kitt picked up another print and looked at it critically. It was himself, on the harbour-side, miming 'surrender'.

'Well, I seriously hope you're not going to use that.' He placed it with the others and returned to the sofa. 'I look like an idiot!' Sitting down, he reached for his wine glass.

'Don't talk rubbish, Kitt.' Chloe joined him, feeling edgy because the progress of a moment ago seemed to be slipping away. Kitt was either being extremely self-effacing, or he was playing a game of reverse-modesty, because even he must be able to see how photogenic he was. 'You look great in photographs and I don't know why you won't admit it. I'd stand a much better chance in the exhibition with pictures of you!' *And I know exactly which ones,* she added silently.

Kitt gave non-committal shrug. 'The Hagan Gallery? Aren't they a bit avant-garde?' He seemed bent on evading the subject of his own camera appeal. 'I've heard that name linked mainly with erotic art.'

'Well, yes . . .' Chloe took a sip of wine as a diversionary tactic. 'They *do* show a lot of nudes and all that. But this exhibition is of less contentious pictures. What you'd call "tasteful", I suppose. It's called "New Sensuality" and it's a showcase for new photographers. Like me!'

'And a load of brickies and some guy acting like a prat at the seaside is "sensuality"?' Kitt's dark eyebrows were raised, and he was clearly trying not to laugh.

'Well, they're sensual to me,' Chloe said firmly, determined not to be baited. 'Both they and you are good-looking, and have good bodies.'

'And you'd be an expert, of course,' said Kitt, sounding vaguely dangerous. 'From your day job.'

'I'm an expert because I'm a woman.'

Kitt appeared to absorb this then, after a second, he smiled. 'Well, I wish you good luck, Chloe, I really do. It sounds like a great opportunity. I hope I'm going to be invited the opening?'

'Er . . . yes, of course.' The sudden, positive response wrong-footed her. She'd been assuming that Kitt wouldn't be interested in the 'New Sensuality' show. That he'd disapprove. Dare she ask him if she could use the 'I Surrender' snap? It would be a huge milestone if he agreed.

But just as she was about to ask, Kitt spoke again, his voice ominously changed. 'Who did these prints for you? They're professional quality.'

Oh no, here we go again. She couldn't lie to him.

'Bobby Smith helped me. It's he who got me

197

in at the Hagan Gallery. The owner's a friend of his.'

She braced herself for an outburst, but Kitt appeared unmoved. At least, superficially. 'I expected as much,' he said.

'He's only helping me because he's a friend, Kitt.' Kitt's restraint was somehow more alarming than anger would have been. 'Surely you realise that? Give me some credit.'

'I hope *he* realises he's just a friend.' Kitt's tone remained even.

'Yes, he does. He's a good man . . . despite what you may have heard about him.'

Kitt took a long, long time to answer. 'Fine. I trust your judgement. You know him better than I do.'

Later, Chloe wondered if Kitt had meant the exact opposite. The mention of Bobby had subtly changed the mood between them, and she'd had to take a firm hold on her emotions when Kitt had suggested an early night—for both of them . . . in their own separate beds. He had been apologetic, almost sweet about it, and he had even kissed her goodnight with a fair degree of passion. But he'd been impossible to budge on the question of them sleeping together.

This is the weirdest engagement ever thought Chloe glumly, curled up in her solitary bed with only Boy for companionship. The tom's instincts had obviously told him that she needed him.

We haven't talked about rings. Wedding details. Anything. But wasn't that her own fault? She was the one who'd said they shouldn't rush. Kitt was only respecting her wishes.

'I can't win, lad, can I?' she whispered, stroking Boy's head and getting a rasping purr in reply. 'When am I going to admit that I'd be better off with you?'

*   *   *

In the next few days, Chloe had a surprise that, for once, had nothing to do with Kitt.

She was selected as the new face of Xaviera, the perfume and cosmetics company she'd done a test shoot for. With all the drama between her and Mitt, she'd completely forgotten about it.

'But what do they want *me* for?' she asked her booker, feeling bemused. 'Didn't they try out all the top girls?'

'But you are a top girl, kid!' her booker had told her, then proceeded to outline again the lucrative details. The fee was monumental. With the earnings from this one major deal, she could afford to give up all her other modelling work. Indeed, they might expect her to. Which would mean masses more time to spend at the other end of a camera.

The downside was that having delayed so long, Xaviera now wanted everything from her

199

immediately. The timetable was murder. Product shoots in America, a video to be made that spanned New York and several major European cities, promotional appearances at key product outlets, not to mention a series of semi-editorials for co-operating magazines. In short, for the time being, her days belonged entirely to a major pharmaceutical and cosmetic conglomerate. When the first push was over though, the job would be money for jam.

A part of her longed to refuse the offer so that she could stay close to Kitt. But she knew that was shortsighted. To be true to Kitt, she had to be true to herself, and the Xaviera job would set her free to concentrate on what she really wanted to do with her life.

To her surprise, Kitt almost seemed to approve of her modelling success, for once.

'I told you that you were a supermodel, didn't I?' he said, reaching across the table to take her hand. They were dining together at 'Lucci', at Chloe's insistence. Neutral ground had seemed better for breaking the news. 'Will you mind being such a well-known face?'

'No, not really.' Chloe thought a moment. 'Loads of people already seem to know me so it won't make that much difference.' She paused again, drawing a pound sign on the tablecloth with her free hand. 'This is just more lucrative!'

A faint shadow passed across Kitt's face,

and Chloe wondered if she'd insulted him somehow. 'Excellent!' he said. Maybe the shadow was imagined? 'I'll look forward to being a kept man then.' He fixed his eyes on her. 'That is, unless they sack you for being pregnant.'

Chloe had considered this. 'Well, if I am, I'm not feeling the symptoms yet.' On the contrary, she felt fabulous physically despite all the emotional dramas. 'And all the major junketing for launch takes place in the next couple of weeks or so. After which, it'll be occasional studio work, often of just my face . . . so there'll be no problem hiding a bump. If I have one.'

What she'd said was true. Chloe had no doubts about being the Xaviera Girl, pregnant or otherwise. It was a walk in the park alongside being engaged to Kitt.

Busy days followed. Days when she and Kitt were separated by work and distance and it hardly seemed as if they were an engaged couple at all.

It was typical of the modelling life that even though Chloe travelled through foreign countries that would normally have fascinated her, she got zero chance to actually explore her surroundings. With deadlines looming and weekends effectively banished, it was a wearying grind of being photographed for hours on end. When that was done, she usually grabbed a meal to make up for missed ones during the day, then fell into exhausted sleep in some luxurious, but anonymous, hotel bedroom. There was never a moment to get out her own camera either—which was doubly frustrating. The only consolation was thoughts of the end product. Financial security and time for herself and Kitt.

Time seemed to be the greatest of their problems, Chloe thought grimly. She was back in London and trying to reset her body clock before yet more travel tomorrow. When she was home, Kitt always seemed to be elsewhere, seeing clients in distant locations. Obviously, he too refused to admit there were weekends. There had been more consultation needed at the Westbourne site, amongst others, and she knew that a return trip to Japan was looming too.

Are you avoiding me, Kitt? she thought, staring at her bedside telephone and recalling a snatched conversation they'd shared earlier. Kitt's voice had been warm, and undeniably affectionate in a jokey sort of way, but he hadn't really spoken of their future.

Uneasy notions chased through Chloe's tired brain. Perhaps Kitt was biding his time? Perhaps he thought that if they didn't get too close, it would be easier to part later? If it turned out that she wasn't pregnant after all . . .

No wonder he never says 'I love you'!

'Well, I'm not having this!' she announced

to Boy, who'd come prowling back from the Pattersons as soon as he'd detected Chloe's return. He was now on her lap. 'When he gets back tomorrow, I'm going to have it out with him!' She sighed. 'Then, if everything does go wrong, at least I'll be back on my way to America and too busy to dwell on things. What do you think?' She stroked the sleeping cat.

But there needn't *be* anything wrong.

She was a grown woman. She loved her fiancé, and she was nothing if not a fighter. She'd get the truth, then she'd handle the situation accordingly. Somehow.

As if she'd summoned it, the phone beside her rang. She snatched it up, hoping it was Kitt again.

'Chloe! Hello at last. How are things going?' Bobby Smith's voice was over-bright somehow, and Chloe immediately wondered why he hadn't contacted her sooner. Then she felt guilty because she hadn't phoned him.

'Fine, although very tiring. As soon as I think everything's sorted—there's another crisis. I've got to fly back to New York tomorrow morning for some reshoots!' She sighed, feeling yet more guilt. 'I'm sorry. I'm so self-centred. How are you, Bobby? How's everything going at the Gallery? I should just about be free for the opening.'

'I'm fine. The show's fine. Well, as fine as these things ever are!' He gave a nervous-sounding laugh. 'Your stuff's all ready to hang, and it looks fabulous blown up to wall size. Streets better than mine.' His voice sounded distinctly odd.

'Is something wrong?' Chloe heard inner alarm bells. Because of her commitments, she'd entrusted Bobby with the task of preparing her photos for the exhibition. She'd told him which ones to offer, but the final selection had been down to Simon Hagan himself. 'Didn't he like my suggestions? Has he chosen the one of Kitt on the quayside?' Against her better judgement and in a spirit of defiance, she'd included the seaside picture. After all, Kitt hadn't specifically forbidden her to use it.

'Not that one. No . . .'

'What do you mean, not that one?' The alarms were deafening now, and she had a horrible, yet almost thrilling, premonition.

Bobby remained silent for a few seconds, then finally spoke. Hesitantly. 'Hagan dropped round to my place, unannounced, and said could he look at the stuff we'd got for the show. He loved the things you'd picked and we'd more or less settled the choices . . . then I went to make some coffee and left him nosing around the studio . . .'

Bobby fell silent, as if he hadn't the nerve to continue.

The alarm bells had stopped now, and all Chloe felt was a state of shell-shocked calm. 'Go on,' she prompted.

'When I came back, he'd put aside the original photos . . . and chosen some others.'

'Oh, Bobby . . .'

Bobby almost seemed to sob, then pulled himself together. 'I'd done additional prints of some of the other photographs . . . experimenting with sepia toning, really, to see the effect. I'd left them drying and Hagan found them and said they were much better than the others and that he wanted them in the exhibition.'

'Which photographs, Bobby?'

'The ones of Kitt by the river.'

It was what she'd expected, but it left her speechless. She couldn't imagine what Kitt would say—she felt as if she were caught in white water rapids with no way to turn back. She could protest, of course, but her objections would just be ignored or her work rejected entirely.

'Bobby, how could you? Kitt will go ballistic! He still doesn't even know that I photographed him. You've got to speak to Hagan and stop this.'

'But he's dead set on them. I said they were just a private thing, but he insisted. He can be a stubborn swine when he wants something and he said if he didn't get those photographs, he wouldn't take anything. From *either* of us.'

She'd been right. Chloe drew a deep breath, realising that she'd been squashing Boy, who was now struggling.

'Then I can't withdraw, can I?' Somewhere inside her, against the odds, Chloe the photographer was rejoicing.

'Yes you can.' Bobby was staunch. 'There'll be other opportunities.'

'Not like this one. And not for ages.'

Bobby thought for a minute, then said, 'Those photographs *are* the best ones. And they're your strongest chance of breaking through. Are you sure Kitt will object to them? He must want to help you.'

This time, Chloe remained silent for a moment 'He does,' she said at last, 'but he's so private . . . he's an unknown quantity in a lot of ways.'

'I'd do it,' said Bobby, his voice more husky. 'I would have posed starkers if I'd thought there was the slightest chance it'd make things happen faster for you.'

Would that be the only reason though?

Chloe chided herself for cynicism. She'd already hurt Bobby Smith far too much.

'Too late now, alas,' she said.

'What are we going to do?' Bobby asked.

'Just let it go ahead and hope that Kitt takes the same altruistic stance that you would have done.'

'He mightn't even find out,' Bobby suggested. 'I mean . . . if he's not a gallery freak. And they are under the name "Chloe Brown" . . . you might get away with it.'

'Bobby, he's asked if he can come to the

opening!'

'Oh! We'd better pull out then.'

'No. I can't do that. Either to you, or to myself. I love Kitt. I love him with all my heart. But I've my own life to lead, and if he's the man I've always believed he is, he'll support me.'

'Let's hope so.' Bobby sounded grim and worried.

Let's hope so, thought Chloe, as she put the phone down.

CHAPTER SEVENTEEN

'That's terrible, I'm so sorry.' Chloe looked out of the window of her room at the Hotel Pierre, and found no inspiration in the New York panorama. She'd been too young to register the only major death in her own life— her father had died when she was a toddler— and she was at a loss as to how to comfort Kitt. He sounded devastated out of all proportion by the sudden loss of Lady Barbara Arrowsmith.

'You're not blaming yourself, are you?' she asked. 'Because of that time when Geraldine arrived and you rowed?' It would be typical though. Most of Kitt's problems seemed to stem from his ex-wife. 'If you are, Kitt, you've got to stop. If anyone's to blame, it's

207

Geraldine!'

'I don't think anyone's to blame.' Kitt's unhappiness and fatigue were as digitally clear as if he'd been speaking to her on the internal phone at home. 'She was very ill. She'd been fighting it for months.'

Chloe cursed the fact that they were apart. If she'd been with Kitt, she could have put her arms around him to comfort him. Told him not to worry about anything, least of all her and his promise to marry her. She'd do anything to take the pressure off him now.

'She was brave. I wish I'd had the chance to see her that Saturday. If only she'd been stronger.' Her words sounded trite and inadequate.

'Yes, she'd have liked that.'

There was a long silence and Chloe almost wondered if they'd been cut off. 'When's the funeral, Kitt?' she asked.

'On Thursday. The service is at eleven, at the local village church . . . with the burial afterwards in the Arrowsmith plot.'

'I'm coming back that day. Would you like me to get an earlier flight, so I can be there?'

The 'New Sensuality' exhibition previewed that evening too, but there was no way she was going to mention it now. She knew she had to confess but this just wasn't the time at all.

'It's kind of you to offer, Chloe, but I don't think there's any need.' His voice was gentler now, filled with what Chloe earnestly wanted to believe was concern for her. 'Funerals are grim affairs. You don't have to feel obligated. Barbara liked you and she knew that you liked her. That's what really matters.'

'Perhaps I won't then.' It was a relief in a way, because her schedule was manic, yet she still felt guilty. 'But could you arrange for some flowers from me instead, please?'

'Yes, good idea,' said Kitt and, wanting desperately to keep him on the line, Chloe launched into an account of some of the trials and tribulations of her stay in New York.

She told him about the Industria Superstudio complex, where the advertising spreads were being shot, and the pernickity attitude of the client. What she didn't tell him about, though, was what the principal photographer had said. He'd photographed her before and he'd remarked that she'd changed, and that she had a new inner glow.

Chloe knew the transformation was because she and Kitt had made love. It *could* be pregnancy, but she didn't think so. The new energy and radiance had come simply from being with Kitt at last. Despite all their difficulties, he'd given her an intrinsic new confidence that transcended all the styling and the 'brand image' moulding. It said 'this is me, this is who I am' and it was almost aggressive. Chloe liked it, but she also found it scary.

Eventually, all her ploys for extending the call were exhausted and they said their farewells. It was an awkward process. If they'd been a true love match, things would have been different, but they weren't, and consequently the words sounded stilted. It was only afterwards that she found herself recalling Kitt's softly spoken, 'Take care, Chloe', and recognising a genuine tenderness.

Looking at her watch, Chloe calculated that it was eleven at night across in England. Had Kitt phoned her from his bed? Immediately, she wished she hadn't thought that . . . the memories were too powerful. She lay back on her own bed, grateful for the anonymity of the room. It had no resonance, despite its sumptuousness. Her own bed at home always seemed to surround her with echoes of Kitt and that was a refined form of torture.

Suddenly it dawned her that she was quite wrong. She was over three thousand miles and umpteen time zones away from him, but she could still—somehow—smell Kitt's cologne and recall the stunning reality of having sex with him. It was so vivid that she couldn't help but cry.

'Oh, Kitt, I love you! Why on earth can't you love me?'

*   *   *

The rest of the week was a blur of faces and vacuous fashion hurly-burly, and Chloe was profoundly grateful when she was finally on her way home. The flight itself was a respite from early morning calls, pop-ins by publicists, and trilling phones but, even so, she could not work out what she was going to say to Kitt when she saw him. Either about the exhibition or the greater issue of their future together.

She arrived back at Willow House with no answers. Kitt was at the funeral and, much as she would have liked to pay her respects, she was grateful for the extra time to think.

Then the phone started ringing . . .

The first call was her mother, enquiring lightly about the Xaviera trip, but really wanting concrete details about engagement rings and weddings. Chloe tried to put her off.

'I don't know, Ma.' Chloe prowled the flat, clutching the cordless phone. 'It might be ages before we get married.' If we ever do, she added silently. 'We haven't even got a ring yet.'

'Well, that's not the impression Kittrick gave me.' Ma sounded exasperated. 'He told me that you'd be getting married quite soon, which is why it's so important to make a start. And I think he's hoping you'll like his grandmother's engagement ring. He's having it cleaned and reset.'

'How do you know all this? When did you speak to him?'

'Oh, just the other day, my dear. He sounds much keener about the engagement than you do, I must say. I don't know what's the matter with you. You should be thrilled to have caught such a lovely man.'

'Caught? What do you mean, "caught"? Women don't say that nowadays . . . and anyway, I thought you disapproved of divorce?'

'I do in most cases, yes, but this is Kittrick. He was meant for you. Geraldine was a mistake. Which is why he never gave *her* his grandmother's ring!'

She's got a point, thought Chloe, feeling suddenly cheered. 'Geraldine probably refused to have a second-hand ring. She's very particular.'

For a few more minutes, Chloe listened to her mother's suggestions, knowing it was cruel to stamp on her enthusiasm when she'd been waiting so long to plan her little girl's wedding. She protested though when Ma spoke of an announcement in *The Times*.

'What? No way, Ma! You've got to cancel it!'

'I'm sorry, my dear, I can't. It's already appeared . . . haven't you seen it yet? I arranged for a copy to be delivered to you.'

With a sinking heart, Chloe recalled seeing a thick newspaper with the heap of post that'd been waiting for her. After her mother had rung off, she retrieved the relevant section and scanned it.

It was a fairly modest entry. *Mrs Prudence Trevelyan is delighted to announce . . .*

But still, it seemed tantamount to carving in

stone something that was dangerously fragile.

Yet, according to her mother, Kitt had been in favour of the announcement. Chloe wished she could phone him at once to get a clarification of his feelings for her, but she knew he'd be in the middle of the funeral party.

When the phone rang again, Chloe snatched it up and said 'Kitt?' but it was Bobby who answered.

'Sorry, only me,' he said, plainly hiding his disappointment. 'I was just ringing to see how New York went, and to ask whether you and his nibs are coming to the opening tonight?'

'New York was mad, as per usual,' she said, the Big Apple virtually forgotten in her concern about Kitt, his possible feelings for her, and how he might react when he found out about the photographs. 'Look, I don't think either of us will be there. Kitt's at a funeral today . . .' She paused, thinking quickly. 'And it might be better if I don't turn up either. I'm too high profile now, and if anyone in the business attends they're bound to put two and two together. There's already been some Xaviera coverage in the papers.'

'But you can't not go!' protested Bobby, sounding almost in a panic. 'How many times do you get an opening night? I know this is small potatoes compared to Xaviera, but I thought your photography was important to you?'

'It is,' said Chloe, wondering why Bobby sounded so aggrieved. But then, he'd worked so hard for this he was entitled to be put out with her. 'Look, I'll have a think and get back to you.' She tried to think things out. 'If Kitt does want to come, I'll have to take my chances . . . and if he calls between now and tonight, and *doesn't* mention the show, I'll come on my own if I can. But just for a short while and I might wear a wig.'

'Come in your ex-army gear,' suggested Bobby, his voice warming. 'Wig. Glasses. Doc Martens . . . nobody will know you!'

Chloe head throbbed at even the mention of a wig, but she agreed to phone Bobby back and then rang off. All that she could do now was to wait and see if Kitt called and, feeling tense and weary, she continued to unpack her suitcase.

The call came a little while later.

'Home in one piece then?' Kitt's voice sounded forced, and Chloe could tell straight away that something was up.

'What's the matter? Are you all right?'

'I've been to a funeral today, Chloe.' His tone was infuriatingly even and Chloe wanted to snap at him and tell him to stop patronising her again, but she knew he had to have been affected by the sadness of the day.

'Yes, I know,' she said, 'did it . . . um . . . go well?'

'I suppose it did really,' he said after a

moment. 'It was a simple ceremony. But moving. At least, I was moved . . .' There was an odd note in his voice and, suddenly, Chloe wondered if Geraldine had been there. Causing trouble again. She daren't ask though.

'Would you like me to come down there?' she said instead. 'I'm too knackered to drive, but Xaviera have put a car at my disposal. I could get the driver to bring me to the Court and then I could come back with you, if you like?'

'There's no need for that, Chloe,' said Kitt quickly. 'I'm embroiled in some legal stuff and it's likely to go on for some time. I'll get back tonight if I can, but it seems pointless you trailing all the way down here when I don't really have time to talk to you. Especially when you're exhausted from your trip.'

What's he avoiding? Red alert clattered in Chloe's consciousness, but she kept her counsel. 'You're probably right. I am a bit bushed. I'll stay in London . . . maybe I'll phone Rose or Florence for a chat, or something. Do you know what time you might be back?'

'It'll be very late,' said Kitt, his tone heavy, reluctant, as if he didn't relish whatever it was that was detaining him. 'Why don't you go out to dinner with your cousins, if you'd prefer not to be alone?'

'Perhaps I will . . .' Chloe wondered if he was feeling guilty at being such an inattentive fiancé. She opened her mouth to say more, but Kitt interjected.

'I've missed you, Chloe,' he said, 'I've really missed you.'

It was the last thing she'd been expecting, and the way he said it was a surprise too. He sounded impassioned, almost distraught, as if it were the truth!

'Me too,' she said. 'I'll see you tonight then or, if not, tomorrow? Are you sure everything's all right?'

'I'm OK . . . don't worry, I'll see you as soon as I can. Take care, Chloe, won't you?'

'You too,' she whispered, adding 'Bye!' just as the connection closed.

Completely unsettled, Chloe didn't feel in the slightest like going to the Hagan Gallery, although she knew she ought to make an effort. If only to see her incredible images of Kitt.

Still not sure what she intended, she picked up the phone again.

*   *   *

'Oh my,' whispered Chloe as she stood in the Hagan Gallery, transfixed. Nothing could have prepared her for the shots of Kitt at near life size.

'They're marvellous photographs, Chloe,' said Bobby from close beside her. 'You caught the perfect moment, the perfect angle, the perfect degree of light . . . everything!' He sighed. 'And, much as I hate to admit it, he's a superb model.' He paused and seemed to ponder. 'Not that you didn't make me look good too,' he continued, sounding apologetic.

Chloe had to admit that she had got the best from her subject—even though he'd been totally unaware of her. She'd made Kitt look primitive and vulnerable, yet still with the elegance of modern, godlike man. Hagan had selected three images, all from the riverside, and shown no others of hers. But these pictures of Kitt, from three slightly different viewpoints, said everything anyone might need to know about her talent. Even the slight graininess due to the extreme enlargement seemed to enhance them.

All the other preview guests clustered with her, around the triptych, were just as blown away as she was.

'What a fabulous man!' cried one woman, waving her half-full wine glass in the general direction of Kitt's naked back and bottom. 'It's obvious that the photographer is in love with him. Just look at the way she's made the light caress him. It's simply breathtaking!'

He *is* fabulous, and I *am* in love with him! Instinctively, Chloe moved away from the pictures, lest her face reveal her. But whether he'll ever love me, if he finds out about this, is extremely debatable . . .

Quite a crowd had gathered around the

217

photographs of Kitt and, seeing the interest still growing, Chloe nodded to Bobby that she was going to circulate. The comments were blush making and she was becoming ever more anxious about being recognised or, worse, her public identity being linked with the photos. She was wearing her old khaki gear with her hair scraped sternly back and gelled, and her plain glass horn-rimmed spectacles for good measure, but there were eagle-eyed *paparazzi* cruising around who were notorious for rumbling disguises.

But, just as she was about to round the next pillar and look at some of the other offerings, the loud voice of the woman with the wine rang out again.

'And she's a supermodel too. The new Xaviera girl. Some people just have to have it all, don't they? Beauty, talent, and a gorgeous bloke. Doesn't it just make you sick?'

Chloe froze to the spot. How did the woman know who "Chloe Brown" was? There was no obvious clue in the name. It had to be a lucky guess.

Moving forward again, Chloe zeroed in on the little white card adjacent to the nearest image of Kitt. Like all the others, it bore the photograph's title if it had one, its catalogue number, and the name of the photographer.

This card said, *Forbidden! #3, Item #46*, and, to her utter horror, the name *Chloe Trevelyan.*

'Bobby?' she demanded, rounding on her companion. His eyes were wide, alarmed, full of guilt.

'I tried to talk him out of it, honestly,' he said, looking more nervous than she'd ever seen any man. 'I pleaded with him. I knew you'd be upset . . . but he said it would be better for you and for the gallery, publicity wise.'

Chloe felt furiously angry and full of a terrible, terrible foreboding. She also felt sorry for Bobby, who appeared genuinely sorry and scared of her. Most people she knew in the fashion business would have tossed aside her objections with little feeling on their own part at all.

'It's my own fault,' Chloe said grimly, feeling her heart sink as she heard more and more remarks about the photographs and the 'Xaviera Girl'. 'I should have insisted that they were withdrawn. I should have seen Hagan myself, instead of leaving all the chores to you. It's my own fault,' she repeated, reaching forward to give him a reassuring squeeze on the shoulder.

It was just at that moment that a flash went off, just a few feet away.

Oh no, it's started, thought Chloe, gathering her mettle and her professionalism, and turning towards the source of the light.

'Hey, Chloe! Brilliant pix, lovie!' cried the photographer, who she recognised vaguely as a freelancer. 'You'll be giving us snappies a run for our money soon!'

'You're not giving up modelling, are you Chloe?' asked another voice as further flashes went off, making her blink because they were too close. 'Who's the guy? Is it someone you're seeing?'

'I'm not giving up modelling just yet,' said Chloe, smiling, as she knew she must, and projecting her most calm and unflappable look. She pulled off the glasses and stuffed them in her pocket. They were useless now. 'And "no comment" to everything else. Absolutely no comment.'

Within seconds, the situation was almost a bear fight, and Bobby put his arm around her and fought his way through to the exit. Unfortunately, photographs were still being taken and Chloe realised that they'd clearly show her being escorted from the gallery in the tender care of a man who wasn't the one in her exhibit. Which was tabloid heaven and something else she'd have to explain to Kitt!

The words 'What have I done? What have I done?' were an inner tattoo as she and Bobby burst out on to the pavement but, luckily at least, they were able to grab a taxi straight away.

'What have I done?' she muttered as the cab pulled away. She felt Bobby's arm around her shoulder still, but it wasn't any comfort.

*　　　*　　　*

By the time they reached Willow House, Chloe had pulled herself together and was able to convince Bobby that she was all right and that he could leave her. The fates were in control now, and there was nothing either of them could do. She felt sorry for Bobby but she had to be alone.

Resignedly, Chloe got ready for bed, trying not to think about the stormy weather ahead. She didn't expect to get much sleep, but she was about to switch off the light and cuddle up with Boy who'd instinctively moved up to comfort her, when there was a loud and insistent rapping at her door.

Kitt! Knocking at the inner door, it could only be him . . .

Pulling on her old dressing gown—it was cool and the kimono had too many connotations—she almost hurdled through the flat to answer his summons.

'I'm sorry if I disturbed you. I shouldn't have come.'

Kitt hovered in the doorway, looking almost as weary and worried as Chloe had felt an hour ago in the taxi. His dark hair was all awry, as if he'd been running his fingers through it, and his green eyes looked dark and heavy, shadowed by care.

'No, it's all right. Come in. I wasn't planning to turn in just yet, just getting comfy,' she lied.

221

Is it the pictures? she thought, leading the way into her sitting room. Surely it can't be? It's too soon for anything to be in the papers . . .

Oh no, what if Kitt's been to the gallery?

But there was no anger in her fiancé's fine-drawn face, just tiredness and unease. Flopping down on the sofa, he flung his black suit jacket over the arm.

'That bad, huh?' offered Chloe cautiously. 'Would you like a cup of tea or a drink or something?'

'No thanks, I'm fine.' Looking far from fine, Kitt tipped back his head, let out his breath and seemed to sag.

Shall I sit down beside him? Shall I ask him what's wrong? Chloe dithered. She was convinced it wasn't the photographs, but there was something more than just the aftermath of a funeral that was chewing away at him, she was sure of it. And he was back so late. What on earth had kept him? Was it the will? Something unforeseen to do with the Court?

'Sit down with me,' said Kitt suddenly, his eyes flashing open as he smiled and patted the sofa. 'I want some nice uncomplicated company. Tell me about New York. I'll bet you're the toast of the town, aren't you?'

Part relieved and part nervous, Chloe described as much of her Xaviera triumph as would be interesting to someone not in the business.

'I'm longing to see the photographs,' he said, slipping his arm around her shoulders and making her jump like a startled hare. Beginning to tremble, she realised he hadn't kissed her yet.

Kitt withdrew his arm, looking a little wounded. 'Sorry,' he muttered, 'I didn't mean to upset you.'

'I'm *not* upset.' Chloe banished her nerves and determinedly drew his arm back around her. This might be their last time together before he became so furious with her that he didn't want to touch her. This might be her last chance to get a kiss . . . or perhaps even more?

'It's been so hectic and all, and I've got into the habit of avoiding contact,' she went on. 'But I don't mind you touching me. I want you to . . .'

Kitt's beautiful green eyes darkened, but not from fatigue this time. Within them was a magical lambent core.

'I meant what I said when I told you I missed you,' he said quietly, inclining his body until he was facing her. He cradled her jaw, staring at her intensely, 'I was missing you before you went away.'

Chloe wanted to whoop out loud with joy—photographs, missing avowals of love, wills and ex-wives were all forgotten. Kitt might not tell her he loved her in words, but he certainly needed her now, and he'd come here because he wanted her. Constraining a wild urge to leap bodily on top of him, she simply leant forward to let him kiss her.

As his arms enfolded her, she felt him groan in sweet relief.

CHAPTER EIGHTEEN

'Damn and blast! Is that the time?'

The body stirring in bed beside her woke Chloe with all the suddenness of a slap or a roll of thunder. It was morning, and Kitt had stayed with her after he'd made love to her last night.

Rubbing her face, she sat up, aware that the nightdress she'd been wearing last night was draped over the end of the bed now, and that Kitt's powerful back, as he bent over and searched the floor beside him, was naked too. Yet, somehow, she still couldn't reach out and touch him.

Kitt straightened and turned to her, clothes in his hand. 'I'm sorry, sweetheart, I didn't mean to wake you.' Dropping his bundle again, he swivelled around and touched her face, then gave her a kiss. 'But I'm late. I expected you to be awake early but . . .' His thumb traced the line of her cheek, '. . . I forgot all about jet lag.'

'I'm sorry.' Chloe fought the desire to press

her face against his hand and smother his palm with kisses. 'I would have set my alarm, but I've got a long weekend off at last. I'm sorry,' she repeated, feeling drained of strength even though a moment ago she'd been ready to leap out of bed.

'Not your fault, Chloe,' Kitt said gently as he got up and started dressing. 'You weren't to know.'

Chloe got up too, even though her limbs felt like concrete. Kitt seemed absorbed in finding his socks, so she shrugged on her robe and padded out of the bedroom intending to make tea. She smiled in irony at how easily she could slip into the role of dressing-gowned wife, rising with her husband to send him off to work. The pleasure faded rapidly, though, when she stepped out into the entrance hall and saw newspapers on the doormat.

Not daring to open Kitt's paper for fear of what she might see—even though it was a quality broadsheet—she folded it, then clutched his mail on top of it.

Back in the sitting room, she found Kitt completely dressed apart from his jacket and tie. With a quaking heart, she held out the paper and the post.

'No time for the papers, I'm afraid,' he said with a slightly wistful look. Chloe got the impression that it wasn't only his morning reading he regretted not having time for. But then again, that could very well be wishful thinking on her part.

'I'll just have a quick look at the post.' He took the envelopes and flicked through them. Some he discarded into the bin and some he saved, but one made his face light up with interest.

'This is addressed to both of us.' He held it out to her. 'Would you like to do the honours?'

Chloe prised open the heavy cream laid flap and took out an invitation. It was from the 'Right to Walk' committee, authorising the entrance of Miss Chloe Trevelyan and Mr Kittrick Maynard to a Charity Ball in aid of the Treatment Centre Fund, to be held at the Storyville nightclub in Docklands. Chloe studied the card, vaguely remembering agreeing to attend the ball, but wondering why the invitation was to her and Kitt as a couple. Come to think of it, why had they received it at all? She certainly hadn't sent any money and, unlike the Garden Party, there would be no freebies for those offering their services. It was strictly cash on the nail and a lot of cash at that.

She looked up at Kitt and found him smiling. 'I got the details a few days ago. I thought it could be our first night out as an officially engaged couple.'

'Officially?'

'Can't get more official than an announcement in *The Times*.' He took the ticket and studied it. 'I think your Ma's angling for Country Life too . . . I'm surprised she hasn't set it up yet.' He looked up again, then winked at her, waggishly.

But what if you don't *have* to marry me? she wanted to remind him. You wouldn't want to be trapped, would you? I'd rather be a valued friend than a hated wife!

'Can you see me in pearls and a twin-set?' she asked, trying to keep things light and dispel her panic.

'You'd look marvellous, Chloe,' said Kitt, his expression warm and genuinely admiring. 'Even if you weren't a model . . . you've got a kind of presence that can't be manufactured.'

Chloe was at a loss for words, but it didn't matter because—giving her another swift kiss in passing—Kitt was already on his way upstairs. 'I have to get changed and be off,' he said. 'I wish I didn't . . . but we've got a major client coming in for a breakfast planning briefing in about . . . um . . . about half-an-hour. It's barbaric, I know, but it's the only time they can meet with us.'

'Don't worry about me,' said Chloe, touched by his sudden desire for closeness. 'Like I said, I'm at liberty . . . I think I might go back to bed for a few hours.'

Something raw and fiery flared in Kitt's eyes, and he sighed. 'You do that, sweetheart. I'll see you later and we'll have a good long chat about things.' He smiled quickly then sprinted up the stairs.

227

Chloe couldn't face another parting so she did as she'd threatened and went back to the refuge of her bed. She also took the precaution of turning on her answerphone, but turning off its speaker. She had a nasty feeling there would be lots of calls this morning, not least of them from her booker, who would be thrilled by any sensational publicity. Chloe knew she needed at least a morning before could deal with the fall-out from the 'New Sensuality' show, so she made sure that her mobile phone was switched off too.

But thoughts couldn't be turned off and, when she got to her bed, the poignant memories drove all sleep away.

Last night hadn't been as mad and new and unexpected as when Kitt had first come to her, but their growing familiarity had an even deeper charm. Chloe had felt more sexual confidence, and she'd dared to take the initiative, and to touch and kiss Kitt's body in ways she wanted to without waiting for guidance. This assumption of control was intoxicating, and it had seemed to thrill Kitt just as much as it did her.

But on one issue Kitt had been very firm.

As soon as they'd reached the bedroom, he'd discreetly set down a pack of condoms on the bedside table. Chloe had thought briefly of horses and stable doors, but she hadn't said anything. It was too contentious.

Protection hadn't diminished their love-making in any way. Roused by Chloe's own willingness and explorations, Kitt had been nothing less than majestic when it had come to the moment of truth. Even now, the mere thought of him made her tingle and, still basking in his glow, Chloe lay back and dozed, feeling that there might be cause for optimism despite the long shadow of those photographs.

*   *   *

To her surprise, it was mid-morning when Chloe woke again to find Boy standing on her chest trying to pummel her into consciousness through the duvet.

'Patience, oaf,' she said, rubbing his head, then rising and climbing into her dressing gown. Hungry cats didn't like to wait.

After feeding herself too, taking a long shower, and dressing comfortably in baggy, jersey trousers and a white T-shirt, Chloe felt better able to face herself, if not the world at large. She eyed the still folded newspaper, and the flashing light on her answerphone, then turned her back on both. She needed a little longer in her oasis of peace before the madness began, so she ignored the radio and the TV too. Brahms on the CD-player seemed like a much better bet and, as she listened, she flicked through some photographic equipment catalogues to distract herself.

But darkroom paraphernalia wasn't as

229

absorbing as she'd hoped. In fact, it made things worse. If she'd been able to develop her own photographs, she wouldn't have been in this mess in the first place. Simon Hagan would never have seen those riverside images of Kitt. But it was too late for 'if onlys'. Kitt's nakedness was a matter of public domain now and she could only pray that the newspaper coverage wasn't too sensational.

Chloe was just about to open the paper and face the worst, when the doorbell pealed. She froze. Had the Press somehow tracked her down? Stealthily, she looked out from behind the curtains so she could see who was at the front door.

Oh no!

Geraldine Van Straten stood at the top of the steps, tapping her well-shod foot as she leant on the bell again. Her smooth face was a picture of displeasure combined, strangely, with a certain gloating quality and, to Chloe's dismay, she was carrying a newspaper along with her attaché case.

'Good morning, Geraldine. What can I do for you?' said Chloe, giving Kitt's ex-wife a cool smile as she answered the door. The other woman was clearly spoiling for a fight, so it seemed pointless to pretend friendship.

'I suppose you think you've been really clever, don't you?' Geraldine demanded without preamble, sweeping past as Chloe ushered her into the sitting room. 'Just whose idea was it exactly? Yours or Kitt's? His, I suppose. I know you've always hung around him like a lovesick puppy but, let's face it . . . he's only taken pity on you now it's expedient for him to do so.'

Without showing a thing, Chloe breathed deeply. She was in danger of stammering and stuttering. Geraldine's anger was confusing, but what she was saying had sickening implications, and Chloe didn't think the newspaper was entirely responsible.

'I don't know what you're talking about, Geraldine,' she said at last, using every bit of her public persona to hide her fears.

'What I'm talking about, you scheming little minx, is my ex-husband getting engaged to you just to get back at me!'

Chloe felt nauseous for a moment, and then her ability to think cut back in again with painful clarity. There was a horrible possible bigger picture here and Geraldine's sense of grievance seemed full of real conviction.

Is Kitt using me? Chloe thought, sickness churning again. His reasons for their engagement *had* sounded insubstantial. She might not be pregnant and, even if she was, single parenthood was almost fashionable these days, especially for someone like her whose finances were good. More than that, she and Kitt could easily have been together *without* actually being engaged or married . . . if they loved each other.

Doubts screamed at her, but still she couldn't believe that Kitt would tamper with one woman's future just to get back at another. He just wasn't *like* that!

Even though she could feel the blood leaving her face, Chloe faced up to Geraldine.

'I'm sorry if the idea of Kitt and me getting engaged has upset you,' she said quietly, 'but we . . .' She stumbled for a moment, realising she couldn't say they loved each other, because Kitt might not love her at all. 'We decided on the spur of the moment,' she went on, retrieving her poise. 'And, as far as I know, *your* wishes were never a consideration. It's nothing to do with you!'

'Nothing to do with me?' The older woman's voice was as smooth as ever, yet Chloe could hear her derision. As could Boy, who went scooting behind the curtains as Geraldine strode further into the room. 'Nothing to do with me?'

Suddenly, Kitt's ex-wife was laughing, her voice both smug and insulting. 'You poor deluded fool! He hasn't told you, has he? Nothing to do with me . . . my dear, your marriage has *everything* to do with me!'

Chloe's knees threatened to buckle, but she stood tall and straight as if she were at the end of a catwalk. She had never needed her height as much as she did now. At least she could loom over her adversary physically, if not emotionally.

'I do wish you'd get to the point, Geraldine,' she said as silkily as she could.

'OK, I will. Kittrick needs to be engaged, before I am, to inherit Arrowsmith Court under the terms of Barbara's will.' A mocking smile twisted the beautiful lines of Geraldine's face. 'The old biddy was devastated when Kitt and I split up . . . she doted on our marriage so much that she changed her will to get us back together again. The Court goes to whichever of us gets engaged first, the idea being that we both want it so much that we'll get back together as fast as we can.' Geraldine advanced, looking less poised now, and glared at Chloe. 'Well, that's what should have happened. Kitt wants the Court and so do I. And we *should* be together. He loves me. He always has . . . he's just being stubborn because I . . . we . . . made some mistakes first time around.' Her eyes narrowed. 'But we're more in tune now—which is something he'll never be with you!'

It was a warm day, but Chloe felt bitterly cold. She clenched her jaw to stop her teeth chattering and defied the urge to collapse into an armchair. Geraldine went on without even noticing, pacing as she spoke.

'Kittrick is a stubborn man. Everything has to be his idea or it doesn't happen!' She spun back to Chloe again. 'Don't you realise that this thing with you is just a blip? You're pretty enough, of course, but deep down it's still *me*

233

he's in love with. He just won't admit it, the swine! He was jealous because I've been seeing other men, and he was furious because I might get engaged and wrest the Court away from him. Barbara told him about this mad will of hers just before she died. Which is why he snapped you up all of a sudden . . . a matter of expediency really, but with fringe benefits. I presume you and he have slept together? Kitt has more scruples than any man I've ever met, but I don't think even *he* would pass up the chance to bed a supermodel.'

That was it.

Wracked by the keenest pain, Chloe still managed to gather her pride. Moving as gracefully as she could, she closed in on Geraldine, taking a grim comfort from being almost six inches taller.

'My fiancé's sex life is no longer your concern, Geraldine, and I'd like you to go now,' she said with great dignity. 'Kitt and I are getting married because we want to. And as for me being a "supermodel" . . . well, maybe I am, but that's not all I am. And Kitt knows that. Now will you please leave, because I've lots of things to do and I'd rather like to get on with them.' Almost as if it were a shield, she picked up one of her photographic catalogues.

Geraldine's eyes flicked to the brightly coloured brochure, then widened. 'Oh yes, your precious photographic career!' she said scathingly, 'well, that's your biggest mistake.' She shook open the newspaper she'd brought with her, and spread it on the table. It wasn't even necessary to look to know what was being featured. 'When Kitt sees this—and he will, because I've already had copies of all the relevant tabloids couriered round to him—I think we can safely say your engagement will be over.' She smiled savagely, her head coming up and, for a moment, she looked almost mad. 'There's nothing Kitt hates worse than being tricked and made to look a fool. So even if he does want you for yourself—which I very much doubt—he won't want you any more when he sees how you've exploited him!'

And with that, the former Mrs Maynard swept triumphantly out of the room without even looking back once, slamming both Chloe's flat door and the front door behind her as she went.

Chloe sat for a few moments staring into space, then suddenly the realisation of what she'd just heard slammed home and sent her running to the bathroom to be ill.

'Not morning sickness, on top of everything else,' she muttered, wiping her face. It didn't feel as if it was though, and she hadn't felt nauseous at all until Geraldine had spouted her poison.

Kitt's determination to get engaged now made perfect sense. It wasn't old-fashioned chivalry over her possible pregnancy that had

235

motivated him at all. He'd been driven by the determination to keep Arrowsmith Court out of Geraldine's hands—and the race had been triggered by his conversation with Lady Barbara on that oh-so-fateful Saturday.

Chloe folded the towel into a precise square, then positioned it carefully on the towel rail. When it slipped off again, she kicked it across the room.

Oh Kitt, how could you do it?

When Chloe returned to the sitting room, it seemed to echo with Geraldine's cutting voice. The newspaper, with its graphic revelations was still open on the table and she scrunched it viciously closed—but not before she'd caught sight of her own smiling face, Kitt's albeit rather smudgily printed bottom, and the headline 'Sexy Chloe's Saucy Snaps'.

But you deserve it, Maynard, you creep, she thought, pushing the paper away from her. I thought you were my beautiful, honourable Kitt. A man I could always believe in—and you're just as low and conniving as the rest of us!

And *you're* an idiot, Chloe! she told herself. Swallowing all that guff about him, being made an honest woman . . . sex—pregnancy even— had never been the real issue. Clever Kitt had used her own hormones against her. He'd tricked her to get what *he* wanted. His precious mock Georgian masterpiece. And silly 'little Chloe' had started to believe he was halfway to loving her.

It was a grim, distasteful scenario and so unlike the Kitt Chloe knew, that it still seemed unthinkable. He'd always been a man whose honesty was as much a part of him as his blood and bones. He'd never said he loved her but he'd treated her with tenderness and affection. He'd made love to her with all the conviction, passion and sweetness of a man who was *almost* in love.

And now there were forbidden pictures of him on show in a trendy London art gallery.

He'll go mad, thought Chloe. We're finished even if this thing with the Court is all a figment of Geraldine's spiteful imagination. It's all a gruesome mess. What can I do? What can I do?

Chloe didn't know how long these thoughts buzzed like hornets in her mind but, after a while, Boy leapt on her knee, purred soothingly, then shot off again when the phone rang and Chloe started wildly. For a fifth of a second, she considered letting the answerphone take it, but then chose immediate pain over the lingering uncertainty of waiting and wondering.

Lifting the receiver, she braced herself for Kitt's cold, angry voice. Then felt almost disappointed at the sound of Bobby Smith.

'Look, I'm probably not one of your favourite people right now, but I was just wondering if either you or Kitt had seen the tabloids yet? You're both . . . um . . . in one or two of them. And I am too.'

'I've seen as much as I need to see,' Chloe said struggling to sound grimly resigned rather than devastated. 'And I understand from my friendly neighbourhood spite fairy—aka Geraldine—that Kitt is also aware of what I've done.' She went on to describe the distasteful visit.

'That was a bit OTT of her.' Bobby's voice sounded odd, as if he too had received a nasty shock. 'Are you all right? Are you on your own? Do you want me to come over? I can easily get away.'

'Yes! No! Oh, I don't know.' Chloe's head was spinning. She didn't know what she wanted. 'Kitt might come storming home . . . I know he's very busy today, but even so. Those photographs are bound to make him mad enough.'

'Then all the more reason for me to be there. It's my fault they went on show,' Bobby said gloomily. 'Hang on and I'll get to you as soon as I can. Even if Kitt doesn't come reading the riot act, I still think you need company. See you in about twenty minutes.' Before Chloe could protest he'd broken the connection.

Angry at her own weakness, Chloe realised she was crying. What a mess! What a terrible mess! She didn't know what to worry about most—Kitt and the photographs, Kitt and the

Court, or Kitt and herself. There didn't seem to be a bright side to any of them.

And Bobby's concern only made her feel worse. It reminded her of the way Kitt used to be. In times of trouble, he'd always been the first with support and help, and now he seemed to be the one who'd betrayed her.

When Bobby arrived, he took one look at Chloe and gave her a hug.

'Oh hell, I feel so responsible for all this,' he said, letting her go. 'I brought something to deaden the pain.' He held up the bottle of wine that Chloe had felt bumping against her back as he'd hugged her. It was red, not her usual tipple, but given the circumstances, she didn't really care.

'It'll just about cap it all,' she said, hunting for glasses, 'if Kitt comes home now and finds us boozing.'

'It's lunchtime,' corrected Bobby. 'A perfectly civilised time for a glass of wine between friends.'

And I'm going to need all the friends I can get now, thought Chloe, accepting her glass and taking an unenthusiastic sip.

'Look, what's the worst possible way he can react to those photos?' Bobby's brow creased and he took a swig of his own wine. Despite her own problems, Chloe once again got the impression that Bobby was disproportionately upset over what'd happened. Theoretically, he should be pleased if she and Kitt were having problems, because it gave *him* another chance.

'It's not just the exhibition—although that's bad enough,' said Chloe. 'It's this other thing, with the Court . . .' She added more details to what she'd told Bobby over the phone.

'So you see, it's double jeopardy!' she said hopelessly. 'Even if Kitt *did* want me, so he could get the Court, even if it was just coincidental, as soon as he finds out about those photographs, he's going to feel just as hurt and betrayed as *I* feel!'

'He might be flattered, you know.' Bobby's words were doubtful. 'I'm tickled pink that you even considered exhibiting those photographs of me . . . I know they didn't get into the show but, even so, the thought counts. And . . .' Bobby hesitated again, real pain on his face now. 'If you're pregnant with his child, there isn't a lot that he won't forgive you, is there?'

'But I might not be pregnant—which leaves no mitigation whatsoever.' Chloe reached for her glass, then wondered if she should be drinking at all. 'It's a no-win scenario.'

Bobby said nothing, but just looked more depressed.

'Those silly pictures!'

More and more, it was her own foolishness that distressed Chloe. Geraldine had probably been twisting the facts, which meant Kitt was innocent. But this only left Chloe herself as the underhand one, the thoughtless idiot who'd thrown a huge barrier up between them 'I

240

could kick myself,' she went on bitterly, 'I couldn't have played deeper into Geraldine's hands if I'd tried. It's almost as if she'd *told* you to let Simon Hagan see those photos!'

Chloe wasn't sure what happened next, except that Bobby seemed to leap as if he'd been stuck by a cattle prod. His glass of wine—which he'd been in the act of raising to his lips—upended and the contents flew everywhere. All over himself and—unfortunately—over Chloe too. The blood-red fluid splattered her trousers and white T-shirt like an angry abstract painting, and described a similar design across Bobby's fashionable cream linen jacket.

'Oh my giddy aunt, what a mess!' cried Chloe, surveying the splashdown site.

Dabbing with tissues was a joke, but Chloe wasn't worried about her own clothes. She suddenly wanted to laugh, long and hysterically, as a release valve. The worst damage seemed to have been sustained by Bobby's jacket, so she tugged at his sleeve. 'You'd better give me this and I'll see what I can do with it.'

Dumbstruck, Bobby complied and she directed him to the kitchen for a cloth and a bucket while she took charge of trying to rescue what was obviously a very expensive garment.

Worrying about wine stains was easier on the heart than brooding, so Chloe abandoned

Bobby to his task and went through to the bathroom to tackle their clothing.

After a copious dowsing with cold water, she managed to get some of the pink out Bobby's jacket, and with specialist cleaning it just might recover—although she was horrified at its expensive designer label.

Her own clothes were a lost cause, and when she stripped them off, she found that the pervasive wine had soaked right through to her cotton underwear. Flinging the whole magenta and white mess into the linen basket, she shrugged on her silky red kimono, cinched it tightly and went quickly back to see how Bobby was getting on.

Obviously quite domesticated, he'd sponged away all signs of the upset and had even got as far as making coffee. 'Are you OK?' he enquired as he handed her a mug.

'Not really,' Chloe replied honestly, 'but I think your jacket might survive. I've given it a good dowsing and if you take it to a specialist cleaners and explain what's happened, they should be able to get the rest of the pink out.' She nodded in the direction of the damp garment, which she'd hung from the hook on the back of the door.

'Sod the jacket!' Bobby replied bluntly. 'It's you I'm worried about. What are you going to do about you and Kitt? Do you think you'll be able to talk him around?' His pleasant face looked white and strained, and Chloe felt quite worried about him.

'I don't know, Bobby, I really don't!' Suddenly, Chloe faced the imminent return of tears. She might be heading for an emotional wasteland before long, but she was damned if she was going to show it! To anyone except Boy, that is . . .

In an action that was as unexpected as the wine-spill, Bobby set his mug down with a clatter and buried his face in his hands. 'I can't bear this!' he muttered through his fingers and, to Chloe's astonishment, his shoulders began to shake. 'It's all my fault! I shouldn't have done it . . . this isn't what I wanted at all!'

'What isn't?' Bemused, Chloe abandoned her own coffee, and slid her arm around him. In pain herself, she understood the value of simple comfort. 'What on earth is it, Bobby? This isn't your fault. I shouldn't have taken the pictures in the first place.'

'It *is* my fault!' Bobby was actually sobbing now, Chloe could see. What on earth was it that was affecting him so strongly? She knew real men could cry, but it didn't happen often. The only time she'd ever seen Kitt's eyes shimmer was years ago, when they'd had to take Patchey—a forerunner of Boy—to the vet to be put to sleep.

'I wish you'd explain.' Chloe stroked Bobby's back in an automatic soothing gesture and it occurred to her that, although they were probably about the same age, Bobby was much younger emotionally.

'I can't! You'll never forgive me.' His voice had steadied a little, but still sounded distraught.

At a loss, Chloe hugged him harder, murmuring clichés like 'Don't worry . . .', 'Take it easy . . .', and 'It'll be all right . . .' She thought back to times when she'd needed TLC like this, then felt a fierce jolt of pain, knowing that it had always been Kitt who'd supplied it.

Her memory flew back across the years, and she tried to believe that it was Kitt's strong, lithe body against her instead of Bobby's more chunky physique. That it was Kitt's fresh, light aftershave she could smell, not Bobby's heavier designer cologne. Breathing deeply, dragging in oxygen, she called up the precious essence of the man she loved . . .

'Am I interrupting something?' enquired a soft, very familiar, yet peculiarly flat-toned voice.

To Chloe's horror, it seemed her invocation had worked!

CHAPTER NINETEEN

As the words hung in the air, Chloe realised that she actually could smell Kitt's fragrance. She wished she could freeze the whole scene—except for herself—and rearrange it. She knew

244

full well how all this must look to him.

Wearing just her flimsy kimono, she'd been caught hugging another man. There was no escape and no hiding place. She couldn't disguise anything with Kitt just a few feet away!

Chloe released the still traumatised Bobby but, other than that, she couldn't move. Kitt's furious green gaze pinned her to the sofa and she couldn't look away from him. She couldn't speak either, and neither, it seemed, could Bobby. When Kitt glared at him, the younger man visibly cringed.

'Smith, would you leave please?' Kitt's voice was so even and polite that Chloe shuddered. There was murder behind those immobile, mask-like features. She couldn't look at Bobby, but she knew he was afraid. Kitt transfixed him, and he was like something small and furry in the path of a top predator. It was several seconds before he suddenly seemed to wake.

'Listen here, Maynard!' Bobby's hand settled on Chloe's arm as if to reassure her. 'I hope you're not . . .'

'Get out of here immediately, Smith.' Kitt was smooth, restrained, totally cool. 'And if you touch my fiancée again, I'll tear your head off. Do you understand me?'

Bobby's fingers slid away from Chloe's arm and he rose awkwardly and stumbled towards his jacket.

'Will you be all right, Chloe?' he asked faintly, hovering for a second, then beginning to back away. Kitt hadn't said another word, but the tiny jumping pulse under his sculpted cheekbone spoke volumes.

'Thanks, Bobby, I'll be fine. Just go, will you!' Chloe was relieved when her erstwhile protector struggled into his still damp coat and did as he was told. She wanted to feel concern, but Kitt's chill, dominating aura meant that Bobby Smith was forgotten almost before he'd disappeared.

'So . . . you get scared by the possible consequences of your actions and, as ever, the faithful Bobby is there to comfort you,' said Kitt when they were alone. His eyes were like chips of matt-green flint. 'In the way he knows best, I presume?'

Chloe shuddered. She was both appalled and angry at Kitt's cold, contained condemnation. His self-control was almost insulting. Especially as he wasn't Mr Perfect either! Confused she lashed out with the first thing that came into her head.

'And what about the consequences of *your* actions, Kittrick? Don't *you* have anything to answer for?'

A spasm of emotion passed across Kitt's face. It was indecipherable, but Chloe was still glad to see it. Anything was preferable to a soul-less mask.

'How do you answer me for *this*!' Kitt threw

a folded newspaper down on to the coffee table. He seemed to be ignoring his own transgressions for the moment.

Chloe studied the 'evidence' and found it damning. In this article, Kitt was named specifically, and all sorts of lurid conjecture was raised about the sexual relationship between Chloe, the 'sylph-like supermodel' and one of Britain's leading industrial architects, a man eleven years her senior. The piece didn't actually say so, but seemed to imply that the writer knew that both the model *and* photographer had been naked during the shoot

'Oh, it's just tabloid rubbish,' she said quickly, flustered by the exaggeration and lies. 'They always make something out of nothing . . . I would have thought you'd know better than to take any notice.'

'Pictures of my naked backside in a newspaper is not "nothing"!' said Kitt, his mouth grim. 'Neither is having those pictures larger than life size in an art gallery!' He turned and strode away, favouring his leg a little—then stomped back again. 'I could have accepted the fact that you'd taken the pictures. We could even have had a private laugh over them. But what I cannot believe is that you'd exhibit them without even consulting me! You've made me look ridiculous . . . both to your precious gallery-goers, and to the great British public at large. What happens if this gets syndicated abroad too? Didn't you stop to think what it might do to my reputation?'

Chloe's anger grew volcanic. She felt as hot with fury as Kitt was icy cold with it. The pictures were beautiful, the best she'd ever taken—how dare he dismiss them and say they made him look ridiculous? How dare he condemn her after what *he'd* done to her?

A part of her wanted to explain and to try and exonerate herself, but the bigger part of her was crying out for justice.

'They're great photographs, if only you could stop being so stubborn and look at them properly!' she stormed. 'You should be flattered. And if you cared at all about me, you'd be delighted that you were helping me launch a new career and be successful and creative!'

For an instant, Kitt looked white and ill beneath his healthy tan. Then his eyes hardened again. 'I wanted to help you. I'd have done anything to help you. But this is underhand.' He waved at the open paper, then flung himself down into an easy chair.

'Oh, and of course, you've never done anything underhand in your shiny-white, oh-so-perfect life, have you?' she raged at him, still standing. She felt herself to be towering over him in a way she'd never done before, not even when she'd been photographing him. 'Never exploited someone . . . never taken advantage of their foolish, misguided feelings

248

to get what you want!'

Chloe's eyes remained on Kitt as he sat there. His body position was as graceful and elegant as ever but, all of a sudden, he looked as if he'd been hit by an unseen wrecking ball. Chloe could not have felt surer of his guilt than if he'd announced it.

'You've been talking to Geraldine, obviously,' he said, and Chloe got no comfort from the fact that he finally seemed shaken.

'She acquainted me with a few pertinent facts.'

'And I suppose you've drawn your own conclusions? Based only on what *she's* told you?'

He wasn't denying it. He wasn't denying it at all. Chloe felt the last of her happiness crumble.

'I've drawn the only logical conclusion. Nasty as it is,' she said, attempting to match Kitt's former *sangfroid*. The balance was tipping now, but she wished it didn't hurt so much.

'Never mind,' said Kitt sharply, 'There's always Bobby Smith to take away the nastiness—or whatever it is he does.'

Chloe's fighting spirit surged. She loved this man, loved him with all her heart and soul but, great as that love was, her pride and sense of fair play ran just as deeply! Drawing on every reserve of poise, she forced him to look at her. Up at her. Into her eyes . . .

'Don't treat me like a half-baked child, Kitt!' Her voice grew stronger. 'And don't start trying to fudge the issue by harping on about Bobby. He's a good friend who isn't afraid to show his emotions. Nothing more than that.' She paused and took a deep breath. '*You*, on the other hand, want Arrowsmith Court, and you need a fiancée to get it. So, hey presto, suddenly you suggest that *we* should get married. Even an air-head like me can work that one out!' She saw Kitt open his mouth to protest, so she rushed on. 'And don't give me all that baloney about the baby. Anyone with your intelligence knows that shotgun marriages based on unplanned pregnancies are always disastrous.' She drew breath again, almost gasping with inner pain, but hoping Kitt wouldn't notice. 'And you also know that I've enough money of my own, plenty in fact, to bring up a child alone.'

'You're talking nonsense.' Kitt's eyes were chilling again.

'No, I'm not. Far from it. The only reason you said we should get engaged is to get the Court.' Chloe glowered at him, challenging him to say otherwise. Her fingers compulsively smoothed the silk of her kimono.

Kitt stayed silent and motionless, with only an infinitesimal narrowing of his eyes as a response. They both seemed to hang in suspended animation for an eternity, then just as Kitt seemed about to speak—his firm lips parted, then closed again—Chloe's temper leapt. She'd had just about enough!

'That's a good enough answer for me, Kitt! You can't lie but you can't bring yourself to admit the truth either, can you?'

For one split second, pain flashed across Kitt's eyes and, if Chloe had felt desperate earlier, the sensation was magnified a thousand times now. It was the pain of guilt she'd seen. He *had* proposed to her for the sake of the Court after all.

'Yes . . .' Chloe's shoulders slumped as the emotion in Kitt's face blanked out again. She'd always known he could hide his feelings but, now, after that brief revelation, the veil was more impenetrable than ever.

Feeling the onset of panic, she began to pace, heedless of the kimono's sibilant swish and the frequent exposure of her long, slim legs.

'But if you only want me for expediency's sake,' she challenged, turning on him again, 'why do you have to come over all macho and possessive? It's the Court you want, not me . . . so why can't I spend time with Bobby? Especially as he and I are only friends.'

For the first time in what seemed like an eon, Kitt moved. Running one long tanned finger down the crease in his trousers, he seemed to scrutinise the action, then look up.

'Is that what you believe?' he asked dully. 'That I want us to get engaged, purely so I can lay claim to Arrowsmith Court?'

On the line, Chloe could only stare bemusedly at him.

'Is it so difficult to imagine that I might want *you*?' It was his turn to demand now. 'Good grief, Chloe, I made love to you, didn't I? No man in his right mind could deny that you're desirable!'

His fierce, almost resentful, tone seemed to kill all the beauty of Chloe's memories. It enraged her.

'My desirability is merely a "fringe benefit" to you, Kittrick,' she hissed. 'A nice little extra, over and above the prime objective!'

'Is that really the sort of man you think I am?' Kitt leapt to his feet, confronting, intimidating.

'I've no idea *what* sort of man you are!' she flung back, holding her ground, but only just. 'I've known you all my life and I'm still no wiser. The closer I get, the further away I seem to be!' She turned, glancing at the abandoned newspaper. 'I've photographed you asleep and naked, I've talked to you for hundreds and hundreds of hours, I've even been to bed with you . . . but I'll never understand you. I don't know if I even want to!'

'This is stupid!' Kitt spun away, presenting his broad back like a column of living antagonism. For a moment, Chloe felt the torment flowing out of him, then it was lost again, burnt off as he turned back towards her, his eyes a hard green wall of armour. 'This is really stupid,' he repeated.

'Yes, it is, isn't it?' Suddenly Chloe was unbearably tired. Her life's most cherished dream was over. 'I think I'd like you to leave me alone now,' she said, with effort.

'Gladly,' said Kitt, his own voice as lifeless as hers. 'I should be at work. I don't even know why I came here.'

Neither do I, thought Chloe miserably—his words still echoing as the door swung closed behind him.

*   *   *

So this is it then? Chloe thought, exploring the numbness. The end of an era. The end of a friendship. The end of the possibility of love . . .

It seemed hours since Kitt had walked out, but she'd barely moved. Her 'engagement' was a meaningless sham, but she had to get on with life. Her own stupid actions, and Kitt's uncharacteristic treachery, had created a huge gulf between them, but wallowing in misery had never been Chloe's style. After dressing quickly in fresh jeans and a T-shirt, and brightening her face with a dab or two of make-up, she took out her personal organiser and picked up the phone.

Sally, her booker, was overjoyed to hear from her although it was very difficult to steer her away from questions about the Hagan Gallery and Kitt. She was also astonished by Chloe's desire for immediate work.

'But you only just got back yesterday,' Sally protested. 'You should be easing off now. You can afford it.' She gave a sigh that was audible even over the usual background hubbub of the agency's booking table. 'And you've got that gorgeous hunk of a fiancé to enjoy too. What a body! I bet he's fantastic in . . .'

'Enough, Sal, what can you get me?' demanded Chloe, fighting the pain. 'There's nothing in my Xaviera contract that says I can't do editorials, is there?'

She could almost hear Sally shaking her head. 'Look, are you sure? Don't you even want some time out to take photographs?'

'I can take photographs anywhere. I don't have to have time off to do it,' said Chloe, aware that she was being curt with someone who had her best interests at heart. 'Now, please, can you get me some work. And soon!'

Sally rang off, but called again only a few minutes later. There was a big magazine shoot in Tenerife the very next day, if Chloe was prepared to travel at the weekend. It was with a major glossy whose fashion editor was over the moon at the chance of getting the new Xaviera girl. The money was way over the odds and there was a whole raft of other juicy inducements. She was a fashion celebrity now, and they'd treat her like a goddess.

Other phone calls were more difficult to make. Ma's voice had featured repeatedly on the answer phone but, when they actually spoke, Chloe found her mother surprisingly not shocked by what she'd seen in the papers.

'Well, it's not exactly what I imagined when you said you wanted to be a photographer, sweetheart, but I have to admit Kitt does have a splendid body. I'm amazed he let you exhibit those pictures though. You did get his permission first, I hope?'

'Sort of,' fibbed Chloe, rushing on to tell her mother about Tenerife and promising a visit— with Kitt—when she returned.

'We have to start making some serious plans, my dear,' her mother reminded her. There was a note in Ma's voice which suggested that she could tell she wasn't getting the full story but, for once, she didn't become insistent. When Chloe rang off, a sense of guilt hung over her.

She was less successful at hiding her subterfuge from Rose and Florence. Both demanded a council of war on her return from the fashion shoot, and both were equally solicitous.

'Take good care of yourself, Chloe,' Rose bade her, anxiety in her voice.

Florence was less circumspect. 'Look, if something's wrong, Chloe, you just have to hang in there and work it out. I ran away too, and it cost me a lot of months when Jacob and

I could have been together . . . and happy.'

Chloe had told each cousin she was fine, lying unashamedly through her teeth.

Keeping busy seemed to help, and when Chloe had packed her bags, she considered getting out into the garden with the Nikon. Her heart wasn't in it though. Every time she looked through the viewfinder, she either saw Kitt, or the whole image blurred with tears. She seemed to see Kitt's face too, cold and angry, as he'd glared at her. His hurt and guilt-ridden face as she'd accused him of a crime just as heinous as her own.

It'll get easier, she told herself, trying without success to banish those dark beautiful features. It *will* get easier! It has to . . . I'll *make* it!

*   *   *

The rest of the day dragged in a way Chloe wouldn't have believed possible.

Bobby seemed completely unreachable, and Chloe suspected that events had got the better of him. He'd been guilty enough to start with, and Kitt's furious reaction had probably made him feel even worse.

In the absence of any better distraction, Chloe returned to her photographic equipment catalogues and spent some time on the phone ordering all the elements of the best and most expensive home darkroom money could buy.

It wasn't until evening that she heard the sequence of sounds she'd been unconsciously listening for since midday. Kitt running up the stairs, then moving around above. Tracking him from below, she heard first the running shower, then the buzz of his razor, and finally the sounds of activity in the bedroom—the opening and slamming of wardrobes and cupboards, the creaking slide of drawers.

He's packing!

The words howled in her brain like a siren. He's packing his bags and leaving! Abandoning her cool survival schemes, Chloe hurtled up the stairs and almost fell into her erstwhile fiancé's bedroom.

Kitt, clad in a pair of dark grey suit trousers and with his white silk shirt as yet unfastened, stopped dead in the act of placing a neat pile of underwear in his flight bag.

Chloe began a silent countdown, and it was 'ten' before Kitt spoke.

'Watanabe's changed his plans. He wants the foundations laid in two months. I'm going back to Japan to look at more buildings.' His words were clipped and lacked inflection, as if he were exerting massive self-control. 'There didn't seem much point in refusing.'

'No. Of course not.' Chloe felt a small degree of hope. He wasn't actually 'leaving her' as such. 'I'm . . . I'm flying to Tenerife tomorrow myself. It's an editorial for "Vivace". They've been begging the agency for a chance to photograph me.'

'That's good.' Kitt sounded slightly puzzled as if she'd undermined the drama of his own departure. Laying the last item in his bag, he zipped it up. 'How long will you be away?' He buttoned his shirt and tucked it in. Against her will, Chloe mourned the covering of his muscular chest. He was fastening his belt as she replied, 'About a week. The Pattersons are happy to watch out for Boy. When do you fly out?'

'In about an hour-and-a-half. So I'll have to get my skates on.' He moved to the mirror, quickly knotting his tie, then smoothing his already tamed curls. He wasn't really doing anything to the shiny black mass, but Chloe sensed that he didn't want to face her. 'I think this might be a good breathing space for us,' he murmured, his voice suddenly less distinct, far less confident.

'You're probably right.' Chloe wasn't sure that she wanted breathing space, but felt profoundly thankful Kitt wasn't making any drastic decisions yet.

Fastening his watch and checking the time, Kitt finally turned towards her.

'Look, Chloe, I've got to leave now or I'll miss my flight. There isn't anything else available for days.' His eyes darkened as he studied her, but not with the chilly fury of earlier. 'Will you be OK?' The words were so soft she barely heard them.

Chloe nodded, not trusting her voice, and offered a small, tentative smile.

'Good girl. Take care of yourself.' Kitt gave her a slight crooked grin of his own. 'We'll . . .' The grin faded, became a more complex expression entirely. 'We'll talk when we both get back. Goodbye, Chloe.'

Like a wooden doll, she stood still and accepted his kiss on her cheek, then watched as he picked up his flight bag and briefcase and made as if to go. At the door, he turned and flicked his fingers at her, then acknowledged her own 'Goodbye, Kitt,' with a brief perplexed frown.

Chloe could still see the strange confused look in his eyes—long after the uneven echo of his slightly limping steps had faded.

*　　　*　　　*

That kiss, and that little frown, stayed vividly with Chloe throughout all the busy days that followed. And despite her worries they burned like tiny flames of optimism.

She flew out to Tenerife fully expecting the photographer to despatch her pale, stressed face immediately back to London but, as luck would have it, a moody-looking model was exactly what they wanted. The clothes were gloomy and Byzantine, and Chloe's slightly drawn expression and darkened eyes added a 'Lady of Shalott' quality that sent the stylist into raptures!

In between being photographed—which, true to form, took place in the most inaccessible parts of the island—Chloe took some photographs of her own. They were nothing special, but at least she felt mildly happy using the camera, and the drama with the photographs of Kitt hadn't killed her enthusiasm which was something she'd feared.

Most of her off-duty hours, Chloe spent alone. Sometimes she tried to read a novel— but hardly took in a single word—and at others she simply thought long and hard about Kitt.

He'd said they were going to talk, and that touch of his lips to her cheek had seemed to suggest to her that not all was completely lost. They would never, she realised sadly, have the romantic, rose-tinted love she'd always dreamed of, but they might still be able to make something of their relationship. And Kitt might well come to appreciate her if not love her—especially if she remained his principal means of keeping the Court from Geraldine's grasp!

But, as the days passed, another reason for their engagement was taken from her. Partly in sorrow and partly in relief, she discovered that she wasn't pregnant. Her feelings were mixed that morning, swinging between relief that at least one complication had been lifted from her, and misery at the loss of something wonderful. *Somebody* wonderful. A baby that would have bound her and Kitt together unequivocally, even if they never actually got married.

But it was no use crying over something hypothetical. Chloe knew she had to move forward, and make the best of what she had.

The shoot took rather longer than anticipated so it was almost a fortnight later when Chloe let herself into her flat on her return from Tenerife.

In theory, at four o'clock in the afternoon, Kitt could possibly have been home early, but Chloe didn't expect to find him. She didn't even know if he was back from Japan. He hadn't contacted her, and she hadn't contacted him.

The silent room mocked her, and even Boy wasn't around for once. Ignoring her disappointment, she dumped her luggage and made her way straight through into the kitchen. In the absence of emotional comfort, a decent cup of tea was her number one priority.

In the kitchen, the first thing that drew Chloe's eye was a white envelope propped against the very teapot she was seeking. It was identical to the one she'd found the morning after she and Kitt had first made love and, once again, it was labelled 'Chloe' in his crisp, decisive handwriting.

With trembling fingers, she tore open the

flap and unfolded the paper inside.

It was a surprisingly long note . . .

Dear Chloe,

I suspect you'll be reading this around teatime, hence the teapot. I know a cup of tea is probably the first thing you'll want when you get in.

Wrong! thought Chloe wryly, because I'm reading this letter instead . . .

I got in from Japan a couple of days ago. Mission accomplished there, but I've been wall-to-wall with catching up since, so I'm afraid I won't be back home again until about half-six. Which is a shame, because there's so much 1 wanted to talk to you about, and tonight—which I'd completely forgotten about, what with one thing and another—is the "Right to Walk" Charity Ball. I know it's a lot to ask, Chloe, but will you still go with me? I wouldn't blame you if you refuse, after the way I've hurt you, but I think it's important that we both be there. You'll find out why later.

I've arranged for a car to collect us at seven, so time will be a bit tight for me when I get in. Please be ready and waiting for me! Please!

Chloe felt a shudder pass through her. The second 'please' was heavily underlined.

I'll just dash in, get showered and changed, then knock on your door when it's time to go.

See you at seven . . .

Forgive me for hurting you so much,
Kitt

262

PS. I fed Boy this morning, but he didn't seem too interested.

I think he's pining for you. I don't blame him.

Chloe had no idea how many times she read the odd but strangely eloquent little message. Afterwards, however, she folded it carefully, clutched it to her heart, and literally to ran her bedroom to start getting ready. Her tea forgotten, she rummaged through her extensive wardrobe, searching for the one dress that would be right for the occasion. If anyone had asked her on the plane whether she wanted to go to a Charity Ball tonight, she would have told them 'no chance!' but suddenly it seemed like a brilliant idea. All she wanted now was to look stunning—but not too outrageous—so that she could make Kitt proud.

His note had given her hopes an injection of strength.

CHAPTER TWENTY

'Hello, are you ready?'

Chloe's heart felt as if it were bouncing against her rigidly boned bodice as she opened the door to Kitt. It was one those moments when a hundred things were thought and felt and seen in the very same instant, and the mass of impressions was almost too great to process.

I love you! she thought, feeling suddenly as light as air. She seemed to soar higher when Kitt's mouth curved into a cautious smile. It only lasted a second, but it was enough. The light in his eyes seemed to validate her hope.

'You look . . .' he paused, as if he was having trouble accessing his vocabulary, '. . . amazing. Just incredible, Chloe . . . incredible.'

Chloe wanted to thank him, but she was having her own problems. She knew she looked spectacular. It was her job to, and a Rose Trevelyan ice-pink satin corset-gown given by her cousin in lieu of modelling fees, made it easy. Kitt, however, needed no special effects clothing to make him look like dream. In a dark, elegantly understated evening suit, he made an impact that stole the breath from her body.

'You found my note then?' Kitt blinked, as if he still couldn't quite believe his eyes either. He seemed too stunned to ask anything more complicated.

'Yes, I got in about four, so I've had plenty of time to get ready.' There was some sort of shadow—Chloe who was making automatic responses because the effort of smiling and acting normally and not throwing herself bodily at the man she loved was enormous.

'You look . . . you look wonderful, Chloe!' said Kitt again, as if he'd forgotten that he'd already told her. 'You've never looked more

264

beautiful.'

'It's just the frock,' she muttered, feeling the automaton falter and the real, unsure, terrified woman blunder from cover. 'One of Rose's . . . anyone would look fab in it.'

'Rubbish, I wasn't talking about the dress! It's you! Are you ready to go?'

'Of course.'

Chloe was confused by his sudden abruptness but, as she followed him and thought about what he'd said, she had to accept that it was a fair comment.

Suffering, it seemed, had refined her somehow, making her eyes look huge, her skin paler and her beauty even more arresting. Her hair, drawn up in a more polished version of her French sex kitten knot, accentuated the high sweep of her cheekbones, and a deep rose-red lip tint added a touch of sensual colour to her softly curved mouth. She knew she looked almost demure, yet as if containing an inner volcano. Like a poised and worldly model hiding a mad, consuming love.

When Kitt put his hand on her back to urge her towards the waiting taxi, both he and Chloe gasped in soundless conspiracy. He wasn't even touching her skin—her boned bustier bodice prevented that—but Chloe could have sworn she felt discreet points of heat from each of his fingertips. For a split second, his hand went limp, yielded, moulded around the curve of her, and Chloe had to bite her lip to keep from crying out. Regardless of all the pain and misunderstanding between them, nothing had altered the simple physical magic. The communication that didn't need words at all.

The taxi ride was trying. That one touch seemed to have primed a very powerful mechanism in Chloe. Her need for Kitt overriding every other consideration. There was so much they had to sort out between them, and yet all she wanted to do was reach for Kitt and kiss him passionately. And, on a deep level, she knew he wanted the same.

The worst thing was that, as soon as they were settled, Kitt had reached out and taken hold of her hand.

It had to be a gesture of conciliation, but the smooth warmth of his palm pressed to hers almost made her angry again. Surely he knew what he was doing? Was he deliberately trying to addle her wits so she wouldn't start asking questions?

They were nearly at their Docklands destination, and Chloe was almost at the point when she would have to speak out or risk going crazy, when Kitt suddenly turned to her, looked directly into her eyes and spoke.

'The photographs. I know it's not your fault they were shown, that you never intended them to be in the exhibition. And I'm sorry for behaving like a pompous, narrow-minded jackass about them. They're a compliment . . .

266

I realise that now.'

Chloe just gawked at him, sideswiped by such an about-turn. She opened her mouth, shut it again, then struggled again for fugitive words. She had almost found them when Kitt offered an odd, apologetic, little half-smile.

'Sorry,' he said, giving a shrug, then squeezing her captive hand.

Chloe forgave him immediately, and sensed that on another level she was simultaneously forgiving him for everything else as well. No matter how much he'd hurt her, he was worth it.

'It's still my fault they appeared.' She met his eyes. 'I should never have taken them in the first place. It . . . it was a form of theft. I stole your privacy . . .'

'But you're a photographer. An artist,' he said, his voice almost scarily sincere. 'You have a duty to seize the moment. Preserve what you think is a meaningful image.' He stopped, grinned broadly, rubbed his free hand down the side of his hip and thigh. 'Even if it is my naked backside in all its glory!'

Chloe laughed too—she couldn't help herself—and she couldn't believe how much better it made her feel.

'Have they . . . um . . . caused any problems for you?' she asked after a moment. 'At work, I mean? I know they're a bit conventional, your lot, aren't they?'

Kitt looked down at their still-joined hands

for a second, then looked up again. He was still smiling.

'Well, actually, there's been quite a surge of interest. We've had approaches from some entirely new clients. Asking for me specifically.' He quirked his black brows at her. 'They must think that if a man's got enough front to pose nude for photographs, he's going to have some pretty radical design ideas too.' He rolled his eyes. 'It doesn't make a lot of sense to me, but I'm not knocking anything that brings new commissions.'

Chloe was about to say she was glad to be of service but, just then, the taxi began to slow in front of the industrial-looking frontage of Storyville. She was just gathering her skirts, whilst at the same time clutching her evening bag, when something occurred to her that she hadn't considered before.

'How did you find out?' she asked as Kitt helped her out of the cab. 'About the pictures . . . about it being a mistake?'

Before Kitt was able to answer, a battery of flash units were going off all around them, and the celebrity snappers were calling out her name, again and again, in an attempt to get that one perfect shot of her. Although she was used to such attention herself, she knew Kitt wasn't and, when she turned to him, she saw that his face was tight and wary. She squeezed his arm and murmured 'Relax, we'll soon be through them.' He forced a smile, grasped her tightly and propelled them forward

'Are you OK?' she asked, once they were safely through security and inside the nightclub. She had heard quite a number of rather vulgar enquiries as to whether 'Kit-off Kitt' would be baring all again soon, and she could quite see how that might make him furious.

But Kitt was laughing. ' "Kit-off Kitt?" I don't believe it!' He shook his dark head. 'It'll go down a storm at the next RIBA dinner!'

Chloe smiled too, wondering what the ladies and gentlemen of the Royal Institute of British Architects would think of having a colleague who was also a nude model. Would it create as much of a stir as it was causing here?

The 'Right to Walk' Ball was a much bigger event than Chloe had anticipated and, for a second, she felt contrite. How many of the other people here—like herself—had lost sight of the prime objective of the Ball? To raise funds for kids and teenagers who couldn't walk, or even stand, much less dance?

As they wove their way through the throng of guests, it seemed that Kitt was at least as much a talking point as she was. They were waylaid dozens of times by the social great and good. The comments were politer than those howled by the paparazzi outside, and Kitt responded with a friendly smile and a classic 'no comment'.

As they reached their table—thanks to the

efforts of a harried PR woman—Chloe could not have felt prouder of her tall, dark companion. This was not Kitt's natural milieu—that RIBA dinner was probably much more his scene—yet he showed no sign of the discomfort she knew he'd felt earlier. He looked completely at ease, totally unfazed and his smile was genuine. It wasn't just his newfound notoriety that was drawing every female eye. In his beautifully cut evening clothes, he was as attention grabbing as a rock star, and he had more charisma, without even trying, than an entire catwalk full of posturing male supermodels.

Face it, Chloe, she told herself, feeling an irrational burst of confidence. If Kitt had turned up in purple loon-pants and a donkey jacket, you'd still think he was the coolest man in the room!

A moment or two later, the arrival of a leading American film actor and his equally stellar wife took some of the pressure off Chloe and Kitt. Almost drooping with relief, she was able to look around and take stock of the event and their location.

Although the ultra-modern club didn't really lend itself to a formal event, Chloe was surprised to find that she and Kitt had been seated at what approximated to a 'top' table. What was more, even though most eyes were now on the movie stars, she could see that Kitt was still a focus of rather more discreet interest. She intercepted a couple of curious stares and some whispered asides, and though it crossed her mind that her own presence might account for them, gut instinct told her that Kitt was the cause of them What on earth was going on?

'How *did* you find out about the pictures?' She returned to her unanswered question as they were served champagne.

'From Bobby Smith.'

'You've talked to Bobby? I thought you wanted to kill him?' Chloe was puzzled. There was no animosity in Kitt's expression. If anything, there was a touch of sorrow as he nodded.

'No, I never wanted that,' he said simply. 'I did feel threatened by him though. Mainly, because he's young, he's talented, and *you* like him.'

'I do like him. But that's all . . . and I'm grateful to him. He's helped me.'

'Ah, well, that's where things get a little complicated.' Kitt took her hand. 'He *has* helped you—but maybe slightly more than you wanted him to.'

'I don't understand,' said Chloe. She did, though, really. Or she was beginning to.

'Don't be angry with Bobby . . .' Kitt's fingers tightened distractingly, their pressure warm and urgent. 'But he was the one who showed Simon Hagan the photographs of me. And he made a point of making sure they were in the exhibition.'

'But I expressly told him that no one was to see them! Why on earth would he do just the opposite?' She knew. She knew. And she felt guilty herself. She'd given Bobby far too much hope . . .

'To drive a wedge between us. To make me think you'd deliberately used me,' said Kitt. 'And then, when I blew up—which like a petulant baby, I did!—he could step in and offer comfort and a whole lot more.'

Chloe took a sip of champagne, barely tasting it. Why hadn't she seen the obvious before now?

'Bobby has been a good deal more obsessed with you than you realise, and for a whole lot longer,' said Kitt, looking uncomfortable. He had released her and now seemed to be drawing a pattern of some kind on the white tablecloth. He was watching his own fingers as they moved in tiny circles. 'Not that I blame him.'

Chloe's heart surged. She shot a look at Kitt's handsome profile. He was still studying the table, still avoiding her eyes, yet there had been a telling roughness in his voice. He *did* feel for her—perhaps even more than she'd begun to hope . . .

'And he had encouragement, of course.' Kitt suddenly lifted his gaze. 'I don't think he'd have done anything that had the slightest chance of hurting you if it wasn't for the intervention of a certain party.'

Pieces of a jigsaw clicked nearly into place.

'Geraldine?' enquired Chloe, vaguely aware that some speech making had begun. The chairman of the Committee, a well-known 'pop culture' aristocrat, was on his feet and addressing the assembly. Under other circumstances, Chloe would have listened attentively, but what Kitt had to say was far more important.

'Who else?' he said, shrugging. 'Apparently, she approached Bobby after that evening at "Lucci" and suggested that, as they both had certain interests in common, they should work together.'

'To what end?'

'I think the objective was to keep you and me from becoming more than just friends and housemates.' He gave her a narrow, roguish smile that made her pulse race and her face and bare shoulders grow warm. 'They failed miserably, didn't they?'

'I suppose so . . . but they did manage to cause a lot of upset.'

'Yes, they did,' said Kitt more seriously. 'But you and I are still here together, aren't we? We're still on speaking terms—and we can't rum back the clock and deny what's happened between us, can we?'

Her inner heat flared, and Chloe wished they were far away from this crowded room filled with eyes that seemed to watch their

273

every move. There were serious issues to resolve, but if they could just be alone again and make love, all could be well again.

'Nobody can take that away from us,' she said quietly, hoping passionately that Kitt would read her meaning. His slight smile seemed to suggest that he had, and the way he took her hand again, holding it lightly and stroking her palm with his thumb, only confirmed it.

'Certainly not those two,' he said, surprising her by looking beyond her bare shoulder and nodding to her to turn and look at something.

Making the least amount of commotion, Chloe looked around—and saw the couple who had caused her and Kitt so many problems. Bobby Smith, sitting very close to Geraldine Van Straten, the ex-Mrs Kittrick Maynard.

Geraldine, as ever, seemed to be networking. She was deep in conversation with a prosperous looking individual at the next table. Her back was both to Chloe and to the companion who sat beside her. Bobby, however, was looking in Chloe's direction, his face revealingly pale and drawn.

Oh, Bobby, I'm sorry, thought Chloe, wishing that she could somehow make him feel better. No one knew better than she did, surely, what it was like to love someone who didn't love you? And yet she couldn't change how she felt. Kitt was the one for her, the love of her life, and there was no way that Bobby could ever be anything other than a friend.

She gave the younger man a smile to show that she didn't hate him, and the effect on Bobby was immediate. He visibly relaxed, and Chloe could almost see the weight of anxiety lifting off him. Returning her smile, he lifted his hand and waved back.

'Lucretia Borgia and acolyte, eh?' murmured Kitt, 'They make an odd couple, don't they?'

'Geraldine could do a lot worse,' said Chloe, turning away from the mismatched twosome. She didn't really want to make eye contact with a woman who hated her so much. 'You know what I mean,' she went on quickly, seeing Kitt's slightly worried expression. 'Does Geraldine know that her little ruse has been outed?'

'Well, I haven't spoken to her myself,' said Kitt. 'I daren't. I felt far too angry when Bobby first told me . . . But I suppose I am going to have to deal with her face-to-face eventually.' His expression said he didn't relish the prospect at all. 'And tell her there really is not a hope of her and I ever getting back together again.'

Really? thought Chloe, so relieved she could hardly breathe. Even if Kitt didn't love her, even if he had asked her to marry him for the sake of the Court and because she might be pregnant, there was no denying he *did* feel something for her. Something that could be a solid basis for more . . . She didn't begrudge him having Arrowsmith Court, after all, and enduring relationships had bloomed out of a lot less than mutual self-interest, hadn't they?

Chloe was so caught up in her resolutions that she suddenly discovered that she'd missed more or less all of what their titled speaker had been saying .

'. . . so you see, Ladies and Gentlemen, subject to a few legal snafus being smoothed out, we won't even have to spend any of the money we earn tonight on setting up the new centre. All the alterations, fittings and initial staffing costs will be covered by a sizeable cash donation that goes with the gift of the house. Yes, Ladies and Gentlemen, this was all a huge bolt from the blue . . . we've got a great property, and sufficient funds to set it up, all in one fell swoop. I think that gives all of us a pretty good reason to party, eh?'

'What's he talking about?' Chloe whispered to Kitt, her attention riveted now, in spite of everything. 'Has somebody donated a house or something?'

'Shush!' Kitt said gently. His eyes were worried again, and his whole demeanour was uneasy. 'You'll see . . .'

'I won't name our benefactor because, one, there are still the aforesaid legal problems to sort out and, two, I don't want to embarrass him . . .' The speaker paused and, to Chloe's astonishment, seemed to flash a glance in Kitt's direction. '. . . But, suffice it to say, a lot of kids who're having a hard time will soon be able to benefit because of him—and the "Right to Walk" Trust is profoundly grateful for the gift of a beautiful house, and a gorgeous little slice of rural East Sussex. So let's hear it for a really cool act of generosity. Hip hip hooray! Hip hip hooray! Hip hip hooray!'

'You've given the Court away, haven't you?' Chloe whispered dazedly under cover of the clapping and cheering. It was so obvious. There was no other explanation.

Kitt's discomfort was even greater now. He looked almost as scared of her as Bobby had done. 'Not exactly,' he murmured. 'Well, not yet at least . . .' For an instant, he closed his eyes, as if he were about to take a giant leap into an unknown and hazardous territory. 'It really rather depends on you, doesn't it?'

Champagne was being topped up now, and food was starting to be served. There was still a buzz of conversation about the announcement, and speculation about the benefactor—but most people were already more concerned with the reason they'd really come to the Ball. Having a good time and being seen doing so.

'Me?' said Chloe. She muttered her thanks to the waiter who had just topped up her glass, but she ignored the sparkling wine. She couldn't concentrate.

'Yes, *you*,' said Kitt, with an emphasis that still seemed to contain a touch of anxiety.

Chloe thought 'why?' and then suddenly, clearly, saw it.

If she didn't stay engaged to Kitt, and most probably marry him too, Arrowsmith Court wouldn't become the much-needed treatment centre. Geraldine was hardly likely to donate it, was she?

She still couldn't concentrate, there were too many variables. Suddenly the room, full of music and voices, seemed to squash her.

'I must get out of here,' she said, rising to her feet, and looking around for an exit. 'I can't think straight . . . and I really feel I need to!'

In a flash, Kitt was up too, and had taken her by the arm. 'Come with me. I know the guy who did the conversion for this place. He showed me the plans.' He drew her forward, his grip gentle yet masterful. 'If memory serves, there's a quiet place outside where we can talk.'

Under cover of the hubbub caused by some late arriving celebrities, Chloe and Kitt made a clandestine getaway from the hot and crowded room. Following him through a maze of corridors, and down a fire escape that presented some problems for her elaborate skirts, Chloe soon found herself outside and in very unexpected surroundings. A secret urban garden looking out on the gleaming Thames.

'Wow!' said Chloe, temporarily distracted by the beauty of this unexpected haven. There was no one around—for miles, it seemed—and she and Kitt might have been the only two people in London that night.

But the hard facts of her situation had to be faced.

'So, I presume I have to marry you, or "Right to Walk" doesn't get the Court?' She wished she didn't have to state things quite so brutally.

'Yes,' replied Kitt, his voice flat. 'That's more or less it.' He went to the ornate iron rail that bounded the little garden, and leant on it as he stared out across the river. Chloe felt a pang of pain at how deflated he suddenly looked.

'But I don't understand you,' said Chloe, following him and standing beside him at the rail. Her fingers ached with the need to touch his arm, to reassure him, but she couldn't quite work out what it was she was supposed to be reassuring him of. 'I know you're not a vindictive man. I know you wouldn't do something like this just to spite Geraldine, no matter how grabbing and acquisitive *she is* . . . but I can't quite see how you've suddenly grown so passionate about the "Right to Walk" cause either.' She paused, pierced again by the increasing tension in Kitt's face. 'I know you care about good causes and people's welfare.

But it's a charity you've only just found out about, isn't it?' She faltered again, knowing what she wanted to say, but not how to. The words were coming out all wrong.

Kitt spun around and took her by the arms. His fingers felt hot against her skin, as if he were feverish and sickening for something. 'I don't know! I can't think straight either!' he said, his voice loud and strangely ragged. 'I think it must be panic. I had to do something or I was terrified I might lose everything!'

'Kitt! What are you talking about?' Once again, Chloe felt the inkling of a light dawning. Something she so wanted to believe but still daren't. Because it was too wonderful . . .

'I'm talking about me being just as desperate and besotted as that poor devil Bobby Smith!' Kitt cried, his fingers like hot metal against her upper arms now, gripping her so hard it hurt. 'I'm talking about doing mad, misguided things in an attempt to get what I can't live without!'

'But you're giving the Court to the "Right to Walk" Trust, aren't you?'

'It's not the Court I've got to have,' exclaimed Kitt, his eyes sparking green fire even though the light in the garden was muted. 'It's you, you little twit! It's you!' He drew in a deep breath, as if he'd just run a marathon. 'I thought that if it turned out that you weren't pregnant after all, you might want to forget about the engagement . . .' His eyes closed for

280

a moment, long lashes sweeping down, then up again, like two black fans. 'And that, I really couldn't bear to contemplate. Not after I'd finally come to my senses.'

Chloe dropped her evening bag. It had been ruinously expensive and would probably be marked, but suddenly her fingers had no strength. Every ounce of attention and concentration in her body was focused on the man before her, the man whose passionate grip would probably leave marks on the fair skin of her upper arms. The beautiful, intelligent, worldly man who looked almost—if her eyes weren't deceiving her—as if he might cry from the intensity of his emotions.

'You love me, don't you?' she said, unable to stop her face breaking into a huge beaming grin of pure happiness.

'Yes. I do,' said Kitt, his mouth quirking on the words as if they were as wondrous to him as they were to Chloe. 'I think I have for a long time . . . but I've been both too stupid and too afraid to acknowledge it.' Releasing her arms, he bent down to pick up her bag and put it on the iron garden table just beside her. 'And I'm still afraid,' he finished, taking her hand and holding it as if it were a piece of rare crystal.

'Why?' It was either ask that, or lean over the rail and yell out in joy and triumph across the Thames. But the sight of Kitt's dear face was infinitely preferable to the darkly flowing water.

'Because I'm older than you are. Because I'm not glamorous, or cool . . . and I've got a wonky leg. Because I'm not sure that you care about me in quite the same way I care about you. Because you might not love me.'

'Of course I love you, you *big* twit!' She shook her hand free, flung her arms around his neck and hugged him. 'I bet I've loved you just as long as you've loved me,' she said, laughing. 'And I've *always* known!' Then, pulling him close with all the power at her disposal, she kissed him hard and made him kiss her back again.

'Good grief, woman, I need to breathe!' exclaimed Kitt after a while, when they briefly drew apart. He kissed her again, much more gently, then looked into her eyes, his own quite serious.

'I've wasted a lot of our time, haven't I?' he said, looking penitent. 'I should have taken notice of all that modern wisdom about women growing up faster than men. I've been keeping you at arm's length all this time when you're probably far more emotionally mature than I've ever been.' His self-reproach suddenly turned to thoughtfulness, then a look of pure surprise, tinged with slight horror. 'Do you know that you're probably the reason I married Geraldine?'

'Getaway! How do you work that out?' If it hadn't made such sudden sense to Chloe, she would have told him he was talking like an idiot.

'Because I had to cure myself of an unsuitable obsession with the girl next door . . . and channel away some even more unsuitable urges.' He rolled his eyes in a parody of lechery. 'I suppose I chose Geraldine because I had to resist the forbidden fruit, and she was more conventionally suitable for a man of my age.'

'Don't worry,' said Chloe, her heart turning over with affection for him. It wasn't that Kitt had ever lacked emotional maturity, she was sure of that, he'd just had an overdeveloped and misdirected sense of old-fashioned chivalry. 'I think we have a few years left before you're confined to a bath chair and can't make love to me any more!'

'Cheeky madam!' said Kitt, before kissing her soundly into submission yet again.

Eventually it was Chloe's turn to grow more serious. She sat down on one of the painted garden chairs—billowing skirts notwithstanding—and encouraged Kitt to take the one opposite her.

'I'm not pregnant, Kitt,' she said quietly, taking his hand. 'Are you disappointed?'

'A part of me is,' said Kitt after a short pause, his honesty more reassuring to Chloe than a total denial would have been. 'There's no denying that I was looking forward to a child of ours . . .' He turned his hand over so that he was doing the holding. 'But I think, on balance, that you need more time before you settle down and have a baby.'

Chloe opened her mouth to tell him she was ready whenever he was, but Kitt gave her a firm look.

'It's not that I don't think you're ready . . . I've no doubt you'll be a fabulous mother.' His thumb began to move delicately against her palm in a way that was devilishly distracting. 'But there are a lot of things that you need to do for yourself first. Especially as a photographer . . . You've got a talent and you ought to give it your best shot, don't you think?'

Chloe nodded, touched beyond measure by his belief in her.

'And, besides that, I think it'd be unconscionably cruel of you to retire from modelling and deny all your adoring fans the sight of their goddess!' he added, smirking archly.

'Too true!' Chloe grinned back at him. 'Not to mention the fact that Xaviera will sue the hide off me if I retire before my contract expires.'

'Well, we'd better not let that happen,' Kitt said. 'I keep telling you that I'm considering retiring myself . . . and becoming a kept man.'

'Is that so?' enquired Chloe, wishing for the moment that the pair of them could retire. At least for the night, to a comfortable bed, back at Willow House. To be able to keep Kitt, in any sense of the word, was all she wanted. 'In that case, I hope you're going to make it worth my while!'

The hot look in Kitt's eyes seemed to suggest that he too shared her views about the preferred way to spend the rest of the evening. Pulling a woebegone face, he said, 'I suppose we really have to go back to this shindig, don't we?'

'It's only polite,' said Chloe, wishing she could be the kind of rude, lawless celebrity who didn't worry about good manners at all. 'But maybe we don't have to stay *too* long?'

'An hour?' suggested Kitt.

'Three-quarters,' amended Chloe.

'Well, in that case, I think you'd better wear this,' said Kitt, reaching into the inner pocket of his dinner jacket and bringing out a tiny pochette made of the softest leather. 'I saw your cousin Rose arrive as we were coming out here—and the other one, Florence, is it?—and they were both staring at me as if I was Godzilla! I wouldn't want them to be getting the wrong idea.'

Inside the little pouch was a ring. The beautiful antique diamond-and-emerald ring that Chloe knew had once belonged to Kitt's grandmother. The rich, green stones were exactly the colour of her fiancé's eyes.

'Well . . . I suppose I'd better do this the proper way,' he said, getting to his feet while she remained seated. Plucking the knee of his trousers, he sank down into the classic pose. 'I know your Ma's already announced it in *The Times* but, as far as I'm concerned, this is the actual moment of truth . . .' Kitt hesitated, swallowed and looked for all the world the very same brave, handsome hero she'd first seen in her mother's garden years and years before. He hadn't aged a bit, and she doubted if he ever really would . . .

'Chloe Trevelyan, would you do me the honour of becoming my wife?' he asked, reaching for her hand and then holding the glittering circlet poised.

'You bet,' said Chloe blissfully—as the ring slid on.